NORDIC BOUND

by

HENRY MORGAN

CHIMERA

Nordic Bound first published in 2000 by
Chimera Publishing Ltd
PO Box 152
Waterlooville
Hants
PO8 9FS

Printed and bound in Great Britain by
Omnia Books Ltd, Glasgow

NORDIC BOUND

Henry Morgan

By the same author:

AFGHAN BOUND

Chapter One

The crack of the sealskin whip was quite distinctive over the spit of pine bark burning on the fire. Orange flames danced and the scent of pine spiralled towards the gap in the log cabin roof. Outside, in the reflected light of fresh snow, the perfumed smoke billowed upwards and in the distance a lone wolf howled at the full moon; a huge shining sixpence that seemed to take up every inch of the velvet sky.

David Harper ran his fingers through the soft fur of a caribou pelt, reclined in its luxury and used the body of an elephant seal for a pillow. Apart from her chubby red face, sown inside the animal skin was Teena, a young, clear skinned Lapp. She had been put naked into the seal while David administered a corporal lesson to her sister, Mishka. The girls had not prepared the cabin for David's return as he had instructed, and now he found himself once more defining the roles of the two who shared his home.

In the light from the fire Mishka's bottom radiated an iridescent glow as evidence of the soft whip that had striped her taut flesh. She remained on her knees until the marks hardened into lifted weals. Seeing this, David left the comfort of the fur-strewn floor and guided the naked girl outside. The strip of warm light from the cabin doorway cut into the blackness forming a shaft of light upon the pure unsullied snow. Mishka was marched to the edge of darkness, each footstep in the deep snow releasing a loud crack to break the silence of the night. David forced the girl down into a squatting position. She resisted, her hot freshly striped bottom remaining an inch or so above the icy rasp of snow.

'Plish,' she begged, using the few English words she had managed to learn from him. 'Plish. Not sit in snow.' Her breath gathered into clouds and was broken up by the cold wind, along with her plea for mercy.

David noticed Mishka's erect nipples, smiled and pushed her down until her bottom touched the freezing crystals and she released a partly stemmed cry of anguish. Away on a rocky outcrop the wolf stopped his howling in sympathy for her, seemingly recognising that Mishka's chilled discomfort masked even his desolate feelings of loneliness.

Satisfied that she had learned her lesson, David took the girl inside. He returned to his place among the dozens of furs on the floor while the naked Mishka placed more wood on the fire. As the flames grew in intensity, the black-haired ebony-eyed girl took her place by his feet. Her lesson was over; Teena's would soon be starting.

David stabbed a toe into Mishka's leg and gestured toward a small trap door in the floor. The girl got up, grimaced at the throbbing of her still smarting bottom and went across. The wooden door covered a hole dug deep into the ground. It was used as a natural refrigerator and contained several cuts of meat and the hind legs of a caribou. There was also a steel container that held David's supply of vodka. Mishka poured him his measure into a cup made from horn, and he motioned for her to sit at his feet again. She did so, her legs tucked underneath her bottom, her back straight, breasts pushed out proudly. David sipped the alcohol, noticing how the liquid moved thick and sluggishly when it was kept in freezing temperatures. A small pool of vodka gathered in a dip he formed in his tongue and he breathed in deeply. The alcohol fumes went straight into his lungs and he felt its effect immediately; his head became light and his eyes failed to focus on the naked girl. He reclined lazily, his head propped against the encased Teena, and he drifted into a light sleep.

On the surface David should have been a happy man. He owned two beautiful Lapp girls, a ski sled, rifles and furs. His cabin was very comfortable and being deep in the forests of Finland's far north, it provided extreme privacy. But he knew it wouldn't last. Sooner or later Justin and Sabrina would seek him out and try to take him back to Britain, and once again put him to stud.

He grew agitated. Mishka leaned forward and took the horn from his hand. She placed it on a low, heavy wooden table and then sat back as David had earlier instructed. As his face distorted, betraying his anguish, Mishka noticed his cock begin to twitch. She knew the dreams that often tormented him had returned. The helmet of his swelling cock pushed against the two small silver balls that were connected to each other by an impaling barbell through his glans. They were a piercing reminder of his past, which was why David refused to remove them. Sometimes, when he watched the girls make love in front of the fire while he smoked loki, a root with similar properties to cannabis, it was easy to forget what they had done to him. It would be simple to forget without the ampallang barbell. He needed that, and he needed the guiche ring, a silver hoop Sabrina had put through his scrotum between his anus and balls.

When Sabrina was putting him to stud she would dress herself up in a short, tight, black dress. Towering on black stiletto shoes, immaculate in her make-up, she would lead David, naked, by a steel lead attached to his guiche piercing. They would enter the room and, after Sabrina had discussed terms with the other woman, he would be forced to mount and pleasure her until she was satisfied. Then he would be tethered, sometimes with other males, while the women smoked and drank late into the night. The humiliation hurt David. He was not to be trained. He was a trainer who had learned his art in Afghanistan and Pakistan and he had brought that art to Britain, where he set up his own training school. A training school for women, where women were re-educated, where they were taught to succumb to the requirements, to the desires, to the needs of their men. How some of them had squealed and begged and pleaded not to feel the tawse again. And how, by the time they finished their education, they willingly lapped his sperm, eagerly sought his praise by offering their oiled vaginas for his stiff cock.

Life was good then; it was ordered, it was right. It had been right, until his one time friend, Justin, had betrayed him with Sabrina, his last pupil. They turned the tables on him, made him the slave and them his master. His anger subsided quicker than usual when pictures of Emily, his first pupil, flooded his mind. How she had taken those men on the snooker table at the newly founded Clifftop Club, without complaint, without hesitation but with total and utter obedience.

His cock grew until it became uncomfortable. In its bid to obtain satisfaction it had woken him like a persistent ache. David opened his eyes and was greeted by Mishka, still naked and waiting by his feet. He nodded at the table and she returned his drink to his hand. The clear liquid provided a stimulating kick to his system and he glanced towards his turgid prick. Recognising the signal, Mishka dipped her head and welcomed the metal-clad member into her mouth. The sensation of her tongue over the silver spheres of the barbell set his cock as hard as iron and it demanded release. Mishka's head bobbed continually, her eyes closed, her bottom pointed beautifully upwards. The girls were such a comfort in winter when the night lasted for almost twenty-four hours. Now that he had trained them they were perfect companions for a man alone in the wilds.

He allowed Mishka several more minutes before he motioned for her to stop. Despite feeling very tired and relaxed he realised that Teena had not undergone her lesson. David was aware that one lapse, one concession, would show a weakness that could be exploited. He couldn't allow that to happen. If the girls lost faith in his dominance they would lose confidence in his ability to control them and their surroundings. David stood up alongside the kneeling Lapp girl. His naked body was well muscled and defined, the consequence of hard living on the run from Justin and Sabrina. It looked good and healthy and David felt that way too. He was covered in a fine sheen of sweat that, he had learned, the girls loved to lick from his body. His solid cock stood up like a pole, the turgid bell-end an inch or so from Mishka's face. He allowed the girl to take some sweat from his thighs then he turned, and she was delighted to lick the sweat from his taut buttocks. He refused her permission to take salt from his balls though, and pointed towards the bed. Mishka flopped onto the raised pelts of various animals, burrowing her legs and arms beneath several of the skins. Comfortable now that her lesson was over she relaxed and prepared for her sister's beating. As she lowered her head a cool breeze wafted over the parts of her body that remained exposed.

Still naked, David had gone outside again. He stood for a moment feeling the intense chill of the Arctic night, steam rising in curls from the heat of his body.

In a few minutes he would suffer frostbite as the blood receded from his fingers and toes to protect his vital internal organs. He pushed his luck, stepped away from the light of the doorway into the darkness and made his way to the top of a small nearby mound. On the other side a short slope fell away into the icy blackness of lake Inan, where the quiet deep waters were cut by a moonbeam. The silence was cloying, heavy and oppressive, yet he loved it. Here there was genuine freedom for a man, the only laws belonged to nature and her first law was only the strong survive. He took several deep breaths and felt the air try to freeze-dry his lungs.

Mishka had sneaked to the door of the cabin and peeped out. She saw David silhouetted against the moon, arms held out to the sides, legs spread, like a great black pentagram on the badge of Satan.

Before David returned Mishka was back on the bed. Seeing her sister run from the door Teena knew that their master was on his way back, and that meant it was her turn. There was nothing she could do. The leather thongs that acted like laces on the sealskin had been drawn tight. The most she could manage was to wiggle her fingers. Escape, in any case, was not an option. From experience she knew that her best plan lay in submission, total deference to his natural authority.

David arrived at the door. The sheen of sweat that had glistened on his body now looked like a fine layer of icy dust. Crystals, like tiny pearls, had formed between the hairs on his body and Mishka's saliva had partially frozen around his semi-erect cock. Teena saw it clearly and knew that her job was to bring his member back to attention as soon as she could. If she succeeded in that, the beating he was about to give her might just be a little less severe.

Once the cabin door had been shut the temperature began to stabilise and slowly increase, despite the fire fading to a dull glow that seemed to pulsate among the embers. The effect threw wild shadows around the cabin, while the stones that marked the boundaries of the fire gave up their heat to the air.

David's shadow loomed ominously over Teena. She could feel the cold from his body suck away the heat that had tormented her in the time she had been sown up inside the sealskin. Strong fingers pulled at the knot and soon her breasts were in view, then her stomach, and finally her young firm thighs. David went across and stood beneath several iron manacles screwed into a ceiling beam. He allowed a few minutes for blood to return to her cramped joints, and then motioned for her to join him. Despite aching limbs Teena stood up. She made sure that her back was straight and her body was displayed to its best advantage; she knew her master would tolerate no slouching or complaint. He called her over and watched the light from the fire reflect upon her smooth skin as she obeyed his command.

'To your knees,' he said.

The words were not alien to Teena. Her English was poor but she recognised the phrases that David used most, and in her new position Teena's face was in line with her master's waist.

'Tongue out.'

She held back her head and thrust out her moist tongue for David to rest his flaccid member upon it. It was still cold from his walk outside, especially the silver barbells, but she remained on her knees until her tongue and his penis were the same temperature. Mishka surveyed the scene from the relative safety of the bed. The two bodies in front of her remained perfectly still – a tableau; her sister on her knees, head

11

back, arms by her sides, tongue out. David stood stock still, legs apart, head tilted slightly upwards, cock on her sister's tongue. Mishka knew what was coming but she dare not interfere. That would only involve her, and her bottom was only just now cooling down from the strapping that had been administered to it earlier.

Now that warmth had returned to his body David leant over the girl, gripped her strongly by the waist and lifted. Teena was up-ended. Her head dangled between David's knees and her cunt was under his chin. Her lips began to separate and David watched as her sex opened wide when her legs fell either side of his face. He manoeuvred the girl until her body faced his, then with one hand around her slim waist, he used his other to push one ankle into a fetter on the beam. Once that was secure he pressed her other ankle into the snap buckle of another fetter. The manacles acted like wide handcuffs. Once a limb was inserted in them a simple locking mechanism prevented it being removed without a key. Teena dangled upside down and David prowled around her, surveying his property. He ran his hands forcefully down her body as if trying to squeeze some imaginary juice from inside her, applying extra pressure when they met her breasts. Teena was younger than Mishka but her breasts were considerably larger. David took hold of one and wrapped a long leather strip around it several times, then tied the other end to special rings screwed into the floor. He did the same with her other breast and then tethered her wrists in the same way.

Teena no longer dangled. She was held, spread-eagled and tight, upside down, her ankles clasped in irons, legs apart, arms apart and held by leather thongs, as were her glorious tits. David took up his vodka and sat on the bed. Immediately Mishka's hand slipped over his thigh and cupped his bloated balls, caressing them. David brushed away her hand and pushed her down between his legs. The girl slavered noisily while David viewed her sister, spread in full glory for his pleasure. He observed her helpless state for some time. It aroused him; it fed his hunger. The image faded, as did the fire and one of the oil lamps, plunging the cabin into semi-darkness.

David motioned Mishka over to the provision chest. In it was numerous large candles. They were long, thick and white. He took one from her and fitted it snugly into Teena's vagina, and then he withdrew a burning stick from the fire and used it to light the candle. At first the flame faltered and lacked life, but then suddenly the tiny minaret of light grew in intensity. It illuminated Teena's creamy inner thighs and provided a cone of light that framed the suspended girl in its inescapable glare.

As the candle burned David pointed out another box to the watching Mishka. The girl nodded and began searching through its contents until she found the items she knew he wanted. There were numerous silver neck rings that grew increasingly smaller until the top ones pinched the throat. She put them on. She also donned the leather shin guards decorated with silver plates and held in place by long leather strips that had to be wrapped around the calves. Similar items were worn on her forearms and her hair was held back by a leather strap, buckled at the back and decorated with amber and silver. David nodded his approval and held up a leather strap of his own design. It was four strands of walrus leather woven together to form a thick handle in the shape of an erect penis, while the other end provided four separate flails. A large, smoothed and shaped piece of amber formed a golden glans at the handle base, while tiny amber beads were threaded into the four flails to provide them with that extra bite. Like the clothes the girls wore, David had instructed them in the designs he preferred. He also forced them to make his correctional tools, and derived great satisfaction from their faces when they realised it was another whip or more restraints that he would use on them.

Mishka fetched more vodka for David, and took the offered whip. Standing behind her sister she noticed that the candle had begun to burn, and several lines of molten wax had travelled down the white shaft like sperm. Mishka drew back her arm and raised the whip. For the most fleeting of moments she considered trying to fake the ferocity of the stroke, but commonsense prevailed and she realised that nothing but a full-blooded swing would prevent her from taking her sister's place. The golden beads of amber bit deep into Teena's back and her involuntary spasm sent gobbets of wax like a burning ejaculation from the fiery candle to splash on her tethered breasts. Another stroke saw the vicious strands sweep around the suspended girl's body like the claws of some Scandinavian dragon sent to devour virgins. Each lash left a raised reminder, each sweep of the whip flashed through the semi-darkness of the cabin, the amber teeth sparkling bright.

On the fourth stroke Teena released a partially stifled yelp, which alarmed her sister. Mishka knew that any noise during punishment would be greeted with further strokes. She looked at David. He was propped against the cabin wall, surrounded by furs and holding a horn full of freezing vodka. He had not heard Teena's yelp because his mind was full of the delights in front of him. He was submerged in a visual frenzy that blocked out his other senses.

Hastily, Mishka reached for a dried strip of leather

and offered it to Teena, who took it in her mouth and bit hard, and as each ferocious lash criss-crossed her white skin she bit harder, until Mishka had administered the twelfth stroke and was allowed to rest.

'Fire,' said David.

The panting girl gathered logs and added them to the glowing embers. The dry wood caught immediately and spat burning sparks as if in temper. Light began to fill the room and David motioned for Mishka to remove the half-used candle from her sister's cunt and take her down. Teena's relief was obvious, but she still recognised her duty. On all fours she crawled across to David and took his swollen member into her mouth. David appreciated the gesture but forced the girl down onto her stomach and called out for the soothing balm.

Mishka brought it immediately. It was a special unguent composed from spermaceti and various lichens. David had been taught how to make it when he lived with a breakaway tribe of Komi who had settled on the island of Ostrov Golguyev, where they eked out a living fishing the Arctic waters. The group had left their original village when the timber forest started to suffer from acid rain. Now they landed their catch at Murmansk, where they had left David to continue his search for a safe hiding place.

The ointment turned out to be almost a cure all that remedied everything from frostbite to the weals of a fresh lashing. It was the latter it was needed for now.

As Mishka massaged the cooling balm into her sister's back David positioned her on her hands and knees and ran his penis deep inside her open sex. The girl took it without murmur and continued her ministrations to her sister. When she finished with the balm Mishka took up a ball of moss and worked it into a square about the size of a handkerchief, which she placed on Teena's back. The girl sighed with relief and fell into a deep sleep, oblivious to the fucking her sister was being given by their master.

Near to exhaustion from his efforts David came deep inside the girl and dropped onto the furs beside Teena. Before Mishka could take her place on the other side of him she first stoked the fire with fresh logs. As a flurry of sparks ascended and vanished through the smoke escape she snuggled alongside the man who owned her. Owned her and her sister. He was hard, yes. But he was fair, and a good strong man who could survive well in the harsh climate around the lake.

Mishka took up her place and David cupped a breast from each girl. There was a long journey ahead of them in the morning and all three were tired. David considered putting the trip off, but it was the Festival of the North at Murmansk, and it started in two days. He needed to trade and he also wanted to enjoy himself, and smiled with anticipation of Murmansk and the nightlife it offered. His firm grip on the girls' breasts disturbed them; both fidgeted and grumbled, but neither woke up. His head reclined upon the pelt of an Arctic fox and his gaze turned to the spiralling smoke. It turned and twisted and made its way to the black hole in the roof and disappeared. David screwed his eyes shut tight and opened them again. The smoke was still there, like the smoke from the stack of the *Piroshka* that had curled skywards over those three long nights on the North Sea. He had watched it vanish on the cold winds when Sabrina was exercising him on the deck, and he thought that like the smoke he had vanished too.

A log slipped in the fire sending a million sparks into the air like the stars that peppered the northern skies. David's eyelids drooped and he remembered how heavy his legs had felt onboard that vessel. Slowly he leant across Mishka and picked up his horn. In one swill he finished off the rest of the vodka and slumped back to wait for sleep, and the inevitable dreams that would accompany it.

The chirpy *tring*! of the galley phone was followed by a loud message from the bridge.

'All clear on deck.'

The sound of Justin's voice both sickened and angered David, but revenge or escape, for the moment at least, was out of the question.

Sabrina replaced the handset and motioned at David with a long sjambok whip. He rose from his place on the galley floor and stood upright. Sabrina admired his naked body and took great pleasure in the power she wielded over him. He was handcuffed, hobbled and gagged – and he was tethered to the galley stove by a chain connected to the ring through his scrotum. He surveyed the whip. It was the one his friend from South Africa had given him, and it had been his favourite for training the girls back at Camelot, his own training school in Cornwall. He had used it on the taut brown bottom of Sabrina, and now the Pakistani girl was using it on him.

'Against the wall and turn around,' she ordered.

David did as he was told. There was no point in dissent; they were in the middle of the sea, he was shackled and no one knew they were out there.

Sabrina admired his firm buttocks and tapped them playfully with the tip of the whip. 'Time for your walk,' she told him, then released his chain and tugged him in the direction of the door. The moment it opened an icy blast engulfed his naked body, inducing goosebumps to pimple his skin, and his reluctance to venture on deck was overcome by a swift stripe of the whip. David stepped gingerly out and immediately felt sea water wash around his toes. He moved out to the middle of the deck and stopped while Sabrina fumbled between his legs to unclip the chain from the guiche ring.

'On you go,' she commanded. 'I want forty circuits.'

David began to jog as best he could around the deck of the lugger, with fear as a close companion. His hobbled legs lost their footing several times as the boat pitched and yawed on the black and troubled sea. Several waves hit the side of the small vessel and broke over the deck, drenching him in freezing salty spray. All it would take was one big breaker and he would be gone, over the side. With his hands and legs shackled he would go under in seconds, food for the cod.

'I want you fit and healthy for when we land,' shouted Sabrina, above the roar of the water. Then she laughed out loud. 'Remember that? Remember telling all those girls how it was their duty to keep a perfect body for their masters? Now it's your turn.'

She lashed out with the whip, catching his freezing flesh just above his left thigh. The cold accentuated the sting and David threw back his head in anguish. Then, through salty, stinging eyes, his gaze caught sight of a figure hanging above the prow. Another wave crashed over him, catching his breath and chilling him further. For a moment the spray abated and David saw it again, swinging violently, it moving one way while the ship went the other.

Crack! Sabrina laid the whip on him again and he was forced to jog. The next time around the deck there was a gap in the waves and David saw it more clearly. A cage, attached to some rigging, and inside it shivered a naked female. For a moment David thought he heard her screaming, but a mountain of water rose up like a gloved hand and slapped away any sound. There was no mistake in what he had seen, though. There, a few feet above the watery abyss Justin and Sabrina had locked a naked female in some sort of elaborate birdcage. As the *Piroshka* rolled back she appeared high in the sky, her body illuminated by the eerie glow of the navigation lights, and when the boat dipped her swinging cage came and went out of view, perilously close to the clutches of the sea.

Now he had a fix on her he listened for her screams, but they did not come. The boiling sea drowned out all noise except for its own fearful crash, and David wondered if it would be long before it drowned them all.

A stroke from Sabrina's whip reminded him to continue his jogging, while another wave reached over the deck and grabbed the boat in its watery grip. This time it deposited dozens of herring onto the *Piroshka*, leaving the confused fish to flap helplessly on the teak decking.

'Get him inside, it's too rough!' Justin had left the wheelhouse and shouted at full voice over the wind and spray.

'What about the bitch?'

Justin picked up a long billhook and motioned to the galley. 'I'll get her. Get him in before we all go over.'

Sabrina laid a savage stroke across David's legs and pointed with the whip, and David acknowledged her and hobbled urgently towards the dry and warm galley. When Sabrina entered he was already in the required position; as taught, he had pushed his penis and balls down until they faced backwards beneath his bottom, then held them in place by squeezing his thighs together. Finally, he had to touch his toes. Sabrina insisted on this because it was easy to reattach the chain to his guiche ring. Once again the girl held him by the leash.

'Over the table,' she ordered. 'You didn't finish your circuits, so now you must face the punishment.'

The anger positively bubbled in David's veins, but he was forced to accept the humiliating beating.

Sabrina was still administering it when Justin entered with the girl. 'Put her over the table, next to him,' she snapped. 'I'll do the two of them together.'

The girl, who looked about nineteen, was forced down alongside David, their bodies touching. She was not screaming or even crying, such was her relief to be away from the cage. The two prisoners looked at each other with empty expressions, and neither flinched when the sjambok came slicing down.

'One stroke does two arses,' laughed Sabrina. 'How's that for energy saving?'

'It's life saving we'll need if this weather gets any worse,' said Justin. 'I'll get on the radio and find out the forecast.'

'Wait!' She brought two more strokes down upon the naked pair. 'I've finished with these two. Chain them up first and I'll get out of these oilskins and prepare some food.'

Justin took the girl into the connecting saloon and strapped her face down over a low table. Then he returned and tugged on David's chain, led him through and tethered him on top of the girl, creating a pornographic sculpture. Satisfied that all was secure, he left to use the radio.

When he returned the saloon looked cosy and warm. A gas fuelled burner designed like a wood burning stove was pumping heat into the compact cabin and a captain's decanter full of ruby port sparkled on the table. Two large steaks, studded with pepper and steeped in sauce, lay invitingly, on either side of the captives. With the surrounding wood panelling it all looked more like a house in the countryside rather than a boat on the North Sea. It was the solid, reinforced portholes that gave it away. That and the not so gentle swell that continually lifted and dropped the vessel upon the waves.

'Would you rather eat on the galley table?' Sabrina asked.

'This is fine,' he said. 'I like the ornaments in here.' He dropped onto a sofa that stretched the length of the cabin wall and Sabrina handed him his dinner.

'How's the weather forecast?' she asked.

'We've seen the worse of it. By tomorrow it'll of cleared up.'

'Thank God for that,' Sabrina sighed. 'At least I can eat my meal without bringing it back up.'

Justin poured them both a drink. 'You can relax for the rest of the night.'

'Good.' She jabbed her fork firmly into David's buttocks. 'Then you and the bitch can entertain us,' she said to him.

'What about food for them?'

Sabrina smiled and ran her knife slowly along David's back. 'Like I just said, they're going to have to sing for theirs. Sing or fuck. Sing and fuck, perhaps. Maybe sing and lick. I'll see how I feel.'

Her meal finished, Sabrina stood in front of the stove and began undressing. Despite the waterproofs she had been wearing her jeans were quite damp. She wasn't cold because the cabin was getting hot, but then she wasn't taking her clothes off for that reason.

It was impossible for David to see what was going on because he had been strapped to the girl with his head facing the opposite way. Nonetheless, he could hear the conversation and knew it wouldn't be long before he was called upon to perform, and the girl beneath him, who was able to see Justin releasing his trousers, had realised that the same applied to her.

Once down to her bra and panties, Sabrina collected a peaked black sailor's cap from a hook. She put it on along with a pair of black high-heeled shoes. Justin noticed the tiny strap of black lacy material that constituted her knickers.

'Not exactly the gear for the North Sea, are they?' he joked.

Sabrina pulled down her knickers and tossed them on the table. 'It's the idea of them that keeps me warm,' she replied, 'not the size of them.' She sat back down and yanked on David's chain, making him wince at the pain. 'Anyway,' she continued. 'It makes it easier to get them down when I want my sex licked.' She leant forward and released the buckles holding David to the table, then pulled once more on the chain, forcing him to turn around on his knees. 'So he better get on with it.' With that she placed a polished shoe behind his neck and pulled him forward. David toppled over, his face falling within an inch of Sabrina's labia. He knew the routine and began lapping at her moist opening straight away.

'Pass my drink Justin,' she said nonchalantly. 'David's busy.'

It was now Sabrina's turn to observe Justin getting undressed. A sight she enjoyed as she sipped her drink and delighted in the expert tongue of her slave. Justin released the bitch, as Sabrina liked to call her, and sat opposite his partner. The timid girl noticed his erect penis and shuffled across on all fours, before stopping in front of him. He flashed a smile of ersatz sympathy and patted her head gently.

'What's the name of that place you're from?' he asked.

'Brynfelinfach,' she replied.

'And where's that?' Justin knew by her accent where it was, but he was enjoying watching her desperate fight to control her fear as he teased her.

'South Wales.'

'And you went all that way from Brynfel-whatever to the big pop festival on your own? You must be a brave girl.'

She said nothing, but he continued. 'Though I know you're not a good girl. Accepting lifts from strangers, telling them all your business. That's silly, isn't it?' She nodded nervously as Justin pressed on. 'And I know you've been familiar with men, haven't you?' She nodded once more.

'Do you know how I know that?' This time he spoke to Sabrina, who was enjoying David's ministrations so much that all she could manage was a shake of her head, so Justin continued to stroke the girl's hair as he answered his own question. 'Because I've tried her out. Haven't I?'

The girl nodded as he continued.

'And how did I know?'

'Because I wasn't very tight,' she whispered.

'Sorry, I can't hear you.'

'Because I wasn't very tight,' she replied again, louder.

'What wasn't?'

'My cunt.'

'Your what?'

'My cunt?'

Justin continued to play with the young girl's fears, arousing himself further as he did so. 'And why was that?' he asked. 'Why was your cunt not nice and tight?'

She knew better than to refuse an answer. 'Because I had sex that morning before I left the campsite.'

'Because you had sex,' he repeated. 'With anyone

in particular? Do you know his name for instance, how old he was? Was he tall, short, fat?'

'I can't remember.'

Justin looked at Sabrina in mock surprise. 'She can't remember, she says. I reckon she's a bit of a slut. It's just as well Carl didn't order a virgin, because two seconds with his cock up her and he'd have known she's had more pricks than a porcupine at a gang bang.'

Sabrina smiled and sighed. 'Well give her another one. One more won't matter.'

David held out his hard penis. 'You heard the lady,' he said, and a moment later the girl took his full length into her mouth and began to suck and lick. As she started her work David's flickering tongue was finishing his by bringing Sabrina to a shuddering orgasm, but despite her release she kept him in position, though she indicated for him to apply a lighter pressure to her sensitive clitoris.

As the two captors reclined in their respective chairs the sea appeared also spent. The earlier crash of the waves had died away, although the heaving swell remained. In its place a strange calm overtook the boat. Justin was having his cock sucked, and Sabrina was still coming down from her orgasm, and the quiet was broken by the strange ephemeral song of a whale somewhere out in the deep. When it passed Sabrina spoke.

'What about the watch?'

'The electronics and the computers will take care of it,' Justin told her. 'We've plenty of time to relax.'

Sabrina stretched out her foot and jabbed a toe in the other girl's sex. When she withdrew it the digit was covered in a slippery film. 'What are you doing to the bitch?' she said. 'She's soaking.'

Justin smiled. 'She's been well trained.'

'And well used by the look of it.' She pushed David

away and pointed to the girl. 'Open her up.'

David turned to the girl who was still crouched over Justin's lap, reached out and eased open her vagina for Sabrina to examine.

'Finger her,' she ordered.

David did as he was told. First with two fingers, then three and four.

'That's better,' Sabrina purred. 'Loosen her up.' She turned to Justin. 'Do you want to fuck her first?'

Justin waved away the suggestion, his face contorted by the pleasure of his impending release. 'She's going to swallow my spunk before I fuck her,' he groaned.

As David's cock slipped smoothly between the girl's well oiled lips Justin fired his jism into her mouth. She struggled to manage it all while behind her David pumped furiously, his pounding hips urged on ever more cruelly with strokes from Sabrina's sjambok.

'Ride her harder,' she ordered coldly. 'You fuck her good and hard or you'll feel this whip across your back. Do you here me? Good and hard... Hard...'

'Hard. You are hard.'

David woke from his dream into a bright sunny cabin to find Mishka's head bobbing in his lap and his erect prick embedded between her lips. The sunlight brought a sense of super-reality that dispersed his dream and calmed his overwrought mind. Mishka's slavering tongue soothed him further and he flopped back down into a somnolent state to enjoy the warmth of her mouth. Outside his dreamworld he was the master, and his was the controlling word.

Despite the approaching summer, daylight was still short and therefore the time available for travel was minimal. The trip to Murmansk for the Festival of the North would take two days at least, and an early start was important. Because of that, David forewent the added pleasure he usually derived from delaying his morning orgasm and ejaculated straight down the Lapp girl's throat. His shudder woke the sleeping Teena.

'Fire,' he grunted as his orgasm subsided. Teena blinked lazily and turned as if to go back to sleep, when David's hand connected with her bottom to emit a sharp slap. 'Fire,' he repeated.

The girl rose and wobbled unsteadily towards the hearth where she prodded and studied the ash in the hope that it was still alight. David smiled at the handprint that stood out as clear as a tattoo on the young girl's behind, and then he administered a similar slap to Mishka's bottom and ordered breakfast.

By the time he had dressed the fire was blazing once more and the table was laden with food. The girls had prepared a fish soup to provide instant internal warmth, along with lightly roasted caribou cubes. They speared the meat on long tines and dipped them in melted reindeer cheese to supply the energy and sustenance for the long journey ahead. The girls drank milk from wooden bowls while David fortified his with a large shot of vodka.

When he had finished eating the girls were then allowed to dress. Although thick furs were required to combat the cold, beneath them David insisted on leather and silver jewellery studded with his favourite amber. Leather strips criss-crossed the length of their legs – from ankles to thighs. Bottoms and vaginas were left without any form of covering for easy access, but tummies and breasts were also constrained beneath tight thongs. Necks were concealed under heavy collars and across their forehead each girl wore a band adorned with a large amber bulb, which held back their black hair.

The fire was allowed to fade and die while the snowmobile was prepared. A trailer loaded with supplies was hooked up and David's rifle was stored within easy reach – an insurance policy against curious and peckish polar bears.

Although the festival was mainly a celebration of the forthcoming summer it brought thousands of revellers to the town, which made for profitable trading. It was here that David made most of his money, and this season looked to be a profitable one. The summer months were spent on the Baltic coast searching for amber, which the girls polished throughout the winter. While they prepared the semi-precious stones David spent his time hunting the migrating caribou, the Arctic fox and other animals – their flesh to eat, their glorious winter coats to trade.

With the girls seated behind him he gave the cabin one last look, and headed into the forest.

Chapter Two

Room eleven of the Hotel Romanov resounded to the swish of a cane being applied to the flawless brown skin of a Pakistani girl.

Sabrina lay face down, spread-eagled and tethered on the high bed, each wrist and ankle held firmly by a silk scarf to a respective post. Justin unleashed another stroke and a stinging red line jumped immediately to view on the girl's taut buttocks. As her body jerked and writhed on the bed, wracked with delicious pain, her moist sex came into view, and Justin tapped it with the tip of the rod. The thin cane parted the puffy lips and slipped easily between the shaven curtains.

'Leave my cunt alone!' barked Sabrina. 'I told you to stripe my bottom.'

Justin brought the tip of the cane to his face and examined the secretion that coated it. It was the result of her excitement and Justin smeared the slick cream on her backside before bringing the cane down once more. She managed to endure two more strokes before shouting, 'Iceberg!' which was the control word for him to stop, so he placed the cane on a sideboard and released her bonds.

She remained in position, her body gently gyrating and pressing into the bed, while he went into the bathroom to relieve himself, and the sound of his piss hitting the porcelain was joined by Sabrina's muffled cry of orgasm.

He zipped his fly and entered the bedroom, to see the girl relaxed almost to sleep on the bed, her hips still rising and falling gently as if she were milking the last droplets of sperm from a lover's cock. He threw the towel with which he was drying his hands and face onto a tall, almost throne-like chair. 'Why do you do it?'

She ignored his question and continued her movements. Justin sat on the edge of the bed, and took a jar of cream from the bedside cabinet. It contained a soothing balm, which he applied to her throbbing wounds. 'Is it the pain?'

She nodded. 'It's the pain.' After a moment she added, 'but not just the pain.'

'Then what?' he asked. 'What makes you put yourself through that?'

The girl reached out for a bottle of vodka, realised it was out of reach and snapped her fingers and pointed for Justin to get it. He poured a large measure onto several ice cubes, added some tonic, and dropped in a slice of lime. She took it from him and quenched the thirst the beating had induced.

'You should know,' she answered. She took another drink, waved away his hand and turned over to sit up. The balm had not taken away all the sting, and the pretty girl winced when her tender bottom pressed into the bedclothes. 'Don't you remember my first night at Camelot, after you'd shaved me?'

Justin looked down to see her sex, which she still kept smooth. Two tigers rampant guarded the exclamation mark that was her vagina, one facing the other on either side of her lips. Justin still remembered David's rendering of Blake's poem as he tattooed her bare mound. 'Tiger, Tiger, burning bright,' he had recited, and all the time the hum of the pneumatic tattooing pump accompanied his words.

'I remember,' he said. 'I was very nervous.'

Sabrina laughed. 'You were nervous? I was stripped in front of two men I didn't know. I was shaved, and I was beaten. It was so humiliating.' She looked down ruefully at her quim. 'You even tattooed my cunt.'

'I didn't,' said Justin defensively. 'David did the tattooing.'

'And you let him,' she countered forcefully.

Justin resented the way Sabrina spoke to him. After all, without him David would have finished her training and she would now be living in Rawalpindi, married to Sunil. Since he had rescued her she'd grown very confident, so much so, she was becoming arrogant and bossy. Nonetheless, he knew she liked the humiliation as much as the pain, and that's why he asked her why she liked being caned.

'From the first stroke of that sjambok,' Sabrina whispered, 'I was hooked. The humiliation of being naked and caned. The way I had no choice but to suck David's cock.'

'I knew you liked it,' said Justin. 'The first time I rubbed the cooling cream into your bottom I noticed you shiver with pleasure.'

The girl shuffled off the bed and jiggled to the bathroom. At the door she bent over, grabbed her ankles and peered at Justin between her legs. He marvelled at her lithe body.

'I never thought I could feel so good,' she said. 'Whether I'm giving it or taking it, I just fucking love it.' With her head still between her legs she blew him a kiss, then stood up straight and carried on into the bathroom where she squatted on the toilet to piss.

Justin was rummaging through his wardrobe when a knock came at the door. Despite the naked Sabrina being clearly visible in the bathroom he called for whomever it was to enter. A young waiter came in carrying two breakfasts on a silver tray, and without being directed he placed it on a table by the large window that looked out over Mandelstam Square.

Sabrina trotted out and snatched a piece of toast, looked down on a fur-clad queue outside a butcher's shop, and turned to the waiter, uncaring of her naked state. 'Do you know where we can find amber to buy?' she asked.

If the waiter enjoyed the sight of the naked girl he didn't show it. 'Amber?' he asked.

'Yes, amber,' Sabrina replied curtly. 'You know, precious stones, Baltic gold, that sort of thing.'

'This is not the Baltic, madam. This is the Barents Sea.'

'Spare me the geography lesson. Is there a place here that sells amber?'

This time the waiter took a long look at Sabrina's body in an attempt to embarrass her for the way she had spoken to him. He allowed his eyes to dwell between her legs for several seconds, but his efforts failed and after a pause he answered her question. 'There is a *Gorky's Trading Post* near the port. You can catch the tram. It will take you there.'

Sabrina dropped the toast and picked up a pair of knickers to put on. The waiter left.

'What now?' asked Justin.

Gorky's Trading Post leant lazily against its neighbours in a rundown street heading to the main port. It possessed a window on either side of the entrance, but if they were intended to offer a tantalising glimpse of the goods inside then an occasional clean was desperately in order. Even the snow that gathered in the corners of the frames was covered in the inescapable grime of the industrial town.

Justin pushed at the door and he and Sabrina entered into a large dimly lit shop. Its main function was as a chandler and the whole interior – walls, floors and shelves – were laden with goods required by the northern seafarers. The pair ambled amongst the ropes, oars and electronic gadgetry searching for signs that David had been in to trade.

'Nothing,' said Justin, 'just bits for boats. I reckon he must have gone south, maybe Moscow. After all, that's where you saw the amber jewellery.'

'That's just where it ended up. It's probably on sale all over the place. But that man in the store knew it came from the north.'

'So what?' Justin put in. 'How do you know it was from him?'

Sabrina pulled the bag off her shoulder, opened the zipper and pulled out the largest piece of amber Justin had ever seen. Light seemed to glow from inside it, sending golden rays against the dim walls. It wasn't just a bulb or cut into a diamond shape; it was worked into the most intricate design and one that Justin recognised instantly; it was two rampant tigers. A perfect facsimile of the two animals Justin had watched his friend tattoo on Sabrina's shaven sex.

'Where did you get that?' he asked.

'Beautiful, isn't it?' She held it up to an oil lamp and admired the swirl of light as the precious stone bent and twisted the soft flame. As her gaze narrowed she smiled faintly and added, 'and accurate.'

Justin repeated his question, disturbed and a little angry that she hadn't confided in him.

'I bought it in GUM's. The moment I saw it my heart missed a beat. I knew David had made it; it's so obvious; as clear as the stone itself. He might as well have left his photograph with the price tag.'

Still put out Justin added, 'So where was I? Why didn't you tell me?'

'Sorry?' she bit back. 'And there is some rule written somewhere which says I have to tell you anything? Some rule I don't know about?'

Justin backed down and said no more.

'I thought not.' She looked into his eyes. 'Not when I make the rules.'

An uncomfortable silence descended, to be broken by Andrei Gorky, the proprietor. 'So, you have the tigers,' he smiled. 'I never thought I would see them again. May I?' He took the golden sculpture and held it up. 'It is so beautiful I could have sold it a thousand times over, but he would only make the one—'

'Who would?' interrupted Sabrina.

Andrei handed back the tigers and threw back a tarpaulin that hung against one wall. It revealed another room stuffed to the rafters with furs, ivories and jewels.

Sabrina entered the Aladdin's cave and ran her hands over a Siberian tiger pelt, while Justin let out a long appreciative whistle. '*Jesus*,' he said. 'Where did all this stuff come from?'

'It's a trading post,' grinned Andrei. 'You work it out.'

Sabrina was rubbing her face into the albino tiger fur looking very pleased with herself. She felt her prey was within her grasp; sooner rather than later David Harper would again be shackled at the end of a leash. 'Who sells the amber?' she asked.

The Russian walked across to a glass cabinet that contained a large display of the golden stones. 'I don't have just one supplier,' he said. 'But I know the man you are talking about.' He picked up a large piece of red amber shaped like a pineapple. 'He supplies me with the best amber I have seen.' He held out the piece for them to admire.

'David, is that his name?' asked Sabrina.

'Yes it is,' said Andrei, surprised. 'Do you know him?'

'We're old friends who lost touch. That's why we're trying to track him down.'

Andrei laughed. 'I hope you are not going to buy his amber. That's my biggest earner.'

'It's not the amber,' put in Justin. 'We want him.'

Sabrina quickly added that they wanted just to see him – to renew old friendships.

'Then I can't help you,' said Andrei.

'We can pay.'

Andrei replaced the pineapple piece. 'I am sure you can, but I simply don't know where he lives.'

'Then how do you do business?' asked Sabrina.

'Whenever he is in town he comes to see me. Otherwise…' he shrugged his shoulders.

'Otherwise what?' Sabrina's short temper was beginning to reveal itself.

'Otherwise, I guess he must be in his place near Lake Inan.'

'Lake Inan?' asked Justin. 'Where's that?'

'Isn't this amber lovely?' said Andrei.

Sabrina recognised his game. 'That's a nice piece,' she said. 'How much is it?'

'In dollars? Two hundred.' He pointed further back in the cabinet and added, 'but that one is an even better piece. Less flaws.'

'How much?'

'Three hundred.'

Justin took Sabrina by the arm and took her aside. 'We've found out what we want to know. He's around that lake he said – Lake Inan.'

'This isn't sunny Derbyshire,' said Sabrina sharply. 'They've got lakes the size of Britain, let alone Derbyshire. What do you expect us to do, walk around the lake in an afternoon looking for him?' She turned back to the Russian. 'That is a nice stone. I think I will buy it after all.'

The exchange was made, and as Andrei handed over the jewel he added, 'maybe you want to find your friend more then I realised.'

'I've paid the money,' said Sabrina.

'And you have the stone.'

Sabrina sighed. 'What more do you want?'

The Russian looked her up and down but said nothing, until Sabrina opened her fur coat, rested her hands on her hips and pushed her breasts forward. Andrei moved to stand squarely in front of her, a hand rose and rested gently on her left breast, his breathing becoming heavy and laboured. 'Amber is so cold and hard to the touch,' he rasped, and then squeezed the soft flesh of her breast hard enough to make her flinch with the pain. 'Flesh is much softer and warmer.'

'Now wait a minute,' warned Justin. 'What the hell do you think—?'

'Quiet,' ordered Sabrina, the discomfort in her breast stirring up familiar urges. 'Andrei and I have things to discuss. Wait outside.'

'I know *exactly* what he wants,' said Justin. 'And he probably doesn't even know where David is.'

Andrei's gaze remained firmly fixed on Sabrina's eyes, but he spoke to Justin. 'You can stay if you want, but you won't put me off this bitch. She needs a good leathering.'

'Get your hand—'

'*Out!*' shouted Sabrina. 'You can wait behind the curtain.'

As Justin, sulking, made his way out of the alcove Andrei called after him, and with a sarcastic tone said he could look after the shop while he was busy.

The curtain dropped, leaving a small gap that Justin felt compelled to peer through. Sabrina's brown suede skirt was already removed and hung from the antlers of a stuffed reindeer, and she was still stood with hands on hips, golden thighs stretching up from knee length boots. A tiny triangle of white knickers covered what

Justin had no doubt, was a sodden sex. Above her briefs a small area of flat tummy was visible before it disappeared beneath a fluffy white mohair top.

Andrei hooked a finger into the top of the cotton knickers and pulled the material out an inch or two, then leant forward slightly and peered inside the girl's underwear. 'Oh,' he said, smiling at her tattoo. 'I see you know David very well indeed.'

'Much better then you could imagine,' she answered.

Andrei stepped back and motioned for Sabrina to remove her coat. She did as he instructed before striking the same pose for him to enjoy, and behind the curtain Justin's breathing matched the rasp of the man about to have sex with his partner.

'Bend over.' Sabrina stretched down to display her firm buttocks, bisected as they were by the tiny strip of her G-string. Andrei yanked the material down her thighs, where it tangled into a knot just above her knees, and Sabrina's prominent sex lips protruded in all their glory. As he marvelled at the girl's body the gruff middle-aged Russian began to undress. He wore no underclothes and his big gnarled prick jumped into view the moment he unzipped his trousers. He took the angry member in his hand and lowered it in line with Sabrina's glistening sex, and she felt the bulb of his cock nudge it's way between her labia. Her moistened cunt offered little resistance to his invading length, her lips widening and contracting as his swollen glans slid into her entrance and began its journey along her sheath. His first thrust threatened to unbalance them as his attempts to steady himself between her legs were blocked by her panties, holding her knees together, but Andrei solved the problem by stretching down and tearing the material in two.

'Over the pelts,' he ordered.

Sabrina shuffled forward, never once allowing his

cock to slip from her vagina. She took her position on the tiger skins and prepared for the onslaught. Andrei didn't keep her waiting. Almost immediately he thrust his bulging, throbbing prick, forcing the girl to yelp with pleasure. Justin could see quite clearly that Andrei had embedded his full length inside her, on her knees with her head resting on the furs. The Russian continued to fuck the girl, stopping only to pull up her jumper and unclip her bra. Once her breasts were free Andrei returned to his heavy thrusts while he milked her, his large rough hands squeezing and pulling at the soft orbs. The aggression sent shockwaves through Sabrina's body and she responded by pushing her hips onto his penis, forcing his heavy rod deeper. His pounding became evermore violent and in his frenzy Andrei snatched up a coil of rope and began beating the girl along her back. The hairy hemp tormented her skin, bringing to it a reddish glow that excited the Russian even further.

Even though Justin had administered numerous beatings to Sabrina he had never seen her endure such a thrashing. Nonetheless, he remained rooted to his position near the curtain, part of him wanting to intervene but another part knowing only too well how angry she would be if he interrupted her pleasure. And another part recognised that he was also excited by the vision of sex that was taking place just ten feet away, and his penis was swelling accordingly. He pulled back the curtain a little further to afford a better view, in time to see Sabrina collapse in orgasmic exhaustion. She lay face down, her legs bent at the knees and swaying with satisfaction. Andrei was already pulling on his dirty work trousers, his prick half bloated and glistening from the juice Sabrina had released.

Andrei looked up and saw Justin spying on them.

He pulled up his zip, laughed loudly in Justin's direction, and left the secret storeroom. As he passed Justin he said nonchalantly, 'I think she needs cleaning up.'

Justin watched the Russian return to the counter, where he took some towels from a shelf and threw them in his direction. Justin picked them up and took them to her. She didn't register his presence, but remained motionless on the furs. Andrei returned and dropped a note in front of Sabrina, who read it through half-closed eyes. When she had taken in the words she turned over and sat up, reached out and picked up her tattered knickers, then shook her head and threw them to one side.

'Fetch my skirt,' she said to Justin, firmly.

Andrei added in forced upper-class tones, 'There's a good chap, what.'

Justin ignored his jibes and gathered up Sabrina's clothes. 'Where is this Ivalo?' she asked. 'Is it near Lake Inan?'

'It is in Finland,' answered Andrei. 'But there is no trouble getting in and out of the country there. David lives with the Saami.'

'The who?' asked Justin.

'The Saami. You probably know them as Lapps.'

'What's he doing with them?'

Andrei smiled at his question. 'Well, I used to think he was trading with them and living the life he wanted. Now, maybe, I think he might be hiding from you two.'

'That is rubbish,' Justin blustered. 'We just want to—'

'Shut up,' ordered Sabrina. 'He's not stupid.' She turned to the brutish man. 'Finland's a big country. Where exactly is Ivalo?'

Andrei guided them to a large map of the area that hung on a wall. 'Like I have already said, it is south of lake Inan, between Inari and the river Lotta. The Saami come and go across the borders. No one stops them. They follow the herds.'

'Well how do we get there?' asked Sabrina.

'You have to live like the Saami, or you will arouse the suspicion of the authorities. There is a road that takes you right to Ivalo, but there are guards at the crossing of the river. You have Russian visas?'

'Yes,' said Sabrina. 'But they don't allow us to leave and re-enter the country.'

'Then you must avoid the guards. Do you have money?'

'Some. What will we need for the journey?'

Andrei busied himself supplying all their requirements for the journey, including food, a tent, a Kalashnikov rifle and a ski sled that he agreed to store for them until they left. Justin weighed the rifle carefully in his hands and turned to Sabrina with a concerned expression, and then the young woman pulled back the firing bar and checked the chamber for debris. It was shining and clean.

'What are you doing?' asked Justin.

'A man's job,' she replied, and then gestured to the fat Russian for ammunition. 'And I'll take that bandoleer.'

'We're not starting some war,' groaned Justin. 'Let's forget David and go home. We make more money supplying the girls, anyway. Why go through all this for someone who doesn't even want to come back to Britain?'

Sabrina forced a single shining brass cartridge into the magazine, and then assembled the weapon with the satisfying snap of precision steel. She pointed the AK47 towards Justin, and without expression made the statement that she was not used to being fucked around with; especially by a man. There was a deafening crack and Justin felt the whoosh of air as the bullet passed by his ear and made a small hole in the head of a stuffed polar bear. Before anyone had time to react Sabrina rolled the rifle in an oilskin, dropped a wad of roubles on the counter and was nearing the door, and then a huge roar of laughter from Andrei broke the stunned silence. He scooped up the mound of notes and thumbed through them.

'Come again!' he bellowed. 'If only all my customers were like you; I'd be a rich man.' As Justin disappeared after his partner into the fading light of a Murmansk evening, a flurry of snowflakes hurried into the shop. Andrei watched the ice turn to water and returned his attention to the wad of money. 'Perhaps then,' he grumbled, 'I can get out of this freezing godforsaken town and move to the Black Sea.'

Chapter Three

Daylight had never really arrived, just a grainy twilight that failed even to reflect off the powdery snow that David and the girls were travelling across. The sled had a bright headlamp, but its powerful beam seemed to break up somewhere out in the gloom. It would soon be dark and travelling through the thick forest would become increasingly dangerous. They were still a day out from Murmansk and they needed to make camp.

David brought the sled to a halt and surveyed the area. To the east were the baroque fjords of Norway's northern coastline, while the vast Karelian forest lay to the south. David had been forced north to avoid the Russian border guards at Nikel. He had learned early on that while the Saami could come and go, his features picked him out easily, and the guards invariably took half his trade in order to turn a blind eye. He had also learned something else, though. Along this unforgiving coast was a wreck of some Second World War battleship, a tank, and heavy artillery carrier that lay stranded on the beach.

He edged the sled slowly forward searching for the ship, the darkness closing quickly. For a while he wondered if the Arctic weather had finally broken the iron hulk to pieces, but it came into view; a huge black mass of tangled metal. The freezing temperatures had preserved the ship well. Rust, the great enemy of all man's machines, had but a few months, sometimes only weeks during the summer when it could attack the vessel.

Happy that he would not be forced to pitch camp in the woods, where wolves and bears could quickly pick up the scent of easy human prey, David accelerated his sled towards the ship. The bow of the vessel, which had once unloaded tanks, lay open and he drove his vehicle straight into the belly of the ship. It looked like Jonah entering the whale as the lamp from the sled disappeared into the once great metal beast.

David dismounted, took up his rifle and motioned for the girls to carry the provisions, then covered the sled with a protective insulation blanket. Light had now all but given way to the inky blackness of an Arctic night. David thrust his hand into the sack over Teena's back, pulled out a flare and set it aflame. The green phosphor hissed and crackled an angry, extremely bright light.

As the three sole occupants of the ship made their way up steps and along corridors three eerie shadows followed. Eventually David came to the door for which he was searching. It was mahogany panelled, although the veneer that still held some polish hid a heavy steel door behind. A copper plate that had turned green stated simply, *Captain*. David leant his shoulder against it, and the door swung open surprisingly easily.

It wasn't a big cabin, though it clearly reflected the distance between captain and rating. The walls were panelled and a heavy leather chair squatted behind a large desk suitable for the reading of maps. There were none on there now. Not because they had been destroyed or removed after the ship had been crippled – they hadn't – but because David had collected them on his very first visit, along with jewellery and other artefacts of the long dead sailors. He sold them all at Gorky's trading post and Andrei had given him a good price. There was time later, David thought, for more treasure hunting, but his first concern was to light a fire and eat. The girls had already begun filling the stove; evidently the ship still had ample supplies of coal onboard when the steel tip of a torpedo had struck her propeller and she was run aground and abandoned.

The satisfying crackle of wood assured the three that the fire was underway, and David was able to light some candles before the flare gave a final desperate flicker and went out. Through the porthole a single shooting star scratched its path across the sky, and all was silent until David heard the sound of liquid tumbling into his cup. He turned to see Mishka holding out his antler horn, brimming with vodka.

'Sit,' she said, and pointed to the captain's chair. David took a sip and slumped into the red leather seat. Near the stove and in the light from the candle Teena was preparing a pipe of loki for her master. While she prepared his smoke her sister threw a slab of harp seal meat on top of the stove. That was for David; the two girls had never been able to eat seal meat cooked.

The small room soon grew warm and the smell of the cooking mingled with the aroma of loki to give the atmosphere a snug and pleasant air. Warm on the outside, the vodka now did the same for his insides. Unusually for him he poured both girls a drink, and then leant back in his chair and smoked his pipe.

David ate his meal off the captain's pewter plates and washed it down with another horn of vodka, and as it was still only mid-afternoon and tiredness had not yet arrived, David tapped the desk and pushed back his chair. In a snowbound country that spent half its time in darkness there were few diversions other than sex. That was why David loved it so much. The two girls stood next to each other at the side of the desk.

'Teena,' he said, his voice breaking the silence like cracking ice. 'Up on the desk.'

She began to obey him immediately, but he stopped her with another order. 'Strip first.'

Teena looked back, unsure of the language until her older sister tugged at her furs and the words registered. With Mishka's help Teena removed her thick silver fox fur trousers and cape. David admired her firm young body adorned with a lattice of leather straps, silver buckles and amber jewellery. When he had satisfied his eyes he motioned with his head to the desk, and Teena compliantly climbed on it on hands and knees.

He turned to Mishka. 'Cunt,' he declared. 'Lick.'

The girl bent forward and dipped her tongue into her sister's vulva, while David took out his prick and stroked it. He timed his movements to coincide with Teena's swinging breasts and was occasionally forced to press his thumb down hard onto his piss hole to prevent himself firing too early, and when his orgasm came too close for comfort he released his prick and leant over to fetch something from his bag.

It was a brass telescope he had salvaged from the wreck on a previous visit. Out here it was an important piece of kit, so David refused to trade it. Along with its magnifying properties it had other uses. Mishka took it off him and knew instinctively what to do, and Teena knew exactly where it was going. The young Lapp parted her knees and her vagina spread accordingly. The cold metal touched the girl's bottom and she withdrew automatically. David pointed towards his mouth, gesturing for Mishka to warm the metal. The girl sucked the instrument like it was a lover's cock, before again trying to insert it inside her sister. This time her bottom didn't flinch and her softening vagina was more accommodating. Mishka pushed in the fat objective lens end, stretching Teena's hole so it could accept the main tube towards the eyepiece. After around six inches had become embedded she looked to David for instructions, so he gripped his cock again and nodded, and at once the Lapp girl began grinding the telescope in and out of her sister. It wasn't a matter of degrading her, for both girls had long since passed the stage of sexual embarrassment. She wanted sex and her sister's actions on the desk indicated she was of the same mind.

This time David measured his strokes, pacing them against Mishka's pumping arm. Teena lifted her head from its submissive low position and looked at him. She was already in the throes of a forthcoming orgasm and grimaced with pleasure.

'Stop,' said David. 'Mishka, strip.'

The older Lapp girl had learned far more English than her sister, and obeyed. Now both girls were wearing nothing but leather, silver and amber. David took Teena by the arm and guided her down from the desk, only to have her bend over it. He took Mishka a step or two away and forced her to bend forward so that both girls now had their bottom's facing each other. He judged the distance almost to perfection, because when he extended the telescope by pulling on the eyepiece, it reached to within an inch or two of Mishka's taut rear.

He returned to his chair and pointed at the older sister, who then reached behind to grasp the now warm brass tube. She held it firmly and slowly shuffled backwards, until she too was impaled upon it. David gave the signal for the two to start fucking, and in perfect synchronism the girls began moving towards each other, stopping only when they were filled, at which point about four inches of brass connected their cunts. David returned to his cock and massaged himself to a full erection while the girls continued their rude display. Teena, who had been close to an orgasm only moments before, released a flow of juice that smeared along the telescope, and the sight of her rapture almost pushed him over the edge.

He stood up and pulled the telescope from Teena's sex and ordered her onto the desk with knees pulled up and apart. The girl's excitement was evident as she continually clenched her vagina, almost as if trying to ensnare any cock that dared come too close. David watched her, and pressed her sister's head down.

Mishka licked the moment she was faced with her younger sister's slick sex. Behind her he closed the telescope but left it deep inside Mishka, and looked at the glorious sight in front of him; Mishka's unblemished back, her glorious black hair tumbling over her face onto her sister's thighs.

'No wonder they call you Lapps,' he said, but the girls didn't respond until Mishka felt his rigid manhood push past her tight sphincter. It complemented the metal in her vagina and she welcomed the extra squeeze, and when David emptied his balls inside her warm arse she had already beaten him by two orgasms, and the sensation of the hot spurting fluid inside her bottom took her to another.

All three required further sustenance to replace the energy lost during sex, so David pulled out three strips of deer jerky from his rucksack. Being freeze-dried it was the Arctic equivalent of the sun-dried favourite of American westerns. It was chewy and rather tasteless, but along with the vodka it refuelled the body.

Once revitalised David motioned for the girls to follow him, and made for the door and a search of the ship. Tomorrow he would be in Murmansk and anything more he could find to trade would give him more money for the needs of next winter.

The ship was in total darkness, and David took up a

length of wood dipped in pitch and set it on fire to act as a torch. He then led the girls down into the bowels of the ship. As the three descended Mishka clung tightly to her sister and both girls stayed close to their master. After three flights of stairs they had travelled lower than David had ventured on any of his previous visits. The temperature plummeted and the sound of slushy iced water slopping lazily against the ship's side informed them that they were below the water level.

Carefully they made their way between bulkheads, and the dancing light of the torch illuminated increasing signs of damage. Pieces of twisted metal occasionally blocked their path, and they had to bend down to pass some ducting that had fallen from the deckhead during the ship's battle for survival. David tried to force some of the hatches, but they were stuck firm. One particular hatch was buckled, and though it would not budge there were some gaps around its edges. He handed the torch to Teena and she held it above his head while he peered through the opening.

The light gave tantalising glimpses of utter carnage. The chamber had been hit badly during the fighting, and there was little salvage to be expected from it. They moved on, surprised to find that the corridor appeared to be rising. It finally terminated in a heavy metal hatch built into the bulkhead. David pushed against it, but it would not budge.

He stepped back to study it. It looked undamaged; there was no buckling, no twisted hinges. It was then that he noticed a faint sign near the locking wheel in the hatch's centre. Fifty odd years ago it would have been bright red, now it was a faded brown. Written across it in white capitals was the word: LOCKED.

He kicked at the heavy catch until the metal bolt gave way and a green sign moved in front of the other one: UNLOCKED.

While David turned the wheel to open the hatch the girls huddled nervously together. Without having to push at all it suddenly swung open and a great gush of icy wind rushed past them. The initial scare over, the three peered out of the back of the ship into a clear sky. A hole the size of a bus had been ripped out of the stern and freezing water had poured in, pulling the ship backwards and down, hence the captain's dash for the shore and his hurried unloading of his cargo. A pool had gathered, rising to within a few feet of the bulkhead, which had been sealed to prevent water flooding the lower decks and sinking the ship.

'That's why the door had been locked,' he laughed. 'I'd thought it was going to be full of gold being shipped out of the country, and it's full of fucking water.' He pointed to the hatch with the torch, but as the girls made to leave both let out a piercing scream.

'What is it?' shouted David. 'What's the matter?'

The girls pointed in unison into the semi-darkness. David turned around, half expecting a bear to be looming over him, but there was nothing.

'On floor,' said Mishka.

Sticking out of the water was a leather boot, and David let out a sigh of relief. 'Fucking hell,' he said to the girls. 'Don't do that. You had me really scared too. It's just a boot – look.' He leant down and pulled at it, but was surprised by its weight. He tugged harder and the body of a man rose slowly from beneath the icy, turbid water. David jumped back and this time let out a gasp before quickly calming down, then again passed the torch to Mishka and proceeded to pull the body from its watery grave.

'Poor bastard,' he muttered. 'They locked you in to save the ship. What a way to go.' He heaved harder and managed to pull the entire body out of the water.

As he gripped the man's trousers his fingers stung with the intense cold, and although the body was slightly bloated it was remarkably preserved. No doubt a consequence of the refrigerator-like conditions. It wasn't touched by fish or other creatures, because the torpedo had weakened the keel and when the ship struck the beach the stern concertinaed into the rest of the vessel and lifted above the waterline.

Once he had him out of the water, David didn't know what to do with him. Until, that was, he saw the gold rings on the man's fingers, and while he stripped the one hand he motioned for Teena to do the same with other. Initially the girl balked, but David spoke firmly. 'Just do it,' he ordered, and there was anger in his eyes at the girl's initial defiance.

The two stripped the body of its jewellery, including a heavy gold necklace with a St Christopher pendant hanging from it. David weighed the charm in his hand, recognising the patron saint of travellers, smiled at the irony, and pocketed it along with the other trinkets.

The body slipped back into the water and David snatched the torch back from Mishka. Waving it above his head he searched the water for more bodies. There were three more, but one of them was stuck beneath some machinery and out of reach. David wedged the torch into the hatch wheel and the three set about their work in the glare of the flame. They stripped the cadavers of any valuables in a frozen version of Dante's Inferno; the girls looking on in horror as David drew his knife and dislodged three gold teeth from the body of one, before releasing it back to its colleagues.

When they left the girls insisted that David lock the bulkhead to stop the men walking the ship in search of their jewellery, and he smiled at them.

'Don't worry,' he reassured. 'You're safe with me.'

The girls didn't understand all the words, but they knew from what they had seen that their master was more than capable of anything.

Back in the captain's cabin the girls curled up in front of the fire while David broke open another bottle of vodka. He watched the light dance across the girls' naked bodies, and settled back in the chair, his feet upon the desk. He fought sleep as he did most nights, and instead of resting and running the danger of slipping into another nightmare, he carried his gaze out of the porthole. The aurora borealis endeavoured to entertain him, at least until he could stay awake no more.

Chapter Four

In room eleven Sabrina was pulling on a tiny pair of black knickers. The lace on the front was so fine that the material appeared almost transparent. The small V of intricate lace gathered under her vagina to reappear as a strap that ran between the cheeks of her bottom.

'Where are my stockings?' she asked.

Justin laid each black nylon out on the bed. 'I've just got them out for you,' he answered.

'And my half-cup bra?'

Justin brought that from the dressing table and fixed the clasps. Sabrina then settled onto the dressing table stool and slowly and purposely applied her make-up. Her black hair had been cut into a neat business-like bob, and glowed with shiny health. It framed perfectly her slightly rouged cheeks, cherry-red lips and sparkling eyes.

'You don't even know this man,' Justin said. 'This Captain Moscow, or whatever his name is.'

'Leskov,' corrected Sabrina. 'Captain Vasili Yaroslav Leskov. What is there to know?' She stood up and smoothed the black figure-hugging dress over her body. It accentuated her curves and made her look incredibly elegant, and then she stepped into a pair of black leather ankle boots. They had sharp heels and pointed toes and a small circle of fur that helped make them snug and warm – perfect for a freezing night in northern Russia. She turned her back towards Justin, who was sitting on the bed, and lifted her dress to reveal her stocking tops. 'Adjust me,' she instructed.

Justin began to run his hands up Sabrina's leg, ensuring her stockings were not even slightly twisted. 'What do you want him for?' he asked. His fingers reached the top of her stockings and ventured further, but Sabrina slapped away his hand and smoothed down her dress. She picked up a thin cane that lay on the dressing table, and pressed the tip to his lips.

'Because, Justin, my naïve little bear. He is not just any old army officer. He is a captain at Severomorsk.'

'So what?' said Justin, through the thin cane. He hated the dismissive way she sometimes spoke to him.

'I will tell you what that means. If he is at Severomorsk then he must be a captain in the Russian North Fleet, and that means he can get hold of arctic equipment; snowmobiles, perhaps helicopters. That should cut our search for David down a bit.' She poked the tip into the centre of his forehead and pushed him backwards onto the bed.

'So what do you expect me to do while you're gone?'

Sabrina whipped the cane down onto Justin's penis, forcing him to double up as the sharp pain bit into him. 'I expect you to fiddle with your limp penis.' She threw the cane by the side of him and pulled on an ankle length coat with fur collar and cuffs. Lifting up the collar she added, 'That's what all you Englishman do, isn't it; play with your soft dicks? They're not much use for anything else.' With that she spun around, her coat rising like a Dervish's skirt, and left.

Justin sat up and rubbed the pain from his penis, muttering, 'David didn't have a limp prick, and that's why you can't stand him being free. I hope he fucks you up the arse!'

Vasili was waiting at the bar when Sabrina entered the hotel lounge. He registered her presence by lifting a glass and flashing a smile in her direction, then he downed the drink in one, slammed the small glass on the bar and waved her over.

Sabrina glided to him, her coat trailing behind like the black wings of a Mig fighter to reveal her knee length dress and stockinged legs. At the bar, circles of vapour spiralled above two shots of freezing vodka. Sabrina rested her hand on his arm and said hello, and the two picked up their glass and downed the alcohol.

'You look beautiful,' said Vasili. 'You are a creation of Nikolay Rerickh certainly; a study of the mystic east.'

'Thank you,' purred Sabrina. She called over the bartender and pointed for two more vodkas, and when they arrived she picked up her glass as if to toast him. 'And you are a very handsome man. That uniform makes you look so strong and powerful. Are you?'

Vasili returned her salute. 'All Russians must be strong. We have many enemies who wait to see us fall. But we have a gentler side, a great culture, men and women renown throughout the world.'

Sabrina sipped her drink. 'Which side are you going to show me?'

Vasili smiled broadly. 'My gentle side, of course. I have much planned.' He knocked back his drink and Sabrina did the same.

'Where are you taking me?'

'I have a car waiting... come,' said the Russian.

Sabrina downed the last of her vodka and followed him. Outside a huge square-jawed soldier stood by a long black limousine. She let out a girlish giggle. 'For us?'

'Compliments of the motherland; a woman of your beauty should walk nowhere.'

The soldier opened a door for her and she slipped into the rear of the car, her exposed leg, elegant and perfectly shaped in its stocking sheath, not missed by the soldier or Leskov.

Vasili issued abrupt instructions to his driver in his native tongue, and Sabrina noted how the Russian voice always sounded as if it was issuing orders. It was commanding and strong.

'Where are you taking me?' she asked, sinking into the soft leather, revelling in the familiar smell of animal hide.

'The theatre,' Vasili answered. He pulled on a polished handle attached to a walnut panel and a small cabinet unfolded to reveal a selection of drinks and fine crystal glasses. 'There is plenty of time. Let us see the city.'

The car pulled off and the two sidled closer to each other. Their glasses chinked together and Sabrina glanced out of the car. Streetlamps and lights from houses and shops seemed to parade past. Many people pointed at them, taking an interest in the unusually long car. Some noticed the small military flag flapping from a chrome pole on the bonnet while others, those with knowledge of what the car meant, turned away and melted into doorways. The reaction wasn't lost on Sabrina; she was in the company of a powerful man, and she liked all things powerful. The sound of a bottle refilling her glass returned her attention to her companion.

'What are we going to see?' she asked.

'Chekov,' said Vasili. 'What else?'

'Where is your woman?' asked the bartender in the lounge of the Romanov. Justin gave him a sneer and picked up his drink, and on the way to a secluded alcove he began grinding his teeth. He only did that when anxious, but noticed he was doing it evermore often. He flopped into a club chair and stared out of the window. Mandelstam Square was deserted except for an occasional person scurrying through the snow as it flurried and gathered here and there in the darkness. He bit into his drink, swallowing the liquid through gritted teeth, and the moment his glass landed on the table the barman was there.

'Another vodka?' He already had a glass in his hand, and he replaced the spent glass with one already charged.

'Keep them coming,' said Justin. He thanked God that Russians drank vodka like the British drank tea, and renewed his thanks that Russian vodka was cheaper than India's favourite infusion. Suddenly there was a loud thud and Justin looked up to see the barman leave a full bottle on his table.

'A man who drinks on his own drinks fast,' said the barman.

Justin reached out immediately and took up the bottle.

'You are alone?'

For a moment Justin thought it was Sabrina, such was the resemblance, but once he had recovered his senses he stammered in the affirmative and the girl sat without being asked.

'You are English?'

'I am English,' said Justin, and then in his mind he added, *and you are about to rip me off*.

'Do you see the sights?'

Justin looked out of the window at the deserted square. 'Yes,' he said with a sigh. 'I see the sights.'

'I am Catherine,' she smiled.

'And you look great,' added Justin.

The girl looked confused. 'Pardon me?'

Justin shook himself out of his torpor. 'No, I'm sorry. I was just being flippant. Would you like a drink?'

Catherine smiled and poured herself a large vodka before Justin had time to reach out and do the honours. 'So,' she beamed, 'what are you doing in Russia?' Her body language had suddenly become animated since the offer of a drink.

'I'm a tourist,' Justin answered. 'Travelling in your country.'

Catherine laughed. 'Tourist,' she grinned. 'No you are not!'

He panicked. 'Why do you say that?'

'Who comes to Murmansk to see the sights? It is rubbish, one big factory, choking trees, smoke, everything is choking. Tourist, it is shit. Is that what you say? Yes, I think it is. Shit, yes?'

Justin started laughing. Her whole manner was open and honest. 'Yes,' he told her. 'I am no tourist.'

'Then what?'

He thought a moment then leaned forward and whispered, 'I am a snow collector.'

Catherine leant back in her chair with a puzzled expression. 'For why?'

He rummaged for a witty answer, but one eluded him. 'Because...' he said slowly '...because in England we have a shortage of snow.' He poured yet another large shot into each glass. 'And everyone in England loves snow at Christmas. Snow in churchyards with red robins on gravediggers' spades. Snow on Christmas trees with candles burning bright.'

Catherine grabbed him by the arm in earnest. 'If you like snow, I show you snow.' She pulled him up and for the first time Justin realised that she was very tall. She was also very beautiful, just like Sabrina.

'Come,' she laughed, her voice loud enough to attract attention, 'let us get some snow. You have money?'

'Yes,' he said, nodding. 'I have some. Not much.'

'This is Russia,' laughed Catherine. 'You do not need

much if you know where to spend it.'

Justin lost all inhibitions, grabbed his coat and bottle of vodka and raced after her. Near the door he looked to the barman and shouted, 'Hey, Boris…' he didn't know the man's real name, but when he looked he pointed at his bottle, 'charge it to room eleven!' and with that Catherine lunged out into the darkness, so he followed.

The girl was already fifty yards away, running and laughing, oblivious to the snow that had turned heavy and was scraping her face with icy nails. Justin raced after her, following the footsteps her leather boots left in the crisp white carpet that paved the streets.

'Where are we going?' cried Justin.

The girl took a right turn and disappeared around the corner. Justin followed, and had travelled a little way when he realised there were no more footprints. He stopped and surveyed the street. The only character he saw was a statue of Anatoly Bredov.

He retraced his steps, feeling deflated. The girl had excited him and offered an opportunity for fun away from Sabrina. She also hinted at danger in the way she suddenly took off after asking him so many questions. He trudged his way back, then saw two sets of prints, his and Catherine's. It was as if she had vanished into the eerie silence of a Murmansk night.

'Hey, English.' It was her. She was standing on some basement steps with a naughty grin on her face. 'You are looking for someone?'

Justin walked across and peered over the rails. 'What are you doing?'

'I want to dance,' she said. 'You come. We can dance together.'

Justin ventured to the bottom of the basement steps and stopped at a large black door. 'What is this place?'

As if in answer the door opened and a blast of heat

followed. A man in a long coat stumbled out, supported by a girl with long blonde hair. She pulled the man to his feet and smiled at Justin and Catherine, before helping her companion to climb the steps.

Justin gazed into the building. Everything inside was dark except for hotspots that were illuminated by dull red lights hanging from the ceiling. Catherine tugged his arm and he found himself being taken inside, where his first reaction was to notice the smell. There was a strong odour of leather mingled with sweat and the unmistakable scent of sexual excitement.

Catherine joined the throng of writhing, dancing people. Her ankle length coat was swirling as she twisted and turned, and Justin saw that above her leather boots she wore only a leather miniskirt and a cropped leopard print bustier that revealed her midriff. As the dance floor thumped to the beat of some northern Russian rock Catherine moved further into the crowd until he lost sight of her.

Aware that he stood conspicuously alone, he pushed his way through the crowd and headed for the bar. By paying for his drink in dollars he secured prompt service whenever his glass required a refill, but Justin was more concerned with the whereabouts of his new companion than the vodka the barman kept throwing at him.

Occasionally he caught glimpses of Catherine as she appeared at his side of the dance floor, but before he could attract her attention she melted back into the mass. He soon realised however, that she was a popular girl. Different men would drape themselves over her but she danced on, impervious to their attention.

When he lost sight of her for the last time Justin decided to check the place over. The cellar, for that was the best way of describing it, was crowded with people and for a moment he pondered how they had all arrived there. Since he had been in Murmansk the largest number of people he had seen was at a bus stop, and they numbered about four. Here there were hundreds of revellers all in various states of abandonment. They were mostly young, but there were a number of older men present who seemed more intent on viewing the spectacle than being part of it.

One man in his late fifties sat at a table in a dimly lit booth. Sat with him were three cronies. Occasionally a young man or girl would approach, speak to him and he would nod. That was the signal for one of the other men to hand over a small foil envelope. You didn't have to be a rocket scientist to guess what he was peddling.

'Enjoying?' Catherine was back.

'Sort of,' said Justin. 'What are we doing here? *Hey…*'

Catherine danced back to the floor, where she was joined by a young man who danced frantically in front of her, running his hands down to her knees and back up her body again. Catherine looked over to Justin and shouted, 'You enjoy; I will see you later,' then she grabbed the young man's head and kissed him strongly on the mouth. A mixture of anger and jealousy washed over Justin. He wondered if Catherine was a user like Sabrina, and he considered leaving, but his thoughts were sidetracked and he was pushed into an adjoining room by two couples. It was unintentional and the four grunted what seemed like an apology, and went off into the gloom.

When the door closed behind him the room fell into darkness. There were a few small ultra-violet lamps, but it was impossible to make out any features. Justin fumbled into the darkness while the muffled thud of the music trailed behind him to be replaced by whisperings in the gloom.

Justin stumbled further into the recesses of the room. Now that his eyesight had grown accustomed to the poor light he found he could make out small alcoves in the walls. Inside each he made out shadowy figures. They seemed to be climbing over each other, forming knots and grotesque shapes. Justin stumbled closer to the alcove nearest him. It was full of people; writhing, pulsating people in sexual congress. There was no shape or order to their movements, no control, no expression other than pure lust. He quickly realised there were three males and one female. She lay above a man on top of a table. His solid cock impaled her. She was on her knees leaning forwards, her breasts swinging freely above his chest. Behind her another man was pummelling her arse, his hefty pole reaming her with each thrust of his straining hips. A third man had a knee placed either side of his accomplice's head so that his balls hung down to almost touch his face, and the girl was sucking hard on the cock that was fucking her face.

Justin was immediately aroused and watched the scene intently, his cock stiffening inside his trousers, the four participants in front of him oblivious to his presence. Their only consideration was to give and receive pleasure, and Justin sensed from their urgent movements that they were obtaining their wishes. It was too dark to discern features, but he could see the silhouette of the female's breasts heaving as she lifted her body to meet the twin prongs embedded in her cunt and anus. The man lying on his back must have had more staying power than his comrades, because the others climaxed simultaneously, the man at her head slumping backwards and completely disappearing into the shadows.

Justin remained motionless. Although he had witnessed and taken part in enough crazy scenes to become indifferent to the morality of such displays, what he hadn't become accustomed to was the intense feelings such sexual scenes aroused in him. He edged forward, hoping to get a closer view, but stopped when a gaunt face leaned out of the shadows. It was the man who had just finished in the girl's bottom, and he looked furious. He spat some words and Justin prepared for the worst. Then the gaunt stranger cursed again and rose to his feet, and in response Justin stepped back a little to give himself space while he checked around the room in search of an escape route. There was little point; it was too dark and he had become disoriented by their lascivious performance.

More angry words issued from the man's mouth, accompanied by a raised hand. Amazingly he was gesturing towards the girl's rear, and although his words still sounded harsh he was now smiling, and his offer needed no translation, so Justin took up position behind the girl. He still had little idea of what she looked like, but it was no matter; his libido was fuelled and his prick required the sheath of a female.

His invading erection appeared not to disturb her; rather she spread herself to accommodate him. Her pursed and pre-oiled sphincter put up little resistance and he found the dome of his cock bullying its way into her back passage. The sensation was incredible, made all the more so by the feeling of the other man's cock still pounding in the adjacent pouch. It intensified his pleasure and evidently did the same for the girl, because she suddenly began moaning and her buttocks pushed strongly back into his groin, and the reason became evident when the man beneath them let out an anguished yell between clenched teeth and fired his sperm into her. Justin actually felt the swell in the other man's penis and was well aware that it pulsated with each furious spurt, and within moments he erupted frenziedly too.

Even before he recovered his senses the Russian who had motioned for him to mount the girl was slapping his back and shouting encouraging words. Unable to understand and answer Justin simply smiled. The man's appetite had returned and he was gesturing for Justin to pull out and stand aside, and the moment he did so the man took up the familiar position and started on the girl again.

Now replete, Justin watched the others in a detached, dispassionate manner. He noticed how the girl willingly gave her body to them. She received another face full of sperm and gratefully lapped up the laces that missed her gaping mouth. That was right, thought Justin. The girl was right; Sabrina had become bossy, arrogant, and dominant. Although she obsessed him, he wished life could return to how it was when he had rescued her from Camelot, David's training centre in England. Although David was now on the run from Sabrina, at least he was free. Justin pushed past the bucking hips of the Russian, who by now was racing to another orgasm.

He wasn't free, he recognised. Sabrina had hooked him and possessed him until he was obsessed with her.

Another couple entered the dingy backroom so Justin saw the light and headed for it. Passing back into the main room he wondered if he possessed the strength to take his manhood back from Sabrina, before she totally emasculated him.

'Hey English, where have you been?' Catherine gave him a playful pinch on the cheek. 'Have you been watching the people? Naughty boy.'

Justin moved with her towards the bar. 'Are you going to run off again?'

The girl circled him as he walked, running her hands

over his face and chest. She was flushed and glowing with perspiration, and she panted with exhaustion. 'Buy me a drink.'

'Why should I?'

'Because,' she said. 'You are an Englishman. And it is right.'

Justin gave an amused grunt.

'And,' she stepped back. 'Because you want to know what my Russian cunt looks like.' The long leather coat opened to reveal her parted legs – long leather-booted legs that vanished beneath a short leather skirt. Justin stared at her erotic pose as she sexily lifted the front of the skimpy leather. Her eyes were fixed on his, but then she didn't need to see what she was doing, just what the effect was having on him.

When the skirt was just an inch above the delicious V of where her shapely thighs met, she stopped. A delicate bulge filled the shiny black patent material, and he could just make out a tiny crease. His breathing became shallow and he watched her watching him. Her eyes never left his, even when several men walked by and took in the sight. It was like there were only two real people in the whole room; others became shadows, voices dimmed, lights faded. Justin simply wanted that cunt.

'Naughty boy.' She released the skirt and the beautifully alluring valley disappeared from sight. 'Now, buy me a drink.'

Catherine called for the drinks and the barman banged two bottles down in front of them. They were tall, elegant bottles filled with a lime-green drink that Justin assumed to be vodka. Catherine clinked her bottle to his and they drank. He was right, but then again, every drink was vodka. This though, had a remarkably fresh, sharp taste, like licking limejuice off a frozen razorblade.

'Good, yes?'

Justin nodded. 'Very good. What is it? It tastes of lemons or limes. I can never tell which is which.'

'They put vodka in a special tub. It is made from arctic pine. Then they put in some polar moss.'

'Is that what gives it the taste?'

'I suppose so,' said Catherine. 'I like to drink it because it makes me want to dance.'

Justin took another sip and smiled, and nodding towards the dance floor he added, 'I can see you like to dance.'

Catherine dipped her tongue into the long neck of the bottle. 'I prefer to fuck,' she said, and gave him that piercing stare that made him nervous. 'First I like to drink, then I like to dance, then I like to fuck. What about you?'

'I'm not too great on the dancing part.'

'You should try it. I will show you.'

Justin took a sip and raised the bottle in a negative gesture. 'It's not for me, thanks. But I enjoyed watching you. You are very good at it.'

'Well,' said Catherine, 'if you will not dance then we must get our fun elsewhere.' She picked up her bottle and headed for the mêlée that were still writhing to the heavy music.

'I told you, I don't dance,' but Justin followed her through the crowd.

'I want you to meet someone,' she told him.

In front of them was the booth with the man Justin had earlier seen peddling drugs. 'This isn't a good idea,' he told her, but Catherine took no notice and sat next to the main man. She patted the seat and called Justin over.

'English, this is Viktor. He sells dreams.'

Justin looked at her sternly. 'I know what he sells.'

Catherine gave him a look of mock hurt. 'Oh,

English,' she said. 'Don't be so stuffy.' She turned to the man and spoke in Russian, then turned back to Justin. 'I need twenty-five dollars.'

'I won't give it to you. Not for that.'

The feigned look of hurt returned. 'Come on, English. It feels good. We will get a whole gram for that.'

Catherine turned to the man, and this time spoke in English for Justin's benefit. 'No, the English will not give me the money. What is that?' She turned to Justin, and then panned her gaze across Viktor's three cronies before speaking again. 'You will give me the dragon if I do what?' Again she looked Justin in the eye. 'If English will not give me money, then I have no choice.'

'What are you going on about?' Justin demanded.

Catherine began shifting in the seat. 'I want the dragon,' she replied. 'Viktor will give me the dragon even if English gives me no money.' She moved down under the table and Justin saw Viktor move slightly as Catherine unbuckled his trousers, and all four men sat in silence while under the table she gobbled on Viktor's prick. Occasionally Justin felt her body move against his leg as she adjusted her position, and it drove him wild to know what she was doing.

Several uneasy minutes passed until Viktor stiffened and signalled that he was pumping into the girl's throat, and a moment later she climbed back up from beneath the table. She took a swig from her bottle as Viktor spoke to her, and she spoke angrily back.

'See,' she said to Justin. 'You don't give me the money, now I have to suck them all.'

'It's not my fault,' he said defensively. 'You want the dragon, or whatever it is, not me.'

The girl shimmied back under the table and began giving the man next to Viktor the same treat. He either had better control than his gangster friend or was having difficulty coming in front of an audience, for Justin watched his blank face. Despite the raucous activity in the club the dim booth was eerily tense, but the sound of Catherine's head bumping up against the underside of the table broke the suspense. She cried out in Russian and for a moment Justin was alarmed, but she reappeared looking more dishevelled than before and sat up next to him. For a short period she was silent, then Justin saw her swallow what was the last of the man's spunk and give a little shudder.

Viktor spoke again and pointed to the next man in line. Catherine smiled and nodded, and told Justin she wanted a drink. Viktor pointed aggressively towards the other man and she nodded again, and was about to slip under the table when Justin interrupted. 'All right,' he hissed. 'I'll give you the money.'

Catherine smiled and reached out to kiss him, but he pulled away, amusing the thugs.

Viktor produced a small silver packet from a pocket, and immediately she pulled over a small candle that had been burning in the centre of the table and unwrapped the package.

As Justin knew it would, the silver wrap contained a white powder, though he didn't know what the substance was. To Catherine it was clearly very precious. She flattened the silver foil in a reverent, almost religious manner, and then pulled a cutthroat razor from her cleavage, Justin making a mental note to remember that.

With the edge of the razor she separated the powder into two uneven mounds. The largest mound she wrapped up again, but with the smaller she made a kind of boat out of the foil. Turning to Justin she licked both sides of the blade to remove some grains that had become stuck to it, then put the larger foil wrap in her pocket. 'For later,' she said.

She then began sailing the silver boat an inch or two over the candle flame, and in a few seconds a white cloud began to lift from the powder, curling upwards. 'See,' she said. 'The dragon.' She leant forward and breathed in deeply, inhaling the dragon's tail and the whole beast into her nostrils. A few claws of smoke escaped, only to be captured by the lungs of the other men. 'Breathe,' Catherine whispered. 'Become the dragon.'

Justin meant to turn away but the dragon caught him. It clawed its way into his head, drying his nose with its vapours. Then it scraped out his brain, leaving only an empty cavity. He felt nothing but the chill of numbness, his mind being cleaned of any thoughts and replaced with a clean white slate.

'I told you I would show you snow,' Catherine whispered into his ear. It took several minutes but the words eventually registered. Justin was beginning to feel again. His eyes flickered and she saw it. 'He comes back,' she gushed. 'The dragon comes back.'

Suddenly Justin's mind exploded into a frenzy of thought and knowledge, of sensation beyond sensation, smells overpowered him, dim lights burned his eyes, and the music smashed his ears. Catherine pushed past him, grabbed his wrist and dragged him to meet other worshippers. Together they twirled, twisted, bumped and swayed in frenzied honour of the all powerful dragon.

Several hundred pairs of gloved hands gave a strangely muffled applause as the players of *Uncle Vanya* took their final bow. The curtain fell and the noise of glove against glove diminished to be replaced by the general bustle of people preparing to leave the theatre. In a box off stage right Vasili Leskov was holding up Sabrina's coat for her to put on.

'Did you like it?'

'Very much,' answered Sabrina. 'Though I don't claim I understood it all.'

'That is what plays are for. To make you think. There is always more to understand.'

'I couldn't make out who Sonja was.'

The captain opened the door for them to make their way out. 'She is the professor's daughter by his first wife, and also Vanya's niece. It is about devotion. To the professor or to whatever. We are all devoted to something; our country, our religion, something.'

Outside the huge soldier was waiting patiently by the car, and within a few moments they were travelling through the streets of Murmansk. When Sabrina saw the Hotel Romanov she thought the evening was at an end, but the car kept going.

'Where are you taking me?' she asked.

The captain offered her a drink. 'I want to show you something,' he said. 'Something special. Do you mind? Is there somewhere you must be?'

Sabrina relaxed into her seat and sipped her drink. 'No,' she answered. 'I have plenty of time.'

The car made a few turns and went on its way. Along one street Sabrina saw a crowd of people climbing into the back of a lorry. Others appeared to be loading it up with boxes and crates. Helping them was Justin. She sat up in her seat, intrigued at what he was doing, but the car turned onto Chelyuskintsev and they headed into the countryside.

Within half a mile the road closed in with pines on either side, and the car was forced to slow down to contend with the heavy snow. The car's headlights tried in vain to punch a hole in the darkness, but were stopped almost immediately by heavy white flakes seemingly intent on blocking their path. Vasili seemed unconcerned, which relaxed Sabrina, so she accepted two more drinks and basked in the warmth of the car's luxurious interior. If she had known she was in a three ton, bombproof military transport she may have felt even safer.

The atmosphere had grown very comfortable and Sabrina couldn't help snatching glances at the handsome captain, replete in his green uniform with red and gold epaulettes. He was quiet and understated, confident and dignified. He caught her looking at him and smiled. 'So,' he said before she had a chance to be embarrassed, 'are you enjoying your stay in my country?'

'Very much,' she said truthfully. 'It is very beautiful.'

'But you are not a tourist.'

She grew alarmed. 'Why do you say that?'

'What tourist comes this far north? Besides, you travel alone. No, I think you are here on business.'

There was no underlying tone to his questions, but Sabrina was cautious. 'A little bit of both,' she ventured.

'Then we must endeavour to help in any way. After all, we are ambassadors for our countries.' He paused, then added, 'We should combine forces, like in the war.'

'That would be nice,' Sabrina smiled. '*Entente cordial.*'

The car began to climb. 'Almost there,' said Vasili, and a few moments later the headlights reached out over a dark, frozen expanse of water. 'Lake Semyonovskaya.'

'It's incredible,' she said in awe. 'It looks like a huge black hole in the earth.'

'It may well be,' he answered. 'The locals say it is bottomless. Fishermen who have drowned in it are never found. Others say that a monster lives there.'

'And what do you say?'

'I say there is much in the world to surprise us. I prefer the monster. We all need monsters; they keep children out of mischief and create order.'

The car continued to climb and the lake melted into the darkness behind them. A few miles further on the vehicle levelled off and Sabrina noticed that Vasili was moving in his seat. 'Almost there,' he informed her, a tinge of excitement to his voice.

The headlights appeared to be cutting further into the night because Sabrina noticed the car was becoming lighter. She looked to the front and saw that the snow was falling as heavily now as it had been earlier. Still the light increased, and then she saw why – the beams from the headlights were being reflected from a huge wall of ice. It looked like a massive iceberg floating on a black cloud, and again Sabrina gasped in genuine awe.

'That is so beautiful,' she whispered to Vasili. 'Now I know why you brought me here.'

He smiled and the car continued onwards until Sabrina noticed that the frozen sheet in front of them was more than a simple wall of ice. There were shapes carved on it and into it; a doorway, windows, steps, balustrades. It was a palace, an ice palace, and it was magnificent. She didn't feel the car come to a halt or see the two men get out. Only when Vasili spoke did she realise he was standing by the opened door beside her.

'Shall we enter?' he asked.

She alighted from the car, and as her foot touched the snow everything went black and the palace disappeared.

'No,' she moaned in honest disappointment. 'I can't see it.' Vasili took her arm to reassure her that all would be all right, and the two stood in the deathly silence and overpowering blackness of a polar night.

Behind them a faint glow revealed that the soldier had opened the boot of the car. He collected some things and joined them, and with the boot closed they were once again cloaked in darkness, but it was broken a moment later by Vasili striking up a flame from a silver lighter. To look at it hurt the eyes, but Sabrina watched as he lit five candles on a huge silver candelabra. The combined flames produced an umbrella of light and the two walked under its glow to the palace, followed by the soldier carrying a large hamper.

They climbed the steps and made their way slowly through the doorway and along a corridor. The whole building formed a giant chandelier reflecting light in every direction, and where the light fell on translucent statues it broke into a kaleidoscope of colour.

'I have never seen anything like this,' whispered Sabrina, in a reverential voice. 'Who? Why? When?'

Vasili never attempted to answer her questions, but led her into the main hall, a cavernous room with walls that looked to be encrusted with light-giving jewels. Along both sides ran statues of Russian Tsars, and the two columns came together either side of a massive window that looked out over the bleak Barents Sea.

Silently, the soldier placed the hamper on the frozen floor and took out a huge sable fur, which he shook out to make a carpet in front of the window. He then laid out a silver bucket containing two bottles of champagne, some silver dishes containing a mound of black caviar, and some fine crystal glasses. When he was done Vasili waved him away. The soldier saluted his captain, turned briskly on his heels and departed, leaving them to gaze out of the window.

'Are you cold?' asked Vasili.

'No, I'm not. Why is that? You'd think with all this ice it would be freezing.'

'Ha,' he laughed. 'Maybe there is some Russian in you.'

Sabrina smiled. 'Not yet,' she answered naughtily, and then walked across to the sable and caressed the warm fur.

Vasili joined her there. He smeared a spoonful of caviar onto a dried biscuit and offered it to her mouth. 'Ice and snow are Russia's friend. They protect us from our enemies and provide us with the source of our wealth.' He lifted the edge of the fur to indicate its importance, and Sabrina ran her fingers through it. The tiny balls of caviar exploded onto Sabrina's tongue and she lay back to enjoy the flavour. The taste was powerful, earthy and full of suggestion, reminding her of a man's sperm.

Vasili interrupted her thoughts by popping the cork on the champagne. The noise reverberated around the palace, then faded back in respect for the moment. He filled the crystal flutes and passed her one, and she sipped it tentatively, allowing the two flavours to interact and produce another.

'They compliment each other well, do you think so?'

'Perfectly,' she answered.

'Like a man and a woman.' He moved closer and placed a hand behind her. 'When they come together they produce something more than themselves.' His lips pressed upon hers and they fell backwards onto the fur.

Vasili slowly undressed her before the frozen stares of the long dead tsars. He was patient and meticulous, intent on enjoying the sight enfolding in front of him. Here and there he planted kisses on the girl's body, tasting her skin and swimming in the aroma of her arousal. When she stood alongside one of the statues he stared in awe, for her body was a testament to the creator's own unsurpassable skill as a sculptor.

'You are beautiful,' whispered the Russian captain. 'Truly beautiful.'

Sabrina graciously accepted the compliment by brushing her hand over Vasili's cock. It was as hard as the frozen palace columns. She released the straining member and felt the heat it generated, felt the blood pounding through the thick vein that ran the length of it's shaft, and felt the need to control it. Tipping forward she puckered her lips and caressed the large domed cockhead, and Vasili stabbed in an uncontrollable instinct to penetrate the female. She allowed it by opening her mouth and lowering herself further. Again he thrust, this time so forceful that Sabrina was forced to move back. Lost now in unstoppable lust, Vasili continued thrusting into Sabrina's luscious mouth, pushing until she was stopped from moving by the frozen blade of Ivan IV's sword, the shock of the cold sending an immediate tingle along her spine.

Another thrust and then another resulted in the sword becoming embedded ever deeper in the girl's sheath. The sensation of heat and cold at either end of her body alarmed and excited her. She began moving in motion with Vasili's thrusts, first sucking on his cock and then sliding along Ivan's sword. The ice on the tsar's weapon had initially gripped her sex, but her heat and lubricant melted its surface and it slipped easily into her body, impaling her as surely as the terrible tsar had impaled many of his subjects all those years ago. When she felt there was no sensation left to experience she sensed the rise of her orgasm. It had begun on the cupola of Vasili's cock and was to end on the sword of Ivan the Terrible. Sweat lifted from her in constant streams of sexual vapour and that which remained was thrown from her flailing body as her orgasm ripped through her like a glacier cracking

73

asunder.

Vasili had not missed the impending climax. He pulled Sabrina off the frozen phallus, forced her to her knees, and there, in front of that huge window, watched by the silent faces, he impaled her upon his own fiery sword, and sent her emotions crashing down in an almighty sexual avalanche.

Justin was amazed at Catherine's lack of concern about the cold. He had watched her and the others unload the truck on the top of the car park and set up a sound system that would do justice to a heavy metal rock band, all with apparent contempt for the constant falling snow. Unlike them, he found himself seeking warmth alongside one of the blazing oil drums that encircled the revellers. His earlier unintentional trip into the realm of the dragon had all but worn off, and he felt strangely alone. Catherine and her fellow dancers were still partying, they had simply changed venue, taking him along with them.

The car park was devoid of vehicles apart from the truck they came in, and Justin had no idea who drove it let alone owned it. He made his way over to a long makeshift table laid out with drinks. He took a bottle of polar vodka and knocked off it's crown top on the edge of the table, then walked away, leaving the Russians dancing.

At the edge of the car park he stopped and looked out over the nearby harbour. An icebreaker was in port for supplies, and an electric arc from a welding jig indicated it was also having some sort of repairs. Beneath the sodium glare of the dockside lamps Justin could make out the night workers huddled inside their storm coats. He envied them their ordinary lives. Somehow, just now anyway, the snow wasn't beautiful, the sea had lost its allure and the chill wasn't exhilarating; it was just cold.

'Why so sad, English?'

He turned to see Catherine swigging from a bottle. She was still moving in time to the music and her smile was as welcoming as ever. Almost immediately his spirits lifted, and she lifted them further by kissing him lightly on the cheek.

'Sorry,' he said. 'I was just thinking.'

'About home?'

'About home,' he confirmed. 'And other things.'

The pair leant against the parapet and Justin returned to his thoughts.

'Do not worry if you are sad,' she reassured him. 'The dragon has a poisonous bite. You must keep away from the dragon until your wounds have healed.'

That amused Justin, and he let out a short but loud laugh.

'Are you making funny with me?'

He laughed again. 'No, I'm not making funny with you. Although I do think you're fun. I've just got a lot on my mind.' He turned towards her. 'I don't know if I've made the right decision.'

Catherine stepped back. 'What do you mean? Do you think you have something to do with me? Have I asked you for anything?'

'Yes, money for that dragon powder shit in your pocket.' He waved a finger at her, then promptly dropped his hand.

'I ask you for nothing. I want nothing.'

'I know,' he said. 'It's not about you... not about you at all.'

'Well then,' Catherine put in. 'Do not make me sad too, because you are sad.'

Justin's frustration almost boiled over. 'I said it is not about you. You're a free spirit, or at least you seem to be. It's about me. I've done a few things I'm not

75

proud of.'

Catherine took a long slug on her drink and laughed. 'Tell me about it,' she grinned. 'I suck cocks to get my fix.'

Justin took a long drink to give him time to think. 'Well,' he said eventually, 'that doesn't sound so bad, considering.' He paused there to watch a trawler land some of its catch and the dockers doing ordinary work.

'Considering?'

'Sorry?' said Justin. He was trying to remember when he once had an ordinary job.

'Considering what?' Catherine repeated. 'You say sucking cocks in return for drugs is not so bad, considering.'

Justin walked away into the darkness and Catherine followed.

'I had a friend once, you see,' he went on, without looking to see if she was still with him. 'A good friend.'

'He is not a friend now?'

'No,' he said. 'Well, I'm still sort of his friend. But I don't suppose he's mine any more.'

Catherine draped a hand around his neck. 'Lot's of friends have fights. You will be friends again.'

'Not us; we can't go back. Not after what I've done.'

'Then you must have been very bad. But I don't think you are a bad person.'

'I'm not... not really.'

She kissed him again and tugged at his arm. 'Well then,' she said. 'All will be okay. Let's go back and dance, or drink some more. You like to drink.'

'No,' he said firmly. 'You don't understand. I betrayed him. He offered me a job and we were going to run a business together, but I tricked him and took the business over with someone else. Now he's disappeared and that's why we're here – to find him.'

'That is good. To make friends again?'

'To take him back,' said Justin. 'Or to kill him.'

Catherine seemed unperturbed by his words. 'Why kill him? You are in England, he is in Russia. You are not friends, yet you travel this far to find him. I don't understand, you are right.'

'It was that business. It was sort of unusual, different…'

Just then a friend of Catherine's came over and tried to drag her away to dance, but she managed to reject his pleas after first pinching a bottle of vodka from him. 'Come with me,' she said to Justin. 'I know where we can talk.' She guided him to the edge of the car park and pointed to a ledge on the other side of the parapet. It reached out about three feet and went around a corner and out of sight. 'Come on,' she said, and then climbed over before Justin could decline.

There were four or five inches of snow on the ledge, which they kicked off as they made their way. Justin edged himself along in the darkness and hoped there would be somewhere safe to sit, but the ledge remained just that – three feet of concrete, and ominously, forty feet below them was more concrete.

Catherine sat down upon the snow and motioned for him to do likewise. 'I come here sometimes, when I want to think or be alone,' she said. 'Don't worry,' she reassured him, 'the snow will not melt when the sky is so cold. You will not get wet.'

Justin sat next to her and peered over the ledge, only slightly grateful it was too dark to see the pavement.

'Here,' she said, offering him a shot of vodka, which he accepted.

'Just what I need,' he said to himself sarcastically. 'To get pissed forty foot up in the air in the middle of a snow storm.'

Catherine took a drink then rested her head on his shoulder and pulled his arm into hers. 'I will look after you,' she smiled quite sincerely. 'Now you must tell me. I want to know everything.'

Justin took a moment to compose himself, pulled his knees up to his chest and huddled into his coat. 'My friend.' He stopped and rephrased. 'My ex-friend, he was a doctor. I was training to be one too but I had to leave university. I had to live or study, I couldn't afford to do both. Anyway, we went our separate ways and then, years later, we met, just by chance. He had this beautiful woman with him. We chatted for a while about old times and then I asked him what he was doing now. He told me he ran a training school and the woman with him was one of his students.'

'He was no longer a doctor?'

'No.'

'Why did he change? A doctor is a good job.'

'He had been to Pakistan to do some voluntary work when some Afghan rebels raided the camp and forced him to go with them over the border. They wanted him to work for them during the war, the one with your country. The problem was, some Russian soldiers caught them and he was accused of helping the rebels. He was given a choice; he could work for the Russian military hospital in Herat, or be shot.'

'In Russia this is a fair choice,' interrupted Catherine. 'Is that why he is in Russia now?'

'No,' Justin continued. 'He escaped back to Britain.'

'To his school?'

'He hadn't set that up then. Anyway, it wasn't a school like you're thinking. It was for adults.'

'Like a night school.'

'Not quite. When he was with the KGB he learned all about torture techniques; how to get people to do what you want, that sort of thing. Mostly he worked with women.' Justin took the bottle from Catherine. While he was drinking a snowflake landed on his open eye. For that split second, before an involuntary blink wiped the flake away, he saw a kaleidoscope of colour through the icy crystal. It reminded him that life, like the story he was recounting, was truly colourful. It made telling the rest of the tale easier, though it didn't ease his guilt.

'So you were going to work in this school?'

'Sort of. But like I say, it wasn't the type of school you're thinking of. It was a training school for women... well, it was for wives.'

'Wives? What, cooking and cleaning?'

'Sex. We trained them for sex.'

'Why do you have to train women to have sex? Are English women strange in some way?'

'No more than anywhere else. But David, that's my friend, he travelled all over the East and he noticed how their women were more subservient than westerners. He just put two and two together. When he came back to Britain he found other like-minded men; men who wanted their wives to be subservient like those in the East. He set up this school and he was taking on clients when I met him. That's why that beautiful woman was with him. He could do whatever he liked with her, all with her husband's approval. He even had a fucking contract, literally. I couldn't believe it. I thought: wow, that's incredible, I wouldn't mind a bit of that. Everything should have been perfect. But I blew it.'

The snow was falling heavily now, covering their footsteps on the ledge. Out on the ocean a foghorn signalled that conditions were deteriorating everywhere.

'Do you want to go back to the party?'

Justin shook his head. 'Not yet. Look, I appreciate you listening to me.'

Catherine gave a nonchalant shrug and recaptured

the bottle.

'David told me all about his studies in training and asked if I wanted to help with his next client,' Justin continued. 'The trouble was, I fell in love with her.'

Yet again the bottle was passed. Justin grimaced. He was at that stage of knowing he had drunk too much, but he was too far gone to do anything about it.

'What is so bad about falling in love?'

Justin slumped down on the ledge. If it wasn't for the bite of the snow on his cheek and the cold vodka Catherine poured over him he would have gratefully fallen into a sleep.

'Come on,' she said through a concerned smile. 'We must go.'

Somehow she managed to get herself and Justin safely along the ledge and back to the car park. Her friends were still there, although some had left and others arrived. She shouted to a young man she knew called Mikhail, and pointed to his scooter. Despite only getting there a few minutes earlier he agreed to take the two of them back to her apartment. Mikhail and Catherine were old friends, and they giggled as they wedged the drunken Justin between them and set off.

It was a matter of a few hundred yards before the scooter pulled up outside a small tobacconist in a grubby area of the city. Mikhail helped Catherine unload her new friend and offered to help her take him inside. She declined, thanked him for his help and guided Justin to the steps that led down to her basement room, and by the time she had opened the door he was beginning to come round. The smell of freshly brewed coffee a few minutes later completed his revival, and he sat nursing a large mug in front of an ancient gas fire.

'I can't remember how I got here,' he mumbled.

'You don't want to know.' She offered him a thick

slice of malted loaf, which he waved away. She persisted, shaking the heavy bread in front of his face. 'It will soak up the vodka. You will thank me in the morning.' She went to turn down the fire, but Justin waved his hand pleadingly.

'Please, I'm just warming up.' She left it alone and he added, 'I thought you said the snow wouldn't make me cold.'

'Wet,' Catherine corrected. 'I said it would not make you wet.'

'Whatever. I know my fingers haven't dropped off because they're starting to tingle, but my toes…' he stamped his feet.

Catherine had already removed her coat, and she took off the black polo-necked jumper too. The sight warmed Justin's mind but his fingers cried out for something more tangible, and as if in answer to his unspoken request she sat down in front of him and began undoing his shoes. In her position Justin could see up her small skirt, which had slipped up almost to her waist, and the delicate mound he'd seen in her panties back at the club was even more visible now.

'Ouch!' She had squeezed his toes hard. 'Not so rough, they really hurt.'

'What are you looking at?' she challenged.

'N-nothing,' he stammered. 'The fire.'

'You were looking between my legs, weren't you?'

'Yes,' he admitted like a scolded boy. 'You look so nice I couldn't stop myself… sorry.'

'Is that what you did to these women?'

'What?'

'Looked at them when you wanted to?'

'I only took part in it all once – well, the female side. I told you, I betrayed David. Then Sabrina, that's the girl who was with us for training, she took over everything.'

Catherine lifted Justin's cold feet and placed then under her armpits. Her movements forced him back in the chair and he relaxed as her warmth transferred itself to his body. 'She became the trainer?'

'Yes.'

'Of men?' Catherine's eyes widened and her breasts lifted with each breath.

'Yes. Men were brought to us just like the women were. Sabrina turned them into submissive slaves for their mistresses. They came and went, but she would never let David go. He was her first and she hated him, but she loved him too.'

'I don't understand.'

Justin placed his feet on the floor and inside Catherine's legs, and then he leant forward until his face was near hers 'She couldn't bear the thought of being controlled, but she craved the physical side of things. She became addicted to being spanked, and worse. She demanded beatings that were so hard you would think they'd harm her. She knew she was out of control and that's why she hated David so much. If I hadn't helped her escape then her training would have been completed and she would have been happy. As it is, she is neither dominant nor submissive. She's in limbo.'

'And you must find David in order for this woman to keep control of the only man who could control her?'

'That's about it. We were bringing David and a girl to Russia, but he escaped the night we delivered her.'

'And no one in your country asked questions about him, where he had gone?'

'He was very secretive because of what he was doing. No one even knew he existed. But he's a clever man. He had lived in the mountains of Pakistan and he learned how to survive. That's why we couldn't find him until now.' He turned his gaze to the fire, squinting into the orange glow. 'Now I don't want to catch him,' he added quietly, almost to himself.

'But this woman, she forces you?' Catherine persisted.

'Yes, I love her. Or I used to. Love, lust, I've confused the two. I just find myself doing whatever she wants.'

'You are confused, I think, because the two of you have upset the balance. You are a man and she is a woman, but you have both crossed over. All this anger, it is just a distraction from the real problems. Leave this David – let him be.' She took the coffee mug and placed it on the floor. 'You must be a man again.'

Justin smiled weakly. 'I think I've forgotten how.'

Catherine stood up. 'I think maybe you have,' she whispered seductively, and then reached back and released her bra. 'I think, as you are a guest in my country, I should do some training of my own.' Her skirt slipped softly to the floor and she kicked it away with her leather-clad foot. Justin had realised earlier that Catherine had little if any inhibitions, even so, he felt unprepared for her bold display. She remained motionless, illuminated only by the gas flames that flickered between the broken pieces of the firebrick. 'You must be a man again. You must take a woman like a man should, with a hard penis that must be satisfied.'

Justin certainly had a hard penis all right, but he remained rooted to his chair, unsure of what to do. Had it really been so long since he took the initiative? Catherine didn't move and the tension grew, but at last his courage returned, slowly. 'Take down your knickers,' he said.

Catherine hooked her thumbs into the flimsy black panties and, without bending her knees, pushed them down to her ankles, and when she straightened up Justin drank in her nakedness, just a sip at first, a taster, a reminder of how it first was when he met David; how Sabrina had been bent over, displayed and shaved.

'Step out of them.' His voice was firmer and her action obedient. 'Stand up straight and put your arms by your sides.' Obedient again. Justin's confidence was beginning its long crawl back, and carried with it the adrenalin surge he had not felt for some time. It made him anxious and seemed to push him into rushing events. But this time Justin would not be rushed; would not be cajoled or ordered. This time he was in charge. He had forgotten how good that felt.

'Step back from the fire,' he said firmly. She did as he said, moving her body in order for him to inspect her in the glow. 'Turn around,' he ordered.

She did as he said. Her back was flawless and her skin like alabaster. Above the moons of her bottom she curved gently inwards before her back flared to support her proud shoulders.

'How old are you?' he asked.

'Twenty-four.' She looked younger.

'Do you have a boyfriend?'

'Yes. Dimitri. He is away with his ship.'

'Does he mind it if you bring men to your apartment?'

'He is my boyfriend. He does not own me.'

'Bend forward, at the waist. Don't bend your legs.'

Catherine reached down and took hold of her ankles for support. Justin sat forward in his chair and watched as her movements pushed her bottom towards his face. The light from the fire illuminated the valley of her sex, and its iridescent glow complimented the colour of her unfolding flower. Above her slightly parted petals the dark bud of her bottom puckered sweetly. To Justin it was the greatest dragon of all; frightening, exciting, all consuming. He stood behind her and placed his hands on her hips, and her bottom pressed back, confirming her desire to be penetrated. She said nothing; the only sound in the room was the insistent hiss of the gas fire. It whispered to Justin to mount her, it said to make love to her, told him to pierce her vagina, demanded that he impale her, screamed for him to fuck her.

He remembered nothing else until his cock was spent. His sole intention had been fulfilled. Catherine had toppled forward onto an old chair, her face pressed into the cushion, her bottom held out in submission. Her cries of pleasure had not registered with Justin, and the frantic movements of her hips went unnoticed as he thrust and pumped his way to an all-embracing climax. Now that his sperm was deposited inside her sheath he noticed that she too had travelled with him. Her sex milked his throbbing cock and she was babbling in her own language. The words required no translation; they were universal, the language of sex.

His cock deflated slowly and Catherine waited patiently for his withdrawal. He did not rush. Instead he enjoyed the feeling of her tightening muscles dismissing his now timid member. It had lost its earlier arrogance if not its confidence. Justin smiled at its final sloppy departure and Catherine returned his affection. When he was free from their coupling he dropped exhausted back into his chair while Catherine remained motionless to enjoy the ebbing moments of her orgasm.

When Justin opened his eyes Catherine was sitting at his feet in front of the fire. She had turned the heat full on and was bathed in a bright orange light. In her hand was a cigarette, and apart from her long boots, she was still naked.

'How are you?' she asked.

Justin smiled and although he rarely smoked, he leaned forward and took the cigarette from between her fingers. He pulled on it and the smoke smoothed his heartbeat to a gentle relaxed rhythm. 'I'm just fine.' He took another tote and handed it back. Catherine steadied herself with a hand behind her bottom and threw back her head. Her movement pulled her breasts upwards, making them stand proud and jaunty. As Justin studied her figure she exhaled a great cloud of smoke towards the ceiling. It relaxed her too, and her knees parted, encouraging Justin to inspect her. A string of sperm hung from her glistening vulva and when she moved she expelled another. He leant down and gently patted her opening with the tip of his finger. She was soft and warm and incredibly wet. His finger made little sloppy tapping noises, the sound of which made her smile – a knowing, naughty smile. He liked that.

Catherine finished her cigarette and sat at his feet. She rested her head on his knee and the two stared silently into the fire. After a moment or two Justin felt compelled to speak. 'Thank you,' he said softly, and ran his fingers through her hair. Her answer was to smile gently and to nuzzle her head into his lap.

'That made me feel really good,' he told her. 'Not the sex… well yes, of course the sex. But I mean the way you gave yourself to me. It did wonders for my confidence.'

'I think you have forgotten that you are a man.'

Justin looked deeper into the fire, past the flames and into the pit from whence they came. He saw himself, naked and hiding behind a rock. Sabrina was calling him out, taunting him. A whip cracked over his head and he was forced into the open, where he cowered and covered his penis with his hands. The whip cracked again and this time wrapped itself around his arm.

Sabrina yanked it. The force pulled his arm away from his body and his penis was exposed. Its appearance was met with laughter and derision. He was ashamed and tried to hide but the whip bit again, wrapping its tail around his other arm. In his lap Catherine's tongue snaked around his penis. Sabrina pulled once more, but now his arm gained strength and began to swell. Catherine's tongue lapped, encouraging him further. Justin grabbed the whip and tugged. Sabrina tugged back and Justin hesitated, his grip began to slip and he grew afraid. Catherine cupped his balls and massaged them, gently pumping his courage to the surface. His cock grew large and his courage returned, creeping higher and higher, preparing to explode in a magnificent display of maleness. It became unstoppable, undeniable, and in one mighty gesture Justin tore the whip from Sabrina's hand, sending it twirling and twisting and spilling over and over into the air.

Chapter Five

The *Piroshka* sailed silently and unannounced into the harbour of Kirkwall. It was four-thirty in the morning but the sun had already broken above the rocks that separated Shapinsay Sound from Wide Firth. When the boat bumped lightly into the row of tyres that lined the harbour walls like some symmetrical Loch Ness monster a middle-aged man called out for the rope. Justin threw it with a cry of ahoy and the man dropped the looped hemp around a cast iron spigot reserved for visiting boats.

When the boat was secured the man jumped onboard. He was tall, and had a weather-beaten face that revealed he spent much of his time outdoors. He shook hands with Justin and turned to Sabrina. She was dressed in warm woollens covered with a waterproofed oilskin.

'Right on time,' he said to them both. 'Any problems?'

'None,' said Sabrina. 'We're just tourists, Carl. Sailing the islands. A couple of eco-tourists looking for whales. Have you seen the harbourmaster?'

'It's all cleared. I paid the dues for a couple of days to give you a chance to rest up.'

'We won't have time for that,' said Sabrina. She opened the cabin door and entered, indicating for them to follow. When they joined her in the warm interior she instructed Justin to get breakfast underway.

'So,' she said, nursing a mug of coffee. 'Where do we do it – here?'

'No, not here,' Carl replied. 'We'll go straight to

my island. I can inspect the merchandise on the way.'

After a breakfast of bacon and eggs the three of them set out for Stronsay Firth, about ten or fifteen miles to the north.

'We'll need diesel,' said Justin. 'Can that be arranged?'

Carl sniggered derisively. 'It's the Orkneys, Justin, not Outer Mongolia. We even have it in pumps, just like a real garage.'

Justin blushed. 'I didn't mean to imply anything,' he blurted, feeling stupid. 'I just thought you might have to order it. You know, I thought it might take twenty-four hours, or something.'

'Not with the number of boats in this part of the world. We've got plenty of diesel – diesel and fish. There's only so much interest in diesel and fish. That's why you're here.'

Carl stood up and shook his empty coffee mug. 'On the stove,' said Sabrina. 'I take it you have the money.'

Carl smiled and his face folded along craggy lines. 'Not on my person – just in case.'

'Do I detect a trace of suspicion?'

The islander sat back down and sipped his steaming drink. 'It wouldn't do to be afloat in these treacherous waters with fifteen grand now, would it? What if I were to have an accident and go visiting a few whales myself?'

Sabrina laughed and went over to a row of keys swinging on hooks by the door. 'I can see your point.' Despite the difference in their years she was not intimidated by Carl, or by the scenario in which they were players. She was confident beyond her years; the time she had spent putting David to stud had seen to that. She chose a key and threw it to Justin. 'Bring her up so Carl can see what he's getting for his money.'

'That's a good idea,' said Carl, quietly rubbing his

hands together. 'I always enjoy market day.'

Justin disappeared into the hold of the boat where a cabin had been made to house the two captives. They were kept together, naked of course, for company. It was the only concession made to them.

'How old is she?' asked Carl.

Sabrina was now reclining in her sweater and slacks and looked every bit the nonchalant businesswoman discussing a deal. 'She's nineteen.'

The door opened and Justin marched the naked girl into the lounge cabin. Carl scanned her body in an instant, gauging her health and considering the merits of his prospective purchase.

'Bring David up as well,' Sabrina commanded. 'I want him to see this.'

'David?'

'Don't worry, Carl, David is the reason we can't stop too long.'

Carl became agitated. 'But you said nothing about another party. Who is he?'

'Relax,' yawned Sabrina. 'He's just more merchandise we've still got to unload.'

'Where are you going?'

Sabrina waved her hand towards the girl as if reminding Carl why they were there. 'We don't need to talk about David,' she said. 'This is why we're here.'

The girl stared intently at the deck until Justin laid the whip across the backs of her legs, whereupon she immediately dropped to her knees and took up the posture she had been taught during the journey; legs tucked underneath her, hands on her knees, back straight and eyes to the front. She also ensured that her long blonde hair was tucked behind her ears; there was to be no escape for her blushes behind her locks.

'I suppose,' continued Carl, 'it's too much to expect that she's unsullied.'

'Too much for sure,' Sabrina answered. 'But you can see she is a very good specimen. More coffee?' He held out his mug and Sabrina refilled it. 'Is she for you?'

'Well,' he pondered, 'it's difficult to say.'

Sabrina poured coffee for herself and sat back down. 'That's intriguing,' she said calmly. 'If not for you, then who?'

Carl's eyes were fixed on the girl's breasts. She was breathing heavily but appeared quite relaxed. Her heavy breasts lifted and fell as if in tune with the waves beneath the boat, and the suggestive movement stirred strong feelings in his groin.

The door to the hold opened and Justin pushed David into the cabin. Carl saw the naked man and realised immediately that Sabrina traded in both female and male flesh. Justin motioned for his onetime friend to take up position by the handrail. David did as he was instructed and waited for the clicks of steel that ensured he was fettered and again helpless. Sabrina all but ignored his presence and returned to Carl for an answer to her earlier question about who the girl was for.

'It's a long story,' he informed them, but he got no further before his curiosity got the better of him. Turning to Justin, he pointed towards the girl's crotch and said, 'Would you mind?'

Justin answered, 'Not at all,' and probed with the tip of his whip between the girl's knees, causing her to shuffle and open her legs until her sex was clearly in view.

Carl nodded his appreciation at the pink parting and spoke again, though he continued to be drawn back to her exposed cleft. 'These islands are dying, as are the old ways. We need some new blood, but the youngsters let us down. The moment they are old enough they leave for the mainland and better jobs.' He snorted his dissatisfaction and took in another glance at the answer to his problems. 'You'd have thought young people would be at it like rabbits, but not one bairn for the last two years. The last few youngsters are all saving up for a move to Aberdeen. They want to see the sights, you see. But I've been to Aberdeen and there's none there, I can tell you.'

'So, what are you saying?' asked Sabrina. 'This bitch is for breeding?'

'We want to restock the island; bring in some new blood.'

Justin glanced at the girl and imagined her pregnant, and wondered at who they had in mind to sire her. Then he realised that she was only one female, and his frown made a question unnecessary. Carl was ahead of him.

'If everything goes to plan we expect to invest in more stock,' he said.

Sabrina let out a low and lengthy whistle. 'You'd need what, another two, maybe three bitches?'

'We reckon six. But we're not rushing things. If we get lucky and she catches straight away and everything goes fine, then we expect to be back in touch.'

Justin looked at his watch and excused himself to check that they were still sailing in clear water. The boat carried a highly sophisticated radar and sonar system. Any object remotely threatening set off an alarm and slowed the engines, but he was still a nervous sailor and he liked to make sure. When he opened the cabin door a whole cacophony of gull screams shattered the quiet mood, so Carl got up from his seat, closed the door, and calm again descended.

'If it's okay with you, I'd like to check things over,' he said, and as Sabrina looked on Carl moved to the girl, took hold of her head with both hands, tilted her back and stared into her eyes.

'Nice and clear,' he announced, before examining her nose. Sabrina was amused. 'Some of these kids get up to all sorts – sniffing solvents or worse; chucking that cocaine mess up their noses. You read about it, don't you?' He proceeded to inspect her mouth, saying that dental fees would have to be considered, but she was free from any oral problems.

'She's grade A,' said Sabrina. 'That's what you wanted – that's what you've got.'

Carl's demeanour became more purposeful. He was used to appraising sheep on his farm and at the market, and to him a nineteen-year-old girl was no different. He lifted her head back again and ran a hand firmly down each side of her neck. When he was satisfied he applied some pressure to her shoulders by pressing down with both hands. She resisted well and he commented that she appeared quite strong. He allowed his hands to travel down her chest, where he cupped each breast in turn. He weighed and checked their size before examining each soft orb. The nipples puckered nicely under his touch, prompting him to say that they were good teats for feeding. He then grabbed the girl firmly, but not angrily, behind the neck and pushed her face down to the cabin floor. For a moment he simulated milking each breast, then straightened up and said that she was obviously ideal for breeding.

'She's a good strong bitch,' he told Sabrina. 'We should get a fair litter out of her.' He moved to the girl's rear end, and added. 'All I need now is to check her nether regions and we should have a deal.'

'Go right ahead,' said Sabrina. 'I'm sure you will be satisfied.'

Carl leant over the girl and parted the cheeks of her bottom. 'She seems clear there,' he said. 'Has Justin been doing anything with her?'

'More than likely,' answered Sabrina. 'But he's not

an animal. She'll be okay.'

From an inside pocket Carl pulled out a stainless steel spoon-like implement, which he used to open the girl's vagina. The bowl of the spoon pressed down part of her canal while opening the rest for inspection. He changed the position of his speculum until he was satisfied that she was totally clean and healthy.

The gulls screamed again as Justin opened the door, and he looked in and saw the naked girl receiving the last of her examination. 'Everything okay?' he asked.

Carl straightened again and returned the spoon to his pocket. 'Perfect,' he answered. 'Just perfect.'

'That's good,' said Justin, as he poured himself another coffee. 'Because it looks like a reception party is waiting for us on the quay.'

'That'll be the committee,' said Carl. He pointed to the girl. 'If you get her ready to travel I'll confirm to my friends that everything is satisfactory.'

On the deck Carl pointed out a man in a hunting cap. 'He has your money. I'll tell him that everything is fine and the handover will take place in *The Bell* over there.' He indicated a squat black and white pub of obvious age that sat about a hundred yards from the quay.

'How will we get her there?' asked Justin. 'This welcoming committee is looking suspicious.'

Carl waved to his friends and each waved back. 'The Sharinsay Investment Committee,' he said to Sabrina with a grin.

Just inside the cabin door and within earshot David managed a muffled and ironic gurgle through the discomfort of his leather restraint collar. In his mind he wondered if they realised that the acronym for the Sharinsay Investment Committee spelled SIC.

A gentle nudge of the boat indicated that they had docked and soon the deck was full of excited middle-aged men. Seeing the general mêlée Sabrina and Justin grew wary of locals coming to investigate the excitement. They called Carl away from several of his friends who were asking him what the girl was like, and suggested everyone went inside until they had decided what to do with her. It was now seven forty-five in the morning and on the island people were beginning to go about their business. Carl looked towards the village and saw Eric the milkman turn his van into the market square.

'You're right,' he said. 'We're getting carried away.' He called across to Fraser, who was holding a light sports holdall containing the money. 'Let's get this thing finished,' he said to him. 'Gather the others and take them over to *The Bell*. We'll get the girl dressed and bring her over.'

Fraser seemed to smile and then swallowed when he realised what Carl had just said. He had his own farm on the far side of the island and he was a quiet, some would say timid, man. 'Y-you mean,' he spluttered. 'You mean, she's in there with no clothes on?' He pointed towards the *Piroshka's* cabin. 'Naked? And you've seen her?'

Carl leaned forward as if speaking in confidence. 'Naked as a Jay bird,' he whispered. 'Like the day she was born.' He flashed his friend a knowing smile. Fraser's occasional nervous tick went into overdrive and he set about gathering the others while telling them that Carl had already seen the goods. Brian, the landlord from *The Bell*, put it into perspective for Fraser by reminding him that Carl had been chosen for that very purpose. It was his job to contact and meet Sabrina and Justin and confirm the girl's suitability before they parted with their money.

'Still,' put in Fraser, as the group left the boat. '*Naked*… Jesus Christ.'

'Please, Fraser,' put in Father MacKay. 'Do not utter the Lord's name so flippantly.'

'Sorry father.' Fraser was genuinely contrite. His simple upbringing had been religious and as a boy the old ways had been firmly instilled in him. That was why he couldn't stand by and watch his beautiful Sharinsay become a wasteland. That was why he had joined the group and that was why he would take his month when it was his turn. It was also the reason why everybody trusted him with the money.

Sabrina ordered Justin inside and Carl followed them. The girl was still kneeling on the deck when they entered, too terrified to move. 'Get her ready, and him,' demanded Sabrina, and Justin checked David's lead was still firmly attached to the handrail, and went below for their clothes.

'What do we do from here?' asked Sabrina. 'I assume sending the entire island out as a welcoming party wasn't your only plan.'

'No,' said Carl. 'I'm sorry about all that. They were supposed to meet in *The Bell* and wait for us there.' He was obviously embarrassed and Sabrina let it drop. 'We've put on a bit of a spread in the back of the pub,' he went on, changing the subject, 'to show our appreciation.'

Sabrina was unable to stifle her smile. Even David, strapped tight to the handrail, could see the humour in the sheer madness of putting on a spread for people involved in kidnap and false imprisonment.

'How quaint,' she said, with more than a hint of sarcasm. 'Chicken wings and ham sandwiches I hope.'

Carl shuffled rather awkwardly and wondered how the hell they had made their island seem even more backward than the youngsters already considered it.

Justin returned with the clothes and set them down in two piles. While the girl dressed in a heavy woollen polo-necked pullover and jeans he connected a chain between the ampallang bolt in David's penis and the guiche ring Sabrina had fitted just below his balls.

'Is he secure?' she asked, and Justin nodded in the affirmative.

'Can't we leave him here?' asked Carl.

'I can't take the risk of someone coming onboard while we're gone.' She walked across to David and slapped his face playfully. 'And I'm not too keen to have him do a Hardy Kruger on me. I've put a lot of work in to David here, and I want the rewards.'

David said nothing. He wasn't going to give her the opportunity to mistreat him. She was sadistic enough without being given a reason to vent her full feelings.

'He's safe enough,' she announced. 'I assume you two men can take control of one man, especially if you've got hold of this.' With a twisted grin she held up the end of the chain connected to his genitalia. 'One tug and I'm sure he'll cooperate.'

David began to dress, and was near finishing when a loud knock came at the door. Through the glass a large man squinted into the cabin, and when his gaze alighted on Carl's his expression changed to a smile.

'It's Douglas from the store. Let him in,' Carl said.

Douglas entered, his eyes surveying the scene, and when he saw the girl he leered. 'I've brought the grocery van,' he said, without taking his eyes from her. 'I thought you'd be trying to figure a way to get her over the road. Who's he?' he nodded aggressively at David.

'That's none of our business,' Carl said. 'But we've got to take him with us. Can you help?'

The big man took his eyes away from the girl's proud breasts for less than a second. 'Trouble?' he asked.

'Not if he leaves the island this afternoon and doesn't do a runner.'

Douglas stood beside David and dwarfed him, and that put paid to David's glimmer of hope. Instead of kicking up a fuss and drawing attention to himself onshore like he had planned, he was resigned, yet again, to do as he was told.

'Out,' said Douglas, in a voice not even considering the faintest hint of a refusal.

Sabrina was pleased to see the van pulled right up to the edge of the quay. Its doors were opened to form a corridor for them to walk into, away from curious eyes. She need not have worried, Douglas's van was at the quay nearly every day picking up supplies or supplying other boats; if there had been anybody out and about that morning they wouldn't have thought twice about them. In fact, the only unusual thing about the unfolding events was that Douglas's van didn't usually leave the quay only to pull up just across the road.

David and the girl were taken out of the vehicle and through a heavy wooden door studded with old iron nails. On the other side of the door a small flight of stone steps led down to the beer cellars that had once been a cowshed. Another small flight of steps led up to the hayloft for the cattle. It was now the backroom of *The Bell* and its ancient timbers were painted tourist board regulation black. Above the stone fireplace, which an earlier tenant had installed, were the horns of an impressive Aberdeen Angus. A Highland Regiment cap dangled from one horn, it's red and white chequered ribbon frayed with age. It was into this room that the two captives were taken. Their entrance made an immediate impact and the room fell silent.

David scanned the room with an almost nonchalant air. This wasn't his show, it was Helen's, the girl from Brynfelinfach. Sabrina and Justin never used her name because they wanted to dehumanise her, to make doing what they did easier for them. They knew that constantly referring to her as the bitch would gradually wear her down too. That would make her more compliant and control could be obtained quicker that way. His show was to come later, on the other side of the North Sea. He had until then to come up with his master plan, or, he looked at Helen, her eyes were bulging and she was trembling, he would endure the same fate as she.

The tension was broken when Father MacKay stepped forward and welcomed them. 'Come on in,' he urged. 'Have some food, a drink.' It was a little before nine in the morning but everyone, including the fully smocked and dog-collared priest, was nursing a glass of whisky. 'Not for us,' said Sabrina. 'We're sailing this afternoon.'

'Very well,' said the Father. 'But you will take some food and sit by the fire with us.'

In all truth, both Sabrina and Justin felt it was a little too early to be eating dressed salmon and trout, but the islanders had obviously gone through a lot of trouble to make them welcome. Sabrina was also anxious for her slice of the extra breeding stock that Carl had spoken about over breakfast, so she accepted the food and signalled for Justin to join her. The Father cast an enquiring glance at David.

'He'll need somewhere to sit,' Sabrina said, by way of an answer. Douglas took David by the arm and led him to the end of the trestle table holding the food. He sat him down on a large oak chair and attached his control chains to one of the cross dowels under the seat. If David wanted to make a run for it he would have to take a solid wooden chair with him.

They joined the others sitting on two high-backed settles that stretched out from the fire. Helen was seated on a simple stool between the two settles, but farthest away from the fire. She was silent, her hands in her lap, her eyes fixed on an ashtray that sported *A Present from the Orkneys* and a dozen or so images of the barren islands around its outside. Everyone appeared deep in thought; the islanders took small nips of their malt and refused to look at each other, and Sabrina and Justin sipped St Mary's Spring water from blue plastic bottles.

'I don't know,' Gordon, a crofter from Leantrow, eventually said. 'Is it right? Is it right?'

'Is it right that we should let the island die?' put in Douglas. 'My family have lived here, been buried here, for generations. And yours, Brian… Fraser. Yours too, Gordon. She,' he pointed to Helen, 'is the answer to our prayers.'

'I agree with Gordon,' Fraser added. 'We shouldn't be praying for such things. What do you say, Father?'

Before the priest could speak Douglas jumped to his feet. 'Look, we've come too far. What do you want to do, ask these people to take her back? They've put themselves through a lot of trouble to get us this girl. We're not buying a fucking car here!'

Gordon admonished his friend for bad language and for a moment both Sabrina and Justin thought the situation was going to turn ugly, but Douglas had a persuasive lever to pull. He stepped behind the girl and yanked her pullover up and off to reveal her bare breasts to the group. Immediately the atmosphere changed and everyone fell silent. Sabrina watched and smiled with amusement at the sight of Brian having to wet his lips by running his tongue along them. Even Gordon was compelled to look at Douglas lifting and displaying the girl's breasts.

'She's built perfectly for what we want,' he told them. 'Heavy tits, good for milking.' He pulled the girl to her feet and yanked down her jeans, and all eyes fell upon her exposed mound. Douglas span her round and forced her over, and she supported herself on the stool while Douglas parted her bottom cheeks. There was now nothing left for the men to see, her puckered anus was stretched and her cleft opened, rose pink.

'I say,' Douglas continued, 'that we finish what we started. We need this bitch to keep our island going. She is mated with all of us until she's pregnant. That way we are all involved.' The men seemed calmer now and more receptive to their original plan. 'When she drops and everything settles we'll bring in another bitch.'

'But she's not a bitch,' Gordon doggedly pointed out. 'She's a woman, not an animal.'

Father Mackay stepped forward and motioned for Douglas to sit the girl down, but before he did so he stripped her naked in order to remind the others of what they were discussing.

The Father walked behind her, paused, and placed a hand on her head. As he did so Sabrina thought she saw a tiny tremor ripple through his body.

'It is written,' started Father MacKay, 'in Timothy. Let a woman learn in quietness and in all subjection. It is her fate to be brought here, her destiny to remain subject and it is our duty to maintain this island in fear of our Lord.'

Sabrina cast a concerned look at Justin, who returned it. Neither of them had expected divine reconciliation for their actions, but that was what Father MacKay was attempting. No doubt, thought Sabrina, Father MacKay had checked out the girl's body and was justifying his right to take it.

'What of the girl, Father?' asked Fraser. 'Has she no rights?'

Father Mackay gripped the top of her head and

brought her to her feet. 'It is in the Book – in Timothy. Do not suffer a woman to teach nor to exercise authority over man, but to be in quietness. These are the laws of God, not of man.' His hand moved down and covered her belly. 'She is as ripe for picking as the apples from Eden. She shall, as Timothy says, be preserved in childbearing.' The hand fell further to her vagina and he massaged her vigorously. 'Let us keep this girl. She has been brought here for a reason. Let us keep her naked, for He has said that women must adorn themselves with modesty and discretion, not with plaited hair and gold or pearls.'

The mood of the group had changed. Everyone was now nodding in agreement. Some had risen from their seats and were gathering around her. The Father lifted his smock and presented his penis to the girl's face. 'She is subject to our will in the name of our Lord. We must save the island for Him.' His speech over, the Father took the girl's head in his hands and forced her mouth over his cock.

'Fucking hell,' said Douglas. 'Father MacKay has shown us the way. There can be no turning back now.' As Sabrina pulled Carl to one side and asked about the money, Douglas was fumbling behind the girl. His hips were already beginning to thrust despite his heavy cock slapping the girl's thighs and missing her sex. Finally his wayward prick connected and was pushed fully home to a yelp of discomfort from the surrounded girl. It was truly too late to turn back now. As each islander took his turn Sabrina and Justin counted their money. Everything was in order.

'May I keep the holdall?' she asked. 'It makes carrying it easier.'

'With pleasure,' said Carl. 'Are you staying for a while?'

Sabrina motioned for Justin to unchain David. 'We

must be going,' she answered, amid the sounds of the islanders' first attempts to enjoy Helen. 'We've got another delivery to make… in Russia.'

'You'd better get a hat then,' Carl called after them, and as the door closed with a heavy thud he added, 'it's fucking cold in Russia.'

An icy blast of air brought David out of his dream-tormented sleep. It seemed to him that not a night went past when he wasn't forced to relive his ordeal at the hands of Sabrina and his onetime friend, Justin. The girls knew how the dreams afflicted him. He would sometimes wake them from their sleep when he cried out or writhed through some unconscious private agony. Mishka had seen the nightmare start and she had gone to the sled to fetch some caribou steaks, cheese and milk for breakfast. She knew he would be tired from a restless night and she wanted to please him.

'Close that door,' said David, more in a grumble than an order.

'Sorry,' Mishka offered. 'I have food.' She held up three frozen lumps of caribou flesh for his approval. David gave a half-hearted nod and she dropped his slab onto the stove, which Teena had just finished stoking. The meat bounced like a stone, and then began to sizzle viciously as the hot metal seared it.

While his meat cooked the girls defrosted their pieces near the stove, finishing the process by sucking and, when it was soft enough, finally chewing it. To help moisten the flesh further they drank caribou milk with it. Like all Arctic mammals a caribou produces very rich milk, almost all cream. The blood mingled with the pure white fluid, curdling it and turning it a beautiful pink colour. David couldn't help but make the connection between the colour in their mouths and the pink slice of their pudenda, and the image developing in his mind did much to compensate for a poor night's sleep.

'Vodka,' he demanded.

Teena left the slab of meat dangling from the corner of her mouth as she fetched his bone cup and filled it with his morning shot of liquid fire. He necked it down in one sour-faced swallow; it was hotter than the fire in the stove and it lifted him out of his seat.

He stabbed his knife into his steak and flipped it over. 'Vodka,' he said again. His cup was refilled, but this time he sipped from it and stood thoughtfully cooking his breakfast. Last night's tormentors had faded into sepia, then to grey, and by the time Mishka began caressing his morning erection they had dissolved into history, although he was only too aware that history had a habit of repeating itself.

He tested the steak with the point of his knife and satisfied himself that it was done to his liking; blood seeped from the small slit he had made. In a restaurant it would be regarded as rare; to the girls it was a cremation.

David returned to the captain's desk and ate his breakfast, while between his legs Mishka continued to massage his swollen cock. When he had taken possession of the girls, one of the first things he taught them was to service the erection he invariably woke up with every morning. Mishka and Teena took it in turns to suck his prick, partly to please him and partly to ensure he was slippery enough to enter the other one. It was a mutually beneficial system for the sisters; if either didn't ensure he was nice and wet then she would find a dry cock tugging and pulling at her vagina the next morning. For that reason the girl doing the sucking always did her best, and the effort was never lost on David.

Mishka was especially diligent this morning. She wanted to make up for his poor night and this was the only way she knew, though she was also sure it was the best method. The way his hips jerked involuntarily whenever her tongue tripped delicately over his bollocks and touched his anus was confirmation of her belief.

David motioned for Teena to get herself ready. The girl stripped obediently and placed herself over the captains desk, where she rested on her elbows and pushed out her young, tight but regularly abused bottom. She was only a few inches from David, sitting in the captain's chair. He took out his pipe and half filled it with loki. When the smoke filled his lungs he felt at peace with himself and relaxed back to enjoy Mishka's mouth and the rounded curves of Teena's bottom. He appreciated how her nakedness was enhanced by the silver torcs around her arms and calves, and how the amber bulb on her head strap imbued her with an almost ancient sexuality. Her proud body provided them with the one undisputable link with the past – the overwhelming need to fuck.

With Murmansk just a few hours away, breakfast over and the girls obviously anxious to please, David was warming to the day. He pushed back into the chair and pulled on the loki. It was almost as good as the sight of Teena's creamy white arse and that dark waiting furrow. Today, he had decided, was going to be good. His cock was thick and swollen and Mishka took it out of her mouth to show him. As she did so Teena wiggled her bottom expectantly, but David was not to be hurried. Mishka seemed a little confused that he hadn't plunged his turgid prick into her sister's waiting sex, but she hurriedly reinstalled the veined member upon her tongue when David motioned for her to do so.

David tugged a few more times on the arctic tobacco, and each time the vapours reined back his straining sperm, preventing their escape and stopping his orgasm. He was having a lazy morning. Today he would not fuck the young Lapp. Mishka would do the work with those pouting lips, and he would simply deposit his package inside her welcoming, accommodating, perfectly open sister.

The moment was not far away. Even a sharp and deep tug on the loki could not prevent his boiling seed from ascending his cock, so he pulled Mishka off and plunged into Teena, firing almost immediately.

David's sled was making slow progress through the fresh powdery snow, but after such a good morning it had little chance of dampening his spirits. He saw the fact that it had stopped snowing some time during the night as a further example of how well the day would unfold. The girls clung eagerly to him and the sun was shining, an incandescent medallion around the neck of fortune.

Chapter Six

Like it always does when you don't want it to, the door of Sabrina's room at the Hotel Romanov shut with a resounding clunk. The noise disturbed but didn't waken Sabrina, but Justin stubbing his foot on the dressing table and knocking over bottles of cosmetics did.

'W-what time is it?' she demanded wearily.

Justin peered unsuccessfully at his watch. The copious amount of vodka he'd drunk last night was obviously blocking his eyes as well. 'It's morning,' was all he managed to grunt.

Sabrina pulled back the sheets and padded through to the bathroom. 'Where were you when I got back?' she asked, between brushing her teeth and splashing her face with water.

'I went out.'

'On your own?'

'No, with a friend.'

'What, you just happened to meet an old acquaintance in the middle of Murmansk? Were they shopping, visiting a long lost aunty?'

Justin knew where this was going. 'Just a friend,' he replied, hoping she would let the matter drop. She wouldn't.

'Name?'

'Catherine.'

'So I take it Catherine is not a man then.'

'No.'

'And I take it you've slept with her.'

Justin nodded, so Sabrina added, 'Take your trousers

107

down and drop your pants.'

Justin wanted to say no and he tried to find the reserve to say that enough was enough, that he wasn't going to let her bully him any more, but his resolve failed him and he released the button on his trousers and let them fall to the floor.

'And those,' she barked, pointing to his underpants. 'I don't want to look at them. Not after what you've been doing. They're dirty.'

Justin finally defended himself. 'It was wonderful. It wasn't dirty.'

She ignored his retort and padded across the bedroom to the whip she kept in the corner. Justin's eyes followed her flawless brown skin and he was unable to prevent himself marvelling at her tight bottom. The firm flesh didn't wobble as many women's did, but remained solid with each step. Sabrina picked up the whip and held it almost lazily. 'Everything you do without my permission is dirty.' She raised the tip of it and lightly tapped between his legs, causing him to rise up on his toes. 'Did she laugh at this?' she mocked.

Justin reacted with thinly disguised anger. 'No, she didn't say anything.'

'Probably too embarrassed,' Sabrina goaded. She knew what she was doing. Her own sexual encounter with Vasili had left her aroused and eager for her own release, and in order to obtain it she needed Justin to be angry, or he would hold back in the power of his strokes.

She flopped on the bed in front of him. 'How could you possibly satisfy a woman with that tiny prick?' she continued. 'Did she feel sorry for it, all small and pathetic?'

While Justin stood on tiptoe accepting Sabrina's verbal abuse she pressed the tip of the whip into his balls, and looked at them pitifully. 'They look like little dates, don't you think?' Justin didn't answer. 'Not like Vasili's, my Russian captain. His were the size of duck eggs, smooth and full of sperm.' She reclined back on the bed to rest on one elbow, all the time tapping his balls with the thin tip of the whip. Her actions were light but they conveyed menace; every three or four taps was followed by a sharper, heavier hit that sent waves of panic to knot his stomach.

'You see, I wasn't alone either,' she went on. 'But I had a real man service me, not a limp-dicked no-balls kid like you.' She held the whip against his thigh and motioned for him to turn around.

When he was facing away from her she began examining his bottom with the end of the whip. 'No, no,' she said dismissively. 'That's a girl's bottom. Vasili has powerful thighs and his arse is like iron. That must be why he could thrust into me so hard, don't you think? Yes, that's why he's a man and you are, well, what are you?'

He remained silent until she dragged the whip viciously across his bottom.

'I asked you a question,' she persisted. 'Why is it a real man can fuck me so hard that I scream with every push, every slap of his balls against my bottom, but you, you don't even get a sniff of my cunt? Why is that, Justin? Why is it I don't let you fuck me?' She wasn't waiting for an answer. 'Why is it you are only useful for licking spunk from me?'

She made Justin turn back around before she positioned herself at the foot of the bed with him directly behind her, then she laid the whip on the sheets so that it ran from the foot to the head of the bed. 'Vasili sent you a little present,' she tormented. 'Can you see it?' She stretched out her hands to grab the frame of the bed and bent forward at the waist. Justin didn't want to play her games, but some irresistible force to peer at her drew him.

'Can you see, little-dick boy? Shall I open up a little bit so you can see better, see what Vasili did to me down there, see what he left for you?' Sabrina spread her legs to their supple extent. 'I was naughty too. He made me do all sorts of rude things. I'm sorry I can't show you the sperm he put in my mouth, but he made me swallow it. Can you see what he left for you down there, though?'

Justin nodded, and through a dry throat managed a strangled reply. 'Yes.'

'Would you have liked to have put that there instead of a hard, solid soldier?' The thick slick of a man's issue was clearly evident, and the smell of recent sex pervaded the room, helped by the heat her excited sex was generating. 'Do you think you'll ever be allowed to put your little thingy in there? Shall I ask Vasili if he'll let you? Maybe after he's finished and has no more use for me, perhaps then he might let you. Shall I ask him for you? I don't think you're brave enough to ask him, are you? He is big, that must be why his cock's so thick. What do you think? Would it be nice to put your little cock in there?'

She wiggled her bottom and Justin's mind went into overload. The words, her body, her spoiled sex, they were all forming into one huge, boiling sexual stew. She was playing him, teasing him, taunting him. 'Is it better than Catherine's cunt? I bet all the Russian boys use her. That's why you could have her, because everybody has her. I know you would like to have me, wouldn't you? Well I'm not letting you, Justin. I don't care how naughty I am and I don't care what you do.'

As she was finishing her sentence Justin reached down and under her belly. It brushed against her mound and she felt it. He was searching for the whip, but to

Sabrina he was seeking the long dark shaft of her lover. He picked it up and slowly withdrew it from beneath her. The finger-thick shaft entered her cleft and he drew it back like a violin bow, and Sabrina shuddered as the tip finally slipped against her pouting pudenda and left her. It would not be long now.

'It's my tight little pouch you want, isn't it?' she hissed, pushing him ever closer to breaking. 'It has always been my pussy, no one else's. You just can't stand it, can you? You can't take it; you can't have me like all those others have. Like Vasili did last night. Pumping my tight little cunt while you diddled with that whore. What are you going to do, piss-dick? You can't have me, you don't know how. All you can do is lick it up, lick it up from the others because you can't give it to me like they can.'

The whip came down with a slashing whoosh that reverberated around the room and faded behind Sabrina's screams; screams that went on and on as Justin's eyes dimmed behind a red cloud of anger and frustration. If he couldn't take her physically he would punish her for the humiliation she put him through. He would thrash her for every prick she had sat on, every prick she had sucked, and every man who had the power to take what he felt incapable of taking.

As his hand moved in a frenzy of thrashing Sabrina created her own sexual world where men would take and women were taken, over and over, again and again. Tied to posts, stripped and humiliated, beaten into sexual submission. When she blacked out under the tremendous weight of Justin's strokes she had no idea that the man she had created and forced into inadequacy in her bed was fucking her harder than any stiff-cocked, muscle-bound Neanderthal she had brought home with which to humiliate him.

The coffee at *Kafe Panoramic* was good, but it did nothing to shake off Justin's guilt and frustration. Sabrina had all but castrated him, and for over a year she had barred him from any meaningful sex with her. He was allowed to stimulate her in any way she saw fit, but ultimately it stopped before penetration. That's why he had taken her when she blacked out; he simply didn't have the courage to take her any other way.

Justin remembered their early days and the intense feelings, sexual and otherwise, which they used to inspire in each other. Then, as the number of girls they trained at David's house in Cornwall grew, she became cold towards him. It was like she couldn't differentiate between him and one of the trainees. Despite the humiliation she put him through, Justin could not pull away from her. Physically she was perfect and he was sure, deep down, that if he remained loyal to her she would see him for the true friend, and hopefully lover, that he was. Life could then return to the way it used to be.

The waitress brought them dishes of severyanka, which looked unappetising but tasted very good. The chowder removed not only the cold but also the sadness pervading Justin's mind. It turned his thoughts to Catherine and the wonderful night of lovemaking they had enjoyed together. She had been so understanding and giving, and in a way it restored his faith in life and relationships. Whoever Catherine's sailor boyfriend was, he was a lucky man. Last night he had opened up to her and told her everything; of how he sometimes hated Sabrina and wished he could just call off this whole adventure to get David back to England, and now, in the cold, or rather freezing light of day, his life didn't seem so bad. Looking out of the *Kafe* window to the snow blanketed countryside and the lights that blinked in Murmansk, even during the day, he wondered how it could be anything but good. He was sure too, that one day soon Sabrina would realise his love for her and would reciprocate.

'It's beautiful here, isn't it?'

Justin broke some bread and dipped it into the chowder. From another window could be seen Lake Semyonovskaya, silent and asleep beneath its sheet of winter ice. 'Very beautiful,' he agreed.

'Vasili brought me here last night, to see the lake and then up to the ice palace, while you were in that grubby flat with that whore.'

'I told you, she wasn't a whore,' Justin snapped.

'Of course she was.' Sabrina continued eating without regard for his feelings. 'Why do you think she was with you? Did you give her any money, buy her any drinks?'

'No,' Justin lied. He threw his bread into the chowder and pushed away the bowl. He wouldn't accept any criticism of Catherine and he didn't want to believe that she had simply given him sex in return for the money he'd given her at the nightclub. 'Why do you say these things to hurt me? What were you doing if not whoring yourself?'

'I'll tell you what I was doing while you had your dick up that whore. I was getting us some proper transport, getting us permission to cross the border without having visas or bunging the guards money to turn a blind eye.'

Justin was intrigued. Sabrina seemed to have limitless energy, and she never ceased to amaze him with her ability to keep going at whatever she was doing, but he had no idea how she could manage to obtain transport and all the other things she was saying when they were in the far north of Russia.

'How?' he asked simply.

'How do you think?'

The woman wearing the fur hat at the next table had a good idea how, but she still leaned closer, rather obviously, in order to catch the details. Sabrina ignored her and continued. 'I gave him what he wanted, and in return he did the same for me.' She looked at the large-framed woman and continued her answer, as if for her benefit. 'You should remember that, Justin. When a woman gets what she wants from a man, she's a lot more receptive to his advances.'

Despite her shoddy appearance – there were some bald patches in the furs she was wearing – the woman was obviously fully conversant in English. In response to Sabrina's response she gave a knowing nod of her head.

'I get nothing from you Justin. That's why you don't get between my legs.' The woman nodded again, but then the door to the *Kafe* opened and she quickly slinked back in her seat and ignored them.

For a moment Sabrina was puzzled, but the sight of Vasili in his military uniform walking towards their table diverted her mind. She rose from her chair and called out his name, pleased to see him. Vasili reached out and the two of them embraced warmly. At the next table the woman hurriedly rolled a chunk of bread around her own bowl of chowder and left, still chewing her food.

'How are you?' Vasili asked politely, then, before she could answer, whispered in her ear, 'I had a wonderful time last night.'

Sabrina looked Justin straight in the eyes and answered, 'I had a wonderful time too, Vasili. Thank you for showing me so much.' The Russian captain then noticed Justin, and Sabrina introduced him, adding that he was a business associate. She then sent Justin to the counter to get more coffee.

The table was empty when he returned but he saw

Sabrina outside, leant against a large military all-terrain truck. She was giggling and kissing her captain, and he was responding in kind. Justin put down the coffee, but was forced to pay for them and the chowder before he could leave and find out what was going on.

By the time he made it to the car park Sabrina and Vasili appeared to be near the point they had left hours earlier. He had his hands inside her long coat, while she rested her hands on his shoulders and whispered her gratitude. Next to the truck were two long sleek black cars. Four men in uniform were sitting in the one furthest away, and two soldiers stood dispassionately alongside the other one. Neither of them spoke, but looked straight ahead.

'Justin, look!' cried Sabrina when she finally acknowledged him. 'Vasili has brought us this truck for our trip to Ivalo.'

'That's great,' he said, rather unconvincingly. The Russian missed his disdain and held out some papers. 'What are these?' Justin asked.

'They are official papers that will let you travel between Ivalo and Lotta as many times as you want for one month,' the officer informed him.

'That's really kind of the captain, isn't it, Justin?' Sabrina's voice was testy and left Justin in no doubt that he had to go along with whatever story she had sold him. 'That's going to make it so much easier to visit the farms we have to see on this visit. Maybe we'll get time to do some sightseeing.'

'I hope so,' the captain said, obviously pleased with himself. 'It is good for Russia that you wish to set up this export business, but you must not think of work alone.' He turned to Sabrina. 'I have to go to Moscow tonight, so I will not see you for some time. If you leave a message for me at your hotel I will catch you when I get back.'

Sabrina smiled, and deep down felt the added satisfaction of a plan that had worked so well. How easy it had been to fool this peasant soldier and make him her slave too. The captain gave her a peck on the cheek and marched to his car, signalling for the two soldiers to follow him. Sabrina ran her hands along the heavy steel wheel arch and raised a leg onto its high bumper. As Vasili pulled away she pulled back her coat and flashed her legs at him, and the captain smiled and waved.

She waved back. 'Bye, captain stupid,' she said, smiling broadly.

'Well,' said Justin, after the two limousines had left the car park. 'Do you know how to drive this thing?'

Sabrina opened the door to the driver's side and climbed into the vehicle. A moment later Justin climbed into the other seat. 'It's all arse about face,' he opined.

Sabrina was concentrating on the controls. Everything was huge and robust, made from steel or heavy plastic, and the interior smelled of oil and old tobacco. On the cabin floor two levers indicated a two or four-wheel drive option, for road or country driving. 'How difficult can it be?' she said, and began pulling some levers. 'It's no different from a Land Rover.'

'Except about twice the size,' added Justin, unhelpfully.

Sabrina turned a knob and stabbed her thumb into a black push button between the two front seats. Immediately the engine barked into life and coughed out an oily cloud of diesel. 'Shit or bust,' she said, and thumped the gear stick into first. The heavy vehicle lurched forward but did not stall, and each looked to the other and smiled as Sabrina took the tank-size truck round the car park, growing more accustomed and confident with each circuit.

'Where now?' asked Justin.

'Back to the hotel to pick up our things,' she told him. 'Then off to Gorky's for that sled. We might need it around Ivalo. Even this monster won't get us through deep snow.'

'So we are going?' Justin asked nervously. 'You're really going to go through with it and track David down?'

Sabrina ground her way through the gears and turned onto Prospekt Lenina. Her knuckles turned white as she gripped the steering wheel, and her face was a mask of determination. 'Of course we are,' she snapped. 'I haven't come this far to turn back now.'

David's braking sled threw up a small storm of powdery snow. He had taken the coastal route north of the road from Pechenga in order to avoid the mountains and forest to the east of Inan. It meant travelling across windswept tundra and crossing a couple of frozen rivers, but it was quicker in the long run. It also avoided the greedy guards stationed at the Lotta border crossing.

The two days of travelling fatigue lifted at the sight of Murmansk spreading out before him. The afternoon sky was failing and the air carried a threat of yet more snow. To the south of the city a large number of Saami were racing reindeer signalling that the festival, or at least parts of it, were already underway. All three passengers on the sled let out a loud whoop and sped down the hillside towards the nearest hotel.

The hotel *Polarny Zony* wasn't the most salubrious of residences but it did have hot water, western mattresses and a toilet to sit on. More importantly, it also had secure lock-ups for ski sleds. David didn't trust hotel safes; this was a working town first and last and receptionists were known to vanish with a guest's property, especially after they had naively publicised their wealth by requesting a safe.

When he was satisfied that his amber was locked away from prying eyes he took the girls upstairs and showed them the possibilities that a shared bath presented. Both girls were hot water enthusiasts, constantly soaping each other as well as David. That was another reason why he had chosen the *Zony*; it had the biggest baths in the Arctic Circle.

A knock resounded at the door and David called out for them to enter. It was room service, and she was carrying a tray holding a silver bucket full of ice. In the ice was a large bottle of vodka and on the tray was an obscenely large Havana cigar, a luxury anywhere in the world, almost unheard of in northern Russia.

David poured a drink for the three of them and allowed Teena to light his cigar while Mishka sucked playfully on his cock. The maid held out a room service check for David to sign without appearing to register the three naked guests cavorting in the tub. The hotel was often frequented by sailors of the Russian northern fleet, or plant workers from the huge Severonikel Kombinat factory at Monchegorsk. They always had money on the hip and that meant business for the hotel and the local working girls. To the maid, only three naked people in the bath was positively decent.

David pulled himself out of the water to sit on the edge of the tub and open the bottle. As he unscrewed the top Mishka continued to lick his hardening prick, helped by her sister's hand softly squeezing his balls. David poured three shots of icy vodka, and while he sipped his he handed the cigar to Teena and watched as she puffed on the long dark tube. It amused him. 'You'd look great with a black cock in your mouth,' he told her. Teena smiled, not understanding what he was saying to her.

When she had pulled on the cigar a few more times

she handed it to Mishka and took her place between David's legs. 'And so would you,' he said, as Mishka's cheeks sucked in the smoke. 'I bet you two haven't even seen a black man, have you?' The girls continued to smile and take turns smoking and sucking, and David took the cigar from them and leaned back against the beautifully decorated tiled wall. He took alternate sips of vodka and puffs on the cigar while the girls took it in turns with his prick. Occasionally they would kiss each other and David noticed that their fingers were busily exploring each other beneath the water.

'You know,' he told them, although neither was listening. 'I think I'd enjoy that; seeing you two with a black dick up you. It's the colour thing I reckon – them being so dark and you being so pale. I wonder how you'd react if I put a black man on you.' He blew a large smoke ring towards the ceiling. 'Not that I'd know where to find a black person up here. Perhaps I'll take you down south after I've traded. It'll be like a holiday. Yeah, we could do with some travelling.'

He looked down to find both girls totally engrossed in each other. Mishka was leaning out of the bath and the water lapped around her thighs, leaving her bottom in full view. It was pink from the hot water and a line of suds ran around her buttocks, only to be stopped by Teena's fingers, bringing her to a slippery, noisy orgasm. 'It looks like you two don't need a cock to have fun,' he mused. 'Black or white.'

He poured himself another shot and allowed the girls to finish, enjoying the noises Mishka was making and the sight of Teena's hand pumping. Water splashed over the sides of the tub and formed pools on the green tiled floor, and soon a wave of steaming suds travelled the bath in sync with Mishka's undulating rear. The rhythm continued to build towards the moment, which arrived with a high squeal punctuated with sudden tight

119

gasps. Mishka threw back her head, her face a mask of tortured concentration, her body tensed and her stomach tight. For a whole minute Mishka maintained her taut pose before losing her ability to control her body, then slumped over the bath and closed her eyes to enjoy the sensuous feelings ebbing between her thighs.

David lowered himself back into the water. 'It's going to be a good festival,' he said to no one in particular. 'And it starts here.' He moved Teena into the same position that Mishka had just modelled. 'Hold this,' he told Mishka, passed her the cigar, and the lovely Lapp relaxed against the side of the bath and took several pulls on it.

She continued smoking and fetched a drink to watch Teena receive David's cock. There was more spilled water, more pools on the bathroom floor, and more orgasms to experience. David looked around and smiled at Mishka as she lazed with the cigar in one hand and a vodka in the other.

'Don't get too relaxed,' he told her. 'You're next.' He pulled Teena's hips back and drove his prick further into her slippery canal. 'I feel fucking great.'

The girls sensed his euphoric state and giggled, and as David fucked Teena over the edge of the bath Mishka flicked water over them and waited her turn.

Despite the Hotel Romanov being one of the more expensive hotels in Murmansk, it was still cheap enough for Sabrina and Justin to keep a room there while they travelled to Ivalo in search of David.

'Just take what we need,' she told Justin as they packed, so he threw several heavy jumpers into a rucksack and announced he was ready. Then he asked if she was sure they were doing the right thing, and Sabrina opened the wardrobe and pulled out the

Kalashnikov in answer to his question. She slid the gun into its case and collected several magazines, which she packed into her own rucksack.

'No one fucks with me and gets away with it,' she growled. 'No one.' She threw the rucksack over one shoulder and picked up the long bag containing the gun and winter survival gear. 'Now, let's get the bastard and get out of this freezing hell-hole.'

There was a large hamper waiting for them in the hotel lobby. Sabrina opened it and inspected the contents. 'Where's the salmon?' she asked the rather timid receptionist.

'It is there, madam,' he answered politely.

'That's fresh.'

'Fresh?'

Sabrina looked at him with contempt and Justin noted how tense she seemed now that they were underway and the excitement of finally doing something was upon them.

'Fresh?' the receptionist repeated.

'Yes,' she hissed at him. 'That is fresh. I asked for tins.'

'Let's take it,' Justin said hastily. 'What's the difference?'

'It'll go off.'

'Go off?' repeated Justin. 'This whole country is like one big fridge.'

'But we'll be in the wagon, won't we?' She pulled the fish out of the hamper and dropped it on the counter. 'Tell your boss I'll pay for one hamper, minus the fish!'

Sabrina was already in the wagon by the time Justin had explained everything to the bemused receptionist. He opened the door and threw in his rucksack. 'What's the point on shouting at him? It was a genuine mistake. They were trying to do the right thing.'

'They couldn't do the right thing if you drew them a map and shoved it up their arse.' She fired up the engine and they pulled away, leaving the hotel choking in diesel fumes. 'Let's just hope Gorky has kept the sled.'

Justin glanced at the long black case behind them. 'Yes,' he muttered to himself. 'Let's hope.'

The *Friedrich Engels* club resounded to the feet of a dozen sailors from the *Petrapavlovsk* dancing and kicking their feet in the manner of their Cossack forefathers. The sailors performed in a circle, and in the centre of that stood an old seadog, an ancient sailor, playing an equally ancient accordion; its keys were of whalebone and its bellows were made from the leather of a polar bear slaughtered by the maestro's great grandfather. He stamped his feet in time with the music and the whole hall joined in with him in celebration of the coming spring.

Around the ring of sailors were numerous other groups, some of only men, some of just women, others of both sexes. David, Teena, and Mishka formed one of the groups and as the music continued to flow, as did the alcohol, so did the number in their party. They danced in the traditional Cossack style, down on their haunches and kicking their feet in time to the music, holding out their folded arms for balance. Occasionally the really good dancers would spin around on one foot before continuing to kick. It was immensely strenuous and extremely exhilarating. Once in a while someone would fall amid peals of laughter, and would then have to pay the forfeit of drinking a shot of vodka before rejoining the dance. Of course, the alcohol would make the dancing more difficult, which would result in more vodka and so one by one the dancing deteriorated, except for the best exponents.

As the afternoon wore on one of the sailors had noticed that Teena and Mishka were with David, but he couldn't work out who belonged to who. He had no particular preference for one girl over the other, he just wanted to get to know a receptive female and both girls appeared very accommodating. Despite that, after being at sea for the last three months he had no desire to choose David's wife or girlfriend and end up in a fight. His confusion was compounded when he saw David kissing both girls, and the only reason the sailor could find for all this was that both girls were single after all, and that both were probably working the festival. He therefore decided to plump for Mishka and made his move by grabbing her waist and leading her to a nearby table.

The moment Mishka felt another man's hands on her body she froze. Although David had allowed other men to have both her and her sister, that was usually when he had taken them hunting and they were in another man's lodge. Very occasionally he would give shelter to other hunters at his lodge, and would share the girls during the night. Always though, he had given his permission first. This time permission had not been granted and David closed in on the sailor the moment he realised what was happening. The sailor recognised his mistake immediately and stepped back from Mishka, and now both girls were behind David and the two men stood face to face. The Russian spoke first.

'I thought she was alone,' he said. 'I did not know she was with you.'

David's smile puzzled and reassured the sailor, and his raised glass was a universal signal of friendship that removed any tension. The sailor's own smile grew into a grin and broadened further into a laugh that attracted the notice of some of his shipmates. Within moments David, or rather his girls, became the centre of attention and soon they were all dancing and drinking together. One of the sailors, a large man called Leonid, picked Teena up in his powerful arms and set her down on a table. He then picked up her sister and did the same with her so that both girls were back-to-back and leaning against each other for support, and while the men clapped their hands the girls continued their Cossack's dance on the table, squatting and kicking their legs straight out. In their knee length fur boots, leather bodices and short leather skirts, it didn't take long before the men noticed that every time the girls lifted a leg, they were treated to the sight of perfect pink sex lips.

The men urged the girls to kick more and to kick higher. David knew what they were doing and added his own encouragement. Soon Leonid crouched down and made no attempt at hiding his gaze, and the other men followed suit and a circle of seated sailors enjoyed the panty-less display of the two Lapps.

Fun and laughter began to give sway to an undercurrent of tension and the beginnings of arousal. None of the men had even seen a girl in several months, and the tantalising peeks between Teena's and Mishka's thighs was taking its toll on them, and many were casting glances at their friend, the one who had initially grabbed Mishka's waist. A few of them whispered to him, and in turn he looked across to David.

David knew what was coming. 'Yes, they are my girls,' he replied to the man's inevitable question. The next query was also expected.

'We,' said the sailor, gesturing with his hand to include the others, 'we take your girls to the back for some fun?' David waved his index finger in the negative and caused a universal moan of disappointment. 'We don't hurt them,' added the sailor. 'We are good men.' The others nodded in agreement.

The dance had now finished and the two girls were sitting on the table dangling their legs over the edge. They had listened to the conversation and were wondering if David would let them go with the eight sailors. They didn't really mind either way, it was not their decision and there was no point getting concerned about it. They kicked their heels idly while David deliberated.

Another song started but no one in the group began dancing; minds were on other things. The mood lifted when David sat between the girls and accepted a drink from Leonid.

'So,' he said to an eager audience. 'You're all keyed up from being at sea?' David's Russian was far from perfected and there was some bemusement among the men. 'You want a piece of my girls?' There was no confusing those words and several of them edged closer. 'Lift your skirt,' he told Teena.

Immediately the girl pulled the fur-trimmed leather skirt up just high enough for the men to glimpse her pudenda. David noticed the coy manner in which she did it, as if she was heightening the experience for the sailors and for him. He looked into her eyes and she smiled sweetly. Teena was obviously growing into a precocious girl.

He told her to release her skirt and the men moaned again, but it was a temporary disappointment because he turned to Mishka and told her to expose herself. Mishka had obviously learned from her sister, because she did the same. David smiled again and she released her skirt, and within seconds there was a flurry of hands in trouser pockets and a huge pile of roubles was thrown onto the table.

'Ah,' said David. 'Now we all understand each

other.' He gathered the money together and set off for the backroom with his arms around the girls' waists. Behind him the eight sailors cheered, grabbed a handful of vodka bottles and followed as if he was the pied piper of Hamlin.

The lounge was small and comfortable. The group sat around two green baize tables near a small stove that leaked fumes as well as warmed the room to a pleasant temperature. The vodka was poured into small one-shot glasses and everyone began drinking and talking. Despite the exchange of money and the implied transaction between David and the sailors, no one made to grab the girls. Given the sailors' enforced celibacy over the past months David found their conduct remarkable, until Leonid pointed out that he was going first on Mishka the moment David had finished.

'Oh,' said David. 'You're waiting for me to go first?' There was an enthusiastic group nod of affirmation. 'I've already been,' he added. 'This morning.' He looked at his watch. 'And besides, I have to be somewhere soon.'

'The girls stay here,' said Leonid, who was obviously worried that David had designs on taking them with him.

'The girls can stay.'

Leonid smiled and reached for Mishka, who was sitting beside him. He squeezed her breast and made her jump with the intensity of his grip.

'But no violence,' added David forcefully.

Leonid and a few of the others lifted their arms in a pre-emptive gesture of collective innocence. 'No violence,' they said.

David poured himself a final drink and watched as Leonid made his move on Mishka. It wasn't subtle, or protracted. The large man simply levered the girl onto her elbows on the table and did the necessary exercise.

Within a few moments her sister joined her on the table, and the two seemed quite happy with the situation and even kissed each other as two men moved into position behind them. As they were penetrated they dipped their backs and threw a comforting arm over each other. The morning's activities in the bath with David had obviously relaxed them and they were more than willing to go along with whatever he had agreed with the Russians.

The tension in the room was joined by the noise from the dancehall as David opened the door to leave, but before departing he turned back and saw that two others were already preparing to mount the girls.

'Be good,' he shouted, and gave them a wave.

The girls waved back and each blew him a kiss, though their movements were jerky with the rear-end pounding they were receiving. Satisfied that his property was safe, he left to return to the hotel *Polarny Zony* to pick up his amber.

Chapter Seven

Snow was again falling and the occasional flake made its way inside the collar of David's coat, to melt and run in slushy rivulets down his neck. It was unable to dampen his spirits, though, and he playfully kicked the occasional small drift into the air.

Always cautious, he checked the leather pouch that contained the season's amber collection. It had been a good year and he looked forward to cashing in the ancient nuggets. One piece in particular was going to be worth a small fortune. It was the largest piece he had ever found and it had become an iridescent tomb for a Mesozoic beetle. Polished and set in a silver clasp it was destined to adorn the neck of some rich Russian lady. Gorky's, his destination, was a short distance away and he returned the pouch into his pocket as he passed the large military all-terrain vehicle parked on the side of the road.

The door to the trading post opened with the usual ching of the bell. The noise caught the attention of Gorky and two customers, a man and a young woman.

Gorky recognised David immediately and shouted, 'Petr!'

The warning was lost on David, who continued into the shop, calling out his true name and wondering why Gorky hadn't remembered one of his best traders.

The other customers were not so slow. The man's face broke into a wide smile of recognition. David saw the welcoming expression and returned the smile, but he was puzzled. The man seemed so familiar and yet he didn't know anyone in Murmansk, and his eyes were still fixed on the man when his thoughts were broken by the grating sound of a firing bar being cocked. The heavy metal snap immediately attracted his full attention and his self-survival system kicked in. But it was too slow.

'Don't fucking move.'

The barrel of the Kalashnikov centred on his stomach, and its threat pinned David to the spot. Sabrina spoke again, this time to Gorky. 'Looks like we won't be needing that sled any more.'

Gorky shrugged nervously and weighed up his chances of reaching for the old Luger he kept beneath the counter for insurance. He decided against it. Sabrina had set the AK47 to automatic, so she wasn't relying on accuracy – she was going for the full spray.

'I've been searching for you, David,' she said dangerously. 'A long, long time.'

Justin nodded at his onetime partner and wondered what had brought them to this meeting, and Sabrina acknowledged the old friendship. 'Just like old times,' she said. 'The three of us together.'

'As I recall,' said David, 'it used to be only Justin and me. You were strapped to the fireplace with no clothes on, waiting on a good fucking.'

Gorky had guessed so much the moment he'd laid eyes on the girl. There was more to this than simple business. It was obviously very personal.

'Why have you followed me?' asked David. 'You must have spent more money tracking me down than I'm worth.'

'Let's just say it's a matter of professional pride.' Sabrina stepped forward in front of Justin. 'Don't be surprised,' she added. 'After all, it was you who taught me the meaning of the absolute. Absolute domination, total submission. I just decided on the former.'

David looked at his friend. 'Does she include you

in that formula?'

Justin shrugged to indicate he had no answer, and then moved as if to speak.

'Shut the fuck up,' Sabrina snapped. 'This isn't a school reunion.'

David made to step back nearer the door, but Sabrina recognised his intention and stabbed the gun into the air as a signal to stop.

'So,' he said, trying to remain calm and buy himself some time to assess the situation. 'Where do we go from here?'

'Back to the future,' smiled Sabrina. 'Back to your destiny. You cost me a lot of money, David. And I mean a *lot* of money. I'm going to have to find you extra duties so I can recoup my losses.'

'You didn't need me to get back your money. You could have found more stock. That's what you did with that girl we left in the Orkneys, wasn't it? You kidnapped her and sold her on.'

'You're a rotten apple, David, about to poison all of us.' Her hands increased their grip on the gun and the three men noticed her beginning to tremble slightly.

'I was about to do fuck all,' David reasoned. 'I'm happy up here. I just want to be left alone.'

'That's not possible. I've come to take you back.'

David threw up his hands and spoke to the ceiling. 'I'm not coming back. Don't you understand? I'm going nowhere.'

The click on the rifle's safety reverberated around the room and the atmosphere rapidly descended to freezing. Justin saw the intensity on Sabrina's face and tried to ease the tension.

'Look,' he pleaded, hoping to defuse her anger. 'We're miles from home. He's not coming back. He doesn't even want to. What damage can he do to us in Britain from here?'

'You're making the mistake of logic, Justin,' David said, the calmness of his voice surprising even him. 'This has nothing to with money. If it did she'd take this amber and let me go.' David offered up his pouch. 'The amber in here is worth thousands back home. Take it and we can all walk away.'

Justin visibly slumped with relief. 'Take it,' he urged her. 'We come out on top and we can put all this shit behind us.'

Sabrina's eyes remained fixed on her quarry. 'I always come out on top. He's coming with us.' She spoke to Gorky without taking her eyes from her quarry, 'You must have some sort of manacles among all this shit.'

Gorky shook his head.

'No rabbit wire for nooses and traps?'

Gorky nodded this time, and added, 'Of course, of course.' He could see the girl was teetering on the edge and the index finger on her right hand had come to rest rather shakily on the rifle's trigger.

'You can see it now, Justin,' David went on. 'Money's got nothing to do with it.'

Justin lifted his hand to gesture for him to be quiet and not to aggravate the situation, but David ignored him.

'She wants me back because I'm the only man who can control her. I'm the only man to make her feel like a woman.' He turned to his onetime sexual trainee and with a smile added, 'Isn't that right, Sabrina?'

Her stern look melted into a faint smile, and in that instant Justin realised that she had never really loved him at all. He turned towards her, dejection written in every language upon his face. 'You mean, we've chased him for a thousand miles because you can't bear the fact he ran away from you? Because you can't live without him?'

'Hurt, Justin?' David goaded. 'She's just a user. When I was running Camelot, the school was there for people who wanted to live that way. It was there to help dominant males and submissive females live how they wanted to.

'But her…' he pointed straight at Sabrina, 'all she ever wanted was money and the power over men. But she knows it's not right. That's why she likes the punishment.'

'How do you know about that?' gasped Justin.

'Shut up,' Sabrina warned.

'Because I showed her how to be a woman,' David went on relentlessly. 'She just didn't realise it at the time. And now she's all fucked up. And she's fucking you up, and now she wants me to pay.'

'I said shut up!' Sabrina cried.

Gorky came back with the trappers wire and placed it on the counter. 'Tie his hands,' she ordered Justin, and he picked up the wire and made his way to his old friend. When he was within a few feet of him he passed between the line of David and Sabrina, and it was the chance David had been waiting for. In that brief moment he reached to his left, pulled over a glass cabinet of hunting knives and bolted for the door. Sabrina let fly with a hail of bullets without warning and by a miracle they all missed Justin, but they also failed to find the intended target. David was gone, and he left the door open on his way out.

'After him!' she screamed, but Justin was rooted to the spot, stunned by the deafening rattle of the gun and the shattering of broken glass.

'My shop!' Gorky wailed. 'Look at my beautiful shop!'

'Did I say to shut the fuck up?' screamed Sabrina. She spun round, waving the gun furiously, and Gorky took that as a signal to hit the floor, awaiting the deathly cough of the gun, but his fears were not realised.

Sabrina rushed past Justin and out of the shop to see David approaching the end of the street, and managed to get off another short blast from the Kalashnikov before he rounded the corner and disappeared from view.

From inside the shop Justin was shouting at the top of his voice. 'What the fuck is going on? What are you doing?' He rushed outside to find Sabrina throwing the gun into the truck and opening the driver's door.

'I'll tell you what's going on,' she spat through clenched teeth. 'I'm doing a fucking man's job because he hasn't got the balls to do it himself.' She slammed the door and stamped on the throttle. Through the roar of the straining engine the first wails of police sirens were screaming closer, and before Sabrina had gone a hundred yards the police were turning into the street behind her. By the time she reached the corner she had clipped a Trabant, almost disintegrating it in the process, and careered into a wall. Two police cars raced past and Justin had no choice but to sidle away. He wasn't stupid, though. If he'd walked in the opposite direction he would have stood out among the throngs of people gravitating towards the excitement. With nerves jangling he made his way towards the wreckage. The Trabant was unrecognisable, as was the driver, who had left his scalp flapping from the broken windscreen. Justin paused long enough to look interested and then went on his way. Passing the damaged army truck his stomach churned at the sight of Sabrina. She was motionless and hanging out of the door, only prevented from falling into the snow by her legs caught around the two gear sticks. His initial reaction was to rush forward, but a familiar voice behind him steeled his resolve. It was Gorky shouting and waving his arms at Justin. In the excitement no one was taking any notice, but Justin knew he would point him out at the first chance he got.

And so, terrified and alone, Justin pulled up his collar and dissolved into the fading light of the afternoon.

David thought he didn't have time to collect his things from the hotel room. He hadn't seen Sabrina crash the truck and he assumed she was tracking him down. He satisfied himself with what he had left in the ski sleds, thanked God that he still had his amber to trade, and set off to pick up the girls.

Mishka and Teena were still entertaining the sailors when David arrived, but he didn't have time to enjoy the scene. Several of the men were drinking and chatting, so David was relieved that they had sated themselves after so much enforced celibacy at sea. It also meant they weren't going to be upset when he pulled the girls away, although the two currently indulging themselves were, and the one screwing Teena refused to relax his grip when David pulled her by the arm, but he was close to ejaculating and his hips juddered as he did so. David sighed; that was one less male to think about.

'Why do you go?' said the large sailor called Leonid. 'We are just resting.'

David smiled grimly, wondering if the sailor had the faintest idea about the complications of people's lives. 'It's a long story,' he said.

'But, we will see you tonight? Here?'

David took hold of Mishka's arm and led her and her sister towards the door. 'I've got to go.'

'Where?'

'Out of here. Out of Murmansk.'

Leonid chased after his newfound friend. 'You are in some trouble. I can see it in your face. Who is after you, the police?'

'Look, it's not your problem. I'd stay well away from me.'

Leonid put out an arm and stopped the trio before they reached the door. 'You go east, west, south maybe?'

David hadn't given any thought to where he was going. All he knew was that he had to get out of there. He paused for thought and Leonid offered him a glass of vodka to calm his nerves.

'I can't go west,' he said, more to himself than to the sailor. 'Gorky must have told them where I am. That's why they were there.'

Leonid and the two girls exchanged bemused looks.

'South is too dangerous. Too near the cities.'

'Then it's east?' said Leonid.

David threw back the vodka and confirmed east.

'Then you are in luck. Tonight my brother sails for Amderma. The breakers have made a path. He will take you.'

'How much?'

'Let's say half the roubles you took off my friends for the girls?'

David looked at the sisters and noted the look of concern on their faces. They had no idea what had just happened but they knew something was amiss. 'Right,' he confirmed to the Russian. 'I need somewhere safe to stay until we sail.'

Leonid went up to the bar and called out to the barman. A brief conversation ensued, during which the barman glanced over several times. Eventually Leonid motioned for David and the girls to join them. As they went across the other sailors cheered and waved them goodbye.

'Everything okay?' David asked anxiously.

Leonid leant forward into his face. 'Georgi,' he said,

pointing to the man. 'He was watching what we were doing with the girls.'

'So?'

'He says no roubles. You give him the younger one and he will hide you until tonight.'

'Is it safe?'

Leonid covered his heart with his large hand. 'Perfectly safe.'

David was not so sure, but then, he had no choice. 'Tell him okay.'

Georgi was all smiles as he pointed the way. The group walked along a sloping corridor that fell away beneath the city pavements. Suddenly Georgi stopped and pulled away a barrel that stood against the wall to reveal a small opening no more than two feet square, and David immediately announced that he was not going into any hideaway. 'You have no choice,' Leonid reminded him, and through a small grimy fanlight that looked up out onto the street a police car could be seen rushing past, siren blaring. 'You have nothing to worry about here.'

'Oh yes?' said David, preparing to enter the small recess. 'And what about you?'

Leonid's expression changed to one of anger. 'I could have smashed your face in the moment we entered this corridor,' he spat, and for a moment David's blood ran as cold as the pavement outside, but then Leonid added, 'But I haven't. That must tell you something.' He paused and turned his hand towards the small opening. 'And you still have no choice,' he added.

David ducked into the cramped room, closely followed by the girls and the two men. There was only just enough room for them, another person and it would be very uncomfortable. Georgi struck a match and used it to light an old lamp that was sitting on a tea chest.

David surveyed the cell, for that was what it looked like. Despite its underground situation it was dry enough, and was also very cold.

Georgi and Leonid said a few reassuring words on their way out, and the two girls looked at David. They were obviously frightened at the way events had so suddenly turned, but the only comfort he could offer was to cuddle them close as they huddled quietly on the small mattress built onto a shelf and stared at the lamp.

The three felt like prisoners, and clung together under the coarse blanket on the mattress. The lamp flickered, but its feeble light was unable to successfully penetrate the gloom of the cell. But it drew their weary eyes to it, as only a flame seems to do, and relaxed them into an uncomfortable doze.

It was two hours before the sound of the barrel woke them. The girls tightened their grip around David as the small door opened and a triangle of light cut the gloom. It was Georgi carrying a tray of soup and heavy bread. He placed the tray on the floor and signalled for them to eat, and then he backed out of the cell.

Just as they had finished eating they heard the grating sound again. This time Georgi came all the way into the cell and David realised it was pay-up time. Georgi placed the tray on the tea chest and motioned for them to move along the mattress. He then mumbled a gruff order for Teena to squat in front of him, and began undoing his grubby trousers.

Teena hesitated, before David nodded and indicated for her to obey. As obedient as ever, the girl positioned herself on the mattress in front of the man, and waited.

The Russian's penis was already semi-erect, and the angry purple helmet was pushing its way past its roll of foreskin in desperate search of the forthcoming pleasure. Georgi turned to his watching audience and gave a satisfied leer. Both David and Mishka looked on with interest, their earlier fears now diminishing as the sexual congress proceeded. Georgi took hold of the girl's head with one hand and presented his cock to her lips, and Teena allowed him access by forming a warm pouch with her willing mouth and sucking him to the back of her throat until the wiry bush of his unwashed pubes touched her nose.

He was in no rush. He had already stroked himself to several orgasms earlier when he had watched the girls being gangbanged. This was the icing on the cake, so to speak, and he was going to hold on to his icing until it was impossible for him to carry on.

David and Mishka slunk into a shadowy corner and pulled the blanket over their legs. As the loathsome man began to increase his tempo David noticed Mishka studying the scene intently, her large dark eyes glued to the gnarled slab pounding her sister's mouth. David smiled and pulled her closer, he was very proud of the girls' substantial sexual appetite, and he was always satisfied with their compliant performances.

For a brief moment the cell fell darker as the light dimmed. David turned from Mishka to see the Russian change position and block out the lamp. He was withdrawing his penis from Teena's mouth and David expected to see it covered with his issue, but he hadn't come. He had decided to savour her generous breasts and pulled Teena to her feet and removed her top. The cold immediately teased out her nipples and he roughly squeezed them into his mouth, crudely fingering between her legs as he slobbered and slavered like a starving pig.

In the shadows Mishka snaked a hand under the rough blanket and sought out David's cock. He allowed her to do it, and relaxed against the wall as a warm glow banished the coldness of the underground cell.

The Russian eventually pulled Teena up from the bunk. He was still clothed except for his trousers, which were a heap around his ankles, and his cock stretched up in silhouette against the lamplight. He took hold of her arm and turned her around to face the bunk, then pushed her forward until she was forced to support herself on the mattress and lifted up her short skirt. Her knickers had been missing since the gangbang, a trophy to some randy sailor. Georgi used a hand to guide his straining prick down and away from his paunch, aiming at the lovely girl's vulnerable fig. He nudged closer and grunted as he felt her open to allow him entry. His hips jabbed, rocking the girl forward and making her squeal as he penetrated her, and then his thrusting increased in power and speed and he slumped on her back and milked her breasts.

Mishka increased her tempo in tune with the brute, and the extra intensity closed David's eyes and mind to everything except the vision of his girl being ruthlessly fucked over the old stained mattress in an underground Murmansk hideaway.

So lost were they all that they missed the dark figure blocking out the faint light of the tiny entrance, and when David did notice the shadow the man was already inside. It was Leonid, and he was grinning from ear to ear at the sight that confronted him. He slapped Georgi's back and was cursed for his pains. Georgi was gripping Teena ever tighter and his face was contorting into a grimace of intensity as he finally jammed his hips forward and ejaculated into her.

'I see Georgi insisted on payment,' Leonid beamed.

David composed himself; his own orgasm subsided and his survival instinct kicked in once again. 'Everything sorted out?' he asked, his voice a little weak after the skilled attentions of Mishka's hand.

'You have no worries,' Leonid confirmed.

David rose from the mattress, quickly fastened his trousers, and told Teena to dress. 'Let's go,' he said.

The two men crawled out of the cell, followed closely by the girls. 'What have you done with my sled?' David asked.

'Nothing,' replied the Russian sailor. 'But I will dispose of it for you, if that is what you want.'

David looked at him with a knowing smile. 'And you will send the money after me?' Leonid smiled slyly, but David added, 'Too bad, my friend. I'm going to need that sled after we land at Amderma.'

Leonid gave an exaggerated shrug, but cheered up when David nodded towards the girls and added that he might compensate them for their trouble on the boat.

The party stepped into the cold and snowy courtyard of the club. It was dark again and an old lorry was waiting to take them to the port. A man jumped down from the cab and Leonid called him over to help load the sled that Georgi had stashed in a disused lean-to against the yard wall.

Within ten minutes the vehicle was loaded and David and the girls climbed into the rear of the tarpaulin covered truck. They were told to lie still and keep quiet. Although the lorry driver didn't know who his passengers were he did know that there was a lot of police activity around by the port. Apparently, he told them, three westerners had been in a shoot-out at Gorky's and the police were treating it as possible espionage.

Behind some containers the three huddled as the lorry jerked and pulled away from the club, and David strained to hear any conversation between Leonid and the driver. There was none, and that worried him. Obviously the scenario with the police was real, and the two Russians were also feeling the tension created by carrying the wanted cargo.

It looked to Catherine like someone had thrown a pile of old rags onto the steps leading down to her apartment. She was cautious. This was a mean town and if something looked suspicious, then it probably was. She decided to approach the clothes carefully and kick it with her boot. She edged closer.

'Catherine!' It was Justin. He was shivering and a tear had frozen at the corner of his eye. 'You've got to help me.'

Catherine looked nervously around and said loudly, 'Who are you? What do you want? I don't know you.'

Justin tried to get up but his knees had locked with the cold and it was a struggle. Catherine scanned the street again. There was no one in sight, so in one swift movement she unlocked her door and bundled the troubled Englishman inside.

'You are freezing!' she said with real concern. 'What has happened?' then before Justin could answer she ran out to the bathroom and turned on the shower, then went back to undress him. He was huddled in an armchair shivering violently. Catherine dragged him in front of the fire and began removing his clothes. As the flesh became visible she rubbed it vigorously with a warm towel to encourage the circulation, then moved on. Suddenly Justin started to groan loudly.

'Does it hurt?' she asked, somewhat unnecessarily.

'M-my feet and my hands,' Justin answered. 'My feet and hands feel like hot pins and needles.'

'That is good,' Catherine told him before yanking his trousers and pants down. She immediately began rubbing his thighs with the towel and Justin saw her giggling.

'W-what's so funny?'

'Your penis,' she chuckled. 'It has grown smaller with the cold.'

'Just what I needed, humiliation and frostbite,' he grumbled.

Catherine kissed the tip of his prick, and then licked his shaft and balls before drawing his whole cock into her mouth.

'Definitely warmer,' he sighed, and then winced as the pain returned to his fingers.

'Well, I don't think you have to worry about your penis falling off,' Catherine told him. 'Now you must have a bath.'

'Can't I stay here?'

Catherine lifted his legs out of his trousers. 'No, you will cook your skin. There is no blood under it. It is inside you.' She made motions up and down her body with her hands, trying to explain that he was suffering minor frostbite, and that his blood and been redirected to protect his liver and other organs. 'Come, in the bath.'

She supported Justin through and helped him into the tub. To him it felt like the water was boiling, his skin crawled with a thousand painful needles and he called out again.

'Try to hold on,' Catherine urged. 'Just a few moments, you will be nice.'

She was good to her word. Within minutes the pins and needles had gone and his body felt as if he was submerged in warm honey. Slowly the feelings came back and within a few more minutes the water began to feel quite cool.

'Good sign,' said Catherine. 'Your senses are back.' She ran some water out of the tub and replaced it with warmer water. Justin's body relaxed and she repeated the process several times until the temperature was raised to that of her normal bath. Then she began to undress.

'What are you doing?' he asked.

She pulled off a pair of white thong panties and threw them on the radiator. 'I am having a bath. You have taken all the hot water.' She laughed and stepped into the tub, her neatly trimmed sex an inch or two from Justin's nose. As she sat opposite him he noted a few tiny bubbles of air in the few hairs she had left on her vagina. Catherine rubbed them with the tips of her fingers and the bubbles rose to the surface and popped. 'I'm sorry,' she said.

'For what? Saving my life?'

'For pretending I didn't know you – outside, on the steps.' She took up the soap and began washing his arms. 'There are still police watching us.'

'Who are *us*?'

'Everyone,' she answered. 'The West thinks we are all free now. That is not so. You surprised me. I did not know why you were here. I thought it was a trap.'

'Well, the police may well come knocking.' Justin shook his head and added, 'I shouldn't have got you involved. It's not your problem.'

Catherine grabbed him by the arm and forced him back down into the water. 'You made it my problem by coming here. The police, they will believe I know something. What have you done?'

Justin looked at her with admiration. 'If I tell you then you will know, and the police will make you talk.'

'If you don't tell me then I cannot help.' She resumed washing his arm again while Justin had time to gather his thoughts.

'It's Sabrina,' he said eventually. 'She went mad in a shop. A trading post sort of place.'

'Gorky's?'

'Yes. She shot a gun and then crashed this vehicle we'd borrowed from some soldier.'

'A gun? You have a gun?'

'Not me,' he answered defensively. 'Her, Sabrina. We saw David.'

Catherine looked surprised. 'That man you were following?'

'Yes. He just walked into the shop while we were getting equipment to go and search for him. It was mad. I told Sabrina not to force him but she was so angry.' He paused and relived those few insane moments in his head.

'She shot him?'

'No, thank God. He escaped but she tried to chase him and smashed into this car.'

Catherine dried her hands and reached for some cigarettes on a shelf. She lit one and blew out the match. 'Why did you come here?'

Justin shook his head pitifully. 'I had nowhere else to go. No friends apart from you. I just didn't know what to do.'

Catherine smiled and drew again on her cigarette. 'That is cute,' she said, as she exhaled. 'Yes, I think that is very cute.'

'Aren't you angry?' he asked.

She paused, as if contemplating the question. Finally she took another tote and answered, 'Too late for anger. We must get you to the embassy.'

'We can't do that,' he said flatly. 'That will just bring notice to who we are, and what we're doing in Russia.'

Catherine stubbed out her cigarette. 'Then we must find out what we can do.' She got out of the bath and drew a towel around herself. 'You stay and I will make some soup.' She left to go to the kitchen.

'And then what?'

She poked her head around the door. 'And then I shall find out what has happened to your friend. But I don't believe *she* is your friend.'

The lorry was stopped at the port gates. The guards were expecting them because the *Olga* was due out in an hour or two for Amderma. They exchanged pleasantries and then David's stomach lurched as he heard one of the guards ask them if they had an Englishman in the back. The guard was so amused at his question that he missed the stumble in Leonid's voice.

'Englishman?'

'You haven't heard?' said the guard.

'Heard what?'

'Two English people, a man and a woman, went mad with a gun. Shot up Gorky's really bad. Hey,' he added as an afterthought, 'you will have to sell those western jeans and music you bring in somewhere else.'

Leonid leant out of the window. 'Know anyone?'

The guard looked at his comrade and received a nod. 'My cousin, Sergei.'

'I'll bear him in mind,' said Leonid, grinding the gears of the truck.

The guard slapped the door and waved them on. 'Make sure you do,' he called after them. 'He'll give you better prices than Gorky.'

Shipside everything was quiet, but Leonid and his mate wouldn't allow David to help unload the sled, so he and the girls were ushered straight onboard. As one of the crew offered a helping hand to the sisters a few of the other sailors passed knowing glances between themselves. The trio were then taken below.

It was an hour before the boat shivered and the engines pushed it away from the harbour wall and out onto the inky black water. It was another half hour before David felt relaxed enough to pull out his pipe and fill it with loki. Mishka offered him a light and he sucked thoughtfully, watching the bowl glow as he inhaled. A day that started so well had turned into a shambles. He pulled the small curtain across the porthole so he could see Murmansk fading as they pulled further away, then he turned to the girls for solace.

Chapter Eight

The van was filled with exhaust fumes and had rattled through the Russian countryside for the best part of two days and nights. It bumped and jolted its way for hours over uneven roads, and Sabrina had no way of knowing how much longer it would go on for. She was kneeling on the van floor, her hands were cuffed behind her back and the cuffs attached to the roof of the vehicle. Around her neck a collar kept her face on the bed of the van, and her head was covered in a black hood. As with all female prisoners the guards had removed her knickers and pulled her skirt up to reveal her sex.

If there had been any windows in the van and if Sabrina had been able to look out of them she may have spotted GUM's as they drove along Nikolskaya Ulitsa, the place where she found the piece of carved amber that had set her on David's trail. She may even have been warmed by the sight of Detskiy Mir, the biggest toy store in Russia. Then again, if she had, she would have recognised Lubyanskaya Ploschad, and she would have known she was on her way to Lubyanka, one time home to the Cheka and now the residence of the KGB and the most infamous prison in the motherland.

As uncomfortable as her position was, she had fallen into torpor from sheer exhaustion. She had not been fed and there were no toilet stops, at least not for her. It was not her fault, therefore, that she hadn't realised the vehicle had stopped. She missed the sound of huge iron gates opening and closing and had no idea that she was deep beneath the pavements of Moscow. Even when the back of the van was opened and three green-uniformed officers, including one woman, stood staring at her exposed urine-stained rear, Sabrina was still oblivious to her situation.

The men grabbed the prisoner and dragged her down a further flight of steps into a reception area that consisted of one table, one chair and a feeble light bulb. The room stank of urine and nicotine. Behind the table sat an officer ranked higher than the others, and the female guard took up her position behind the seated interrogator while the men forced Sabrina into the centre of the room and took a few steps back.

'You are?' said an English voice with just the hint of an eastern lilt. It was the first words Sabrina had heard since they left Murmansk.

She remained silent.

'You are?'

Still she said nothing, so the officer spoke again. 'Let me rephrase that,' he said calmly. 'You are,' he paused, 'in deep shit.' He nodded to one of the two men behind Sabrina, who stepped forward and tore the skirt from the prisoner, leaving her naked from the waist down.

'Oh,' said the officer without changing the pitch of his voice. 'How unusual.' He had spotted the rampant dragons tattooed either side of Sabrina's naked sex and leaned closer to examine them.

He stood up and remained directly in front of her. Sabrina could now sense his presence; she could smell the strong odour of stale coffee on his breath and when he spoke again she felt the blast from his mouth disturb the cloth of the hood. She was though, too terrified to answer, and she kept her eyes screwed tightly shut in case some unseen object was poked into them.

The one thing she wasn't worried about was being

naked. She was well aware how sexual embarrassment was used to break down prisoners, especially females. She had used the technique herself, including on David, and she knew it was effective. She also knew that its efficiency lay mostly in the prisoner's strength of character and their feelings about sex. In that department Sabrina was stronger than most.

But if her mind was powerful her body remained that of a female, and when a clenched fist struck her in the stomach she crumpled and landed heavily on her bottom. The blow had driven the wind out of her and she dropped her head between her parted knees to gasp for air. The interrogators appreciated the view and smiled at each other.

'Pick her up!' snapped the chief guard.

The two male guards dragged Sabrina to her feet and presented her to their boss. 'Your courage is admirable,' he told her. 'But you will tell us everything we want to know.' The boss ran a finger against Sabrina's sex. She didn't flinch and that made him smile again. 'I shall look forward to breaking you.'

He turned to the guards and told them to take her to the bathhouse. She was grabbed immediately and dragged away.

With her arms locked behind her back and partially lifted from the floor Sabrina part-ran, part-walked, and mostly stumbled along between the two burly men, when suddenly her body hit a pole fixed in the centre of the corridor and she fell backwards in both shock and pain. The two guards had purposely marched the unsuspecting and hooded girl into it as a form of welcome, which they extended to all the new inmates. After picking her up and taking her along several other corridors they stopped and Sabrina heard the sound of a heavy door being opened. It was the bathhouse.

She was guided inside and immediately felt the icy

chill in the air, especially around her exposed thighs. She began to shiver.

A woman's voice barked and the female guard answered before pushing Sabrina further into the room. There was another exchange of words and the hood was suddenly pulled from Sabrina's head. Her eyes remained tightly shut because she was afraid the light would hurt them after two days of total darkness. She was also terrified of what she would see. But she need not have worried about the light, because the room was very dimly lit by several dull lamps bolted to the walls. Some niches and corners were in total darkness, while the rest of the room was in shadow or half-light.

'Welcome,' said a large Russian woman sat behind a table that was on a raised platform. She was looking into a bluff coloured folder, which she promptly put down in order to look at the prisoner. 'I see we know nothing about you,' she added, before getting out of her seat, and Sabrina saw that the woman's size was due to physical exercise, and not an over enthusiasm for food.

The interrogator, for Sabrina was in no doubt that she was just that, walked slowly around the table, her eyes fixed permanently on those of Sabrina. Despite her heavy build she stepped lightly down from the raised area and stood directly in front of her new prisoner. New prisoners were always a joy to Yelena Nesterov. Most were terrified from the start, and that was good. A few, and Sabrina looked to be in that company, entered Lubyanka with confidence and would have to be broken, and Yelena liked that too.

Too frightened to return her gaze, Sabrina looked over Yelena's shoulder. The room was completely tiled from floor to ceiling and several stalactites of what looked like some sort of salt descended like the encrusted teeth of a dragon.

Yelena gripped the heavy material of Sabrina's shirt and ripped it into tatters as if it was paper. Sabrina was too scared to be impressed. The Russian leaned forward and their eyes met, but Sabrina saw not one glimmer of humanity. Her captor was a robot of the motherland, an automaton prepared to carry out any instruction she was given. She was as cold as the room.

Without emotion she slipped her hands under the cups of Sabrina's bra and tore the garment in two. Apart from the rags of her shirt hanging from the handcuffs Sabrina was now naked. At the movement of Yelena's hand the guards directed Sabrina towards a passageway that was even darker than the rest of the room. She made her way in some trepidation, her feet pitter-pattering on the cold tiles as she followed behind the broad Russian.

After about ten feet or so Sabrina detected freezing water around her feet. It was so cold it was at the stage of slush and Sabrina wished she was wearing the heavy serge uniform of the prison guards.

The small party of two men, two women and Sabrina entered another gloomy room. This one was even colder than the other, and Sabrina noticed an open trough that was fed by a large tube running with icy water. The other end of the trough emptied through a hole in the wall on the opposite side of the room. There was a walkway running along the trough, with a rusting handrail above from which hung rubber tubes terminated with a steel attachment, and before Sabrina could hazard a guess at their intended employment she witnessed them in use.

At one end of the trough two men were bent over the handrail. They were naked and their bottoms forced high. Behind each of them stood a woman, their uniforms protected with leather aprons, feeding the tubes into the anus of each man. Once fitted the women pulled a lever and the men flung back their heads in obvious discomfort and pain.

The guards were about to drag Sabrina across to take her place over the rail when Yelena stopped them. She wanted to build up the fear in her new prisoner, and letting her watch what was happening was a good way to do it. And it was having the desired effect on Sabrina, who watched wide-eyed as the hoses were removed from the men's behinds and replaced with rubber plugs. One of the women, a stunningly beautiful Slavic blonde, almost six feet tall, then kicked the first man in his distended abdomen. He yelped pitifully in severe pain, but the girl was oblivious. She kicked his legs wide apart and slapped a wooden paddle into his scrotum. He screamed again and tried to bring his hands to his groin, but was stopped by chains holding them to the floor. The blonde then wrenched the plug from his arse and laughed as a great arc of water and effluent emptied from his bowels into the running trough.

It was already enough for Sabrina. She had trained both men and women for their dominant partners but she was out of her league here, where there was obviously no compassion and leniency was a foreign word. 'I'd like to speak to someone,' she said quickly.

'Sorry,' Yelena answered.

'Someone in authority,' pleaded Sabrina.

The phrase seemed to irritate the Russian. 'When you are in the bathhouse,' she replied angrily, 'I am the only authority.' She nodded at the guards, who began dragging Sabrina towards the trough.

'No!' she pleaded. 'I'll tell you what you want… anything!'

'We already know that,' laughed Yelena, and the other guard grinned at the certainty of the comment. Sabrina was forced to the other side of the rail just as the second man's freezing enema gushed from his arse into the trough. Horrified, her eyes followed the flight of greasy waste until it hit the water, and the horror continued as in the shallow water she saw a naked girl pegged just at the waterline. Her skin was translucent and she appeared to be dead, frozen in the icy filth that washed over her body.

Sabrina's pleas became hysterical. Even when one of the guards unchained the young woman in the trough and dragged her out to revive on the freezing floor Sabrina was still begging to be allowed to see someone, anyone, who could help her, but he hand of the blonde that whipped across her face and returned to grab her hair silenced her cries.

In one move Sabrina was bent over the rail, her cuffs removed and her wrists locked into the floor shackles. Intent on keeping the hose out of her rectum she clenched her buttocks tightly together. It was a wasted effort; the second leather-aproned woman stepped to the side of her and pulled her cheeks apart to expose the puckered star of her anus. Then Sabrina felt the steel-tipped hose bully its way into her back passage and her bowels were flooded. The cold water immediately chilled her insides and threatened hypothermia. In all the weeks she had been in Russia she had never felt so cold. The added pressure ballooned her tummy and Sabrina watched it grow as the savage blonde allowed more and more water into her private chute. Only after the pain had grown so intense and the cold chilled her insides did Sabrina's eyes begin to roll upwards and Yelena called for the blonde to stop. Sabrina was then plugged and Yelena nodded to the tall blonde to pull up the prisoner's head so she could talk to her.

'Why are you in Russia?'

'Please,' gasped Sabrina. 'Release me and I'll tell

you everything.'

Yelena motioned to the female guard who had first escorted Sabrina to the bathhouse. 'I want the belt.'

At the sound of those words Sabrina's stomach began to fold continuously over itself, forcing her to retch. She had used the belt on her own, albeit willing, prisoners. Now she was to face it from a vicious Russian KGB guard, or so she thought.

The belt turned out to be a large leather harness that ran around her stomach. It also had a separate length that passed between her legs and over her lower back to hold the bottom plug in place. While she was being harnessed the two men and the unconscious girl were taken back to their cells.

Yelena spoke again. 'Why are you here?'

'Please,' said Sabrina. 'Stop this…'

Yelena nodded and the Slav pulled the harness one notch tighter. The pressure increased, as did the pain. 'No more!' Sabrina wailed.

Another notch slipped through the buckle with an obvious result. 'You will have noticed,' said Yelena, 'that speaking out of turn, or answering a question I haven't asked, will mean Svetlana will tighten the harness.'

The belt slipped another notch.

'Ahhh…!' cried Sabrina.

Another notch.

This time Sabrina remained silent, and the three remaining female guards smiled.

'I see you have the message,' Yelena said calmly. 'Let us try and get through this as pleasantly as we can, shall we?'

Sabrina nodded in defeat.

'Why are you in Russia?'

'I-I'm chasing someone – a man,' Sabrina panted. 'The one I tried to shoot in Murmansk.'

'And?'

'That... that's it.'

A nod from Yelena meant another notch and Svetlana dutifully obeyed. Sabrina's stomach felt as if it would burst and she found herself almost unable to speak. 'Please,' she mumbled. 'It's the truth. I was chasing him because he ran away from me.' The cold was numbing and Sabrina gratefully felt herself slipping out of consciousness as the excess pressure began to squeeze her arteries, but Yelena saw her prisoner begin to fade and ordered the harness and plug to be removed, and with only one possible exit the release of so much pressure found expression in a fountain of foul slurry.

The relief was instantaneous and Sabrina found its aftermath to be actually pleasant. She experienced the most wonderful sensations of weightlessness and the rush of blood returning to her head brought with it the snap of clarity, as did the freezing water being hosed over her body.

'What have we discovered?' asked the interrogating officer from the reception room, who had entered unnoticed.

Yelena snapped her heels together and replied that the prisoner claimed to be pursuing a male.

'Is that all?'

Yelena answered that it was, and that she was forced to abandon her questions when the prisoner began to faint.

'Take her to the cells. We shall begin the interrogation properly tomorrow.'

Still naked Sabrina was dragged, for she was too exhausted to walk, out of the bathhouse. Her head felt too heavy to lift and she watched the floor swim beneath her as she was led along dingy winding corridors accompanied by the squeals of pain and anguish from other inmates.

At last they stopped outside a cell, which was opened and into which she was thrown. It was tiny, windowless, cold and illuminated by a dull light. She landed on a bare mattress. There was no blankets, no furniture, and a soiled pot in the corner was the only concession to civilisation. The guards departed without a word and the door slammed shut.

Sabrina couldn't prevent a small smile coming to her lips. She had survived her introduction to Lubyanka. 'Welcome to hell,' she said to herself, and then made a promise to do whatever it took to survive.

Her solitude was short-lived. At the sound of keys in the lock of the door she drew her legs up under her chin and wrapped her arms around her shins. The door opened slowly to reveal an obese giant of a man. He wore no uniform like the others she had seen, just an old pair of trousers and a ripped vest. No doubt his massive bear-like bulk kept him warm in the cold subterranean temperature.

The man entered, his gait more of a shuffle than a purposeful walk. He was carrying two buckets, which he placed on the floor to either side of him. Sabrina said and did nothing. He tapped one of the buckets with his foot. Sabrina leaned forward, unconcerned by her nakedness, to peer into the zinc pail. It contained semi-rotten apples, lumps of cheese and some bread, all mouldy. She made to take some but the brute pushed the bucket away. He spoke no English, but he made himself quite clear with a grunt and a nod of his head to his groin, so Sabrina, too hungry and weary to protest, rose to her knees and pulled at his zip. It was difficult because the trousers were so old and there were several teeth missing from the zipper, but when she did eventually manage it she revealed a pair of underpants that matched the brute's vest in that they were torn and soiled too. His semi-turgid cock poked rudely from the front, and he thrust his hips towards her as a sign of his impatience.

She peeled back his foreskin and took his prick between her lips. Even in the rank hellhole of Lubyanka she could smell his unwashed genitals. Hygiene was obviously not one of his strong points – but sex evidently was.

His cock grew rapidly and to an enormous size. Sabrina sucked avidly, desperate to end the ordeal. In return he bent and roughly squeezed her breasts, and she responded by increasing her action, hoping to bring him off quickly. She felt him tense and his cockhead swell, but he pulled out of her mouth in order to pick a lump of bread. She wondered at his behaviour, but he pulled her face back towards his prick and she was forced to continue fellating him.

A few moments later she sensed the familiar swell and again she was pushed away, but this time the monster continued to stroke himself until he ejaculated strings of gluey sperm onto the bread. Immediately understanding his intent she looked at him with contempt, but was forced to accept it. The leering brute indicated for her to eat it, reluctantly she pushed it into her mouth, and he grinned broadly as he watched the new prisoner chew on the coated dough, then he put his hand behind her neck and pushed her head to the floor.

As Sabrina continued to eat with her bottom raised he took a lump of cheese out of the bucket and pushed it into her vagina. He then left a steel cup of water on the floor, stepped back to admire his sculpture, and left.

Sabrina removed the cheese and sat back against the wall. It wasn't the best dinner she had been served, but it was probably the most welcome. She scraped away some mould from the cheese, placed it on the sperm-soaked bread, and ate it. In a few more days, she thought to herself, she would have the brute eating out of her hands, just as she had done with Justin. She would suck and fuck him like he'd never been sucked and fucked before. She would become his favourite, and for the second time since arriving at Lubyanka she smiled, then drank to wash down her meal.

Only then did she realise that the brute had pissed in the water.

The click of the door echoed through the apartment, waking Justin and startling him enough that he contemplated hiding, but the sight of Catherine entering the bedroom allayed his fear. In the light from the passageway he saw that she had already removed her skirt and was wearing just a pair of knee length boots, a mohair jumper and a pair of black knickers; not a particularly sexy pair, but on Catherine any item of clothing became erotic. She saw he was awake and dropped onto the bed, where she sat against the headboard and lit a joint of marijuana.

'Where did you get that from?' he asked.

'Viktor.'

'You've been to the club?'

'Of course.' She took another hit and slumped down before handing Justin the spliff. He took it from her, propped himself up on one elbow and sucked. The smoke was relaxing.

'I made dinner,' he sulked.

Catherine looked at him. 'Sorry,' she apologised. 'Nice?'

'Not really.' He returned the joint after another hit. 'Anything happening in the great outdoors?'

She blew a smoke ring towards the bedroom ceiling and pushed her finger through the middle of it before wafting it away with her hand. 'They look for you still. Gorky said to police that there was a man and a woman. I see they look for you. There are men I haven't seen before. They want us to think they are here for the festival but they do nothing but walk and watch.'

Justin flopped onto his back and entwined his fingers behind his head. 'Shit, how am I going to get out of here?'

She took a last draw out of the joint and stubbed it out, and then she lifted her leg into the air and unzipped her boot. 'You stay here until they are fed up. Then I will get you home.'

'How?'

'Viktor will do it,' she answered, and pulled off her top.

He admired her breasts and added sarcastically, and not a little jealously, 'Yeah, I bet he will.'

'He has many friends,' Catherine continued. 'And he is very powerful. He is trying to find out what has happened to your friend Sabrina.'

'Why should he do that?'

Catherine turned over to lie on her tummy, picked up another joint from the bedside table and lit it. 'Because I asked him to, and because he likes me.'

Justin grew concerned. 'You don't have to do anything for me. You've already done more than I should ask.'

She swung her feet in the air in an almost childlike manner and continued to smoke. 'I know I don't have to,' she told him. 'But I want to. I like you. But you won't be here forever. So I do this thing for you now. And Viktor will help.'

'I know his sort. He'll want something back in return.' Justin reached for the joint and hoped she recognised the sincerity in his voice.

'What do you think, that Viktor is a monster?'

Justin sat up in the bed. 'I know he sells drugs. I know he has apes for bodyguards, so he's obviously up to no good.'

Catherine laughed and kicked her feet again. 'And you,' she said. 'You who have chased a friend – not an enemy, a friend – to Russia, tricked a Russian captain, and no ordinary one at that, to give you a truck, and shoot at people in the street. You… you are a good man?' She destroyed him with logic.

'But I *am* a good man,' he insisted.

'Do I say again?'

Justin shook his head. 'Point taken. But it doesn't stop me being uneasy about you asking for favours on my behalf.'

Catherine pulled the sheets down just past Justin's groin. His cock reclined there, limp and without intent. 'I think you are jealous of Viktor,' she told him. She flicked his penis with a finger. It jumped to rest on his right thigh before slowly returning to its natural position on his left. She flicked him again. 'You think Viktor wants to fuck me? You think I should not fuck him back, don't you?'

Justin knew he was on dodgy ground and had no right to demand anything. 'It's not for me to say,' he answered meekly. 'I hardly know you.'

Catherine took the joint away from him and sucked on its root. 'That is right,' she said indignantly. 'You hardly know me and yet I help you. I ask for nothing from you. But you… you take my help and want to control me.' She rolled over onto her back and Justin marvelled at her slim frame, her flat tummy and her lovely breasts. 'You are not fair, Justin.'

He had gone too far and he knew it. 'I'm sorry,' he said. 'I have no right—'

'But I like the way you worry,' she interrupted him.

'It makes me feel wanted.' She stared dreamily at the ceiling. 'But I must not be a fantasy.'

Justin smiled at her choice of words. 'Too late for that,' he told her, and she looked at him with a confused expression. 'Sorry,' he said. 'I was just being silly.'

'I know you will go and I will still have a life here, so I must remember to keep my friends, or I will end up alone.' Once again her logic was flawless. She extinguished the second joint, stood up shakily and removed her knickers. She was a beautiful sight and Justin knew that among all the trouble he was in, he was still with the most gorgeous girl in the Arctic and for that he counted his blessings. He moved across the bed and pulled back the sheets so that Catherine could join him.

'Mmm,' she purred. 'You are nice and warm.'

'And you,' said Justin, 'are so fucking hot.' He lifted the bedclothes and ducked underneath them in search of her neatly trimmed sex. He loved the way she had shaved off all but the smallest line of pubic fur while underneath, between her slim and smooth legs, she was completely denuded. He found her familiar lips and poked gently with his tongue. She was wet, and there was a definite wave of heat emanating from her. He moved his nostrils closer and breathed in the musky odour of her, and when his head was swimming with the sweet scent of her vagina he lifted his head and spoke.

'You know, I think you're one of the most beautiful women I've ever known. Beautiful, yes, but not just in that good-looking sort of way,' he continued. 'I mean, beautiful inside.' He patted his chest, just above his heart.

Catherine accepted the compliment with a smile, then pushed his head beneath the sheets. 'Shhhh,' she cooed. 'No talk… you are busy.'

Chapter Nine

The constant lap of the water on the hull of the *Piroshka* seemed to David to be as cruel as any Chinese water torture. He had endured it for many nights as the small boat traversed the North Sea, bobbed across the Skagerrak and pitched, rolled and yawed its way over the Kattegat and into the Baltic.

Some of the storms had been terrifying for David, chained as he was below decks. On more than one occasion he had felt the boat roll so far over he never expected it to right itself. But every time it did and a great sense of relief washed over him as powerful as the very waves surging against the sides of the old trawler.

The few times Sabrina had ordered Justin to give David some exercise he had felt like a condemned man reprieved as the axe began to fall. As wonderful as it was to walk the decks and see Copenhagen fade in the dying light of a northern sky, he had considered throwing himself into the black icy waters to escape the clutches of his tormentors. Sabrina, though, had seemed to read his mind; maybe she had seen him staring at the waves, waiting to choose the one that would take him to the mud in one great sweep of spray and foam. She had barked out her orders again and Justin brought up a small chain that she connected to the guiche ring just behind his balls. The other end she connected to a cleat and David was left in fear of losing his feet and tearing his scrotum. As he concentrated on timing his body to move with the boat he saw Sabrina with a triumphant grin that said she had beaten him; that she was his mistress; that he was broken.

'Bitch!' he screamed through the leather strap covering his mouth. 'Bitch! You fucking bitch, you fucking bitch, you fucking bitch! You...'

'Wake up. Wake up, plish. You are dreaming.' Teena began to shake him, slowly at first because she didn't want to irritate him. But as his distress grew she decided to risk his anger and shook him violently. David sat up with a start, his face streaming with sweat. Teena draped her arms around his neck and held him tight. He appreciated that.

'You dream again,' she told him. 'You always dream. Bad dreams.'

David squeezed his Lapp girl and Mishka joined the two in a three-way embrace.

'No more dreams,' Teena added.

David stared at the porthole. It was a black circle; nothing shone through it, no distant lights, no moon, no stars. Nothing to say they weren't floating in space, except the familiar lap of the water.

The door opened and interrupted the moment. It was Leonid. 'We are clear,' he said. 'No more worries.' He indicated for them to follow him. 'Come with me. My brother Nicholas, he wants to see you.' David stood and Leonid added, 'bring the girls.'

As they made their way forward David mentioned his concern that Leonid had joined his brother's ship.

'My ship is in dry dock,' Leonid answered. 'We don't sail for two, maybe three weeks. So I come along for the ride with my brother, the captain.' He smiled broadly and put his arms around the girls. 'Up the steps,' he continued. 'The bridge is there.'

Nicholas was waiting when they entered the bridge, a shadowy figure sitting motionless on a high chair and wrapped in a large serge coat despite the warmth that was being generated by the numerous instruments. It was the light from various dials and screens that illuminated the room; outside it was pitch black, but occasionally a flurry of foam spat against the windows that ran the width of the ship. Leonid said something in Russian and Nicholas replied, before rising from his chair and pulling his staring eyes away from their search of the darkness.

'Good evening,' he said. He extended a hand of greeting but remained in front of his chair, and resumed his scan over the sea. David moved across and took his hand, and then joined the captain in surveying the water without knowing why.

'Everything okay?'

'Very good,' answered Nicholas. 'I am watching for the Northern Fleet. They are exercising in the area. The subs have hit more than one ship in my time on the seas. Some have come up right under the boat and turned her over.'

'That's a comforting thought for bedtime,' David said, with a grim smile.

The captain smiled back and added, 'If the sea has a special time for you then she will come one day, and you must go.' He returned to his seat and picked up a mug of hot chocolate. 'Until then it is best to keep an eye open and not steal someone else's place.'

A quiet moment of contemplation descended and all eyes on the bridge peered out through the thick glass. No one was even aware that just fifty feet below them and a hundred yards behind, hidden in the cavitation of the *Olga*'s propellers, the typhoon class *Kudryavtsev* was trailing and using them as a training target.

Leonid took the girls to the map area at the rear of the bridge and poured everyone a mug of chocolate.

The girls handed one to David and a fresh one to Nicholas, then they collected their own and went to stand near the windows. It was the first time the two had been on such a large ship, apart from the wreck they used for a camp on their way to Murmansk.

'You have something for me?'

David pondered for a moment, and then realised Nicholas meant money. He pulled out the fat wad of roubles he had taken from the sailors at the *Engels* club and divided it up. He gave the one half to Nicholas and returned the rest to his pocket.

'Thank you. And the rest.'

Those were the words David was dreading, if expecting. He shrugged and pulled out the now smaller roll of notes.

'Please,' said the captain. 'You misunderstand.' He nodded towards the unsuspecting girls, who were looking silently out at the sea. 'Leonid told me you had such fun in Murmansk. You shared the girls with other sailors. That was very good.'

David sighed with relief. The Barents Sea on a stormy night is no place to discover your captain is no more than a pirate. 'I see,' said David. 'Do you have a preference?'

'A preference?'

'One or the other.'

The captain surveyed the girls' bottoms and allowed his eyes to travel the strong curves of their backs. 'Perhaps both,' he said.

David would have smiled had he not been so tired. Instead, he gave a nod to indicate he understood and called the girls over. They responded immediately and gathered in front of the captain, where they seductively sipped their chocolate. He was pleased and spoke to Leonid.

'Did you?'

'Both,' was the reply.

The captain rose from the chair that dominated the bridge and wrapped an arm around each girl's waist. He pulled them close and the sisters held hands behind his back. Nicholas walked them to the window and all three stared out into the blackness, and the quiet was broken by a plume of spray breaking against the window like some enormous ejaculation. The girls jumped at the power and sound of the water thumping against the glass, and a second later it had all run away in tiny rivulets of foam and the darkness returned. Teena and Mishka squeezed the captain tighter, and he responded by smoothing his hands over their tight curves until he reached the perky swell of their buttocks.

Looking at the flickering lights from a small fishing village on Ostrov Kolguyev, Nicholas spoke. 'The men know you are aboard.'

'Is that bad?' David asked.

'It might be. They have heard the rumours about an incident in Murmansk. The police are after some people. They speak English. You speak English. The men think there may be something in it for them.'

'I have very little money left,' said David.

'Then you must find some other way to pay them.'

'With what?' The captain squeezed the warm flesh in his hands, and David smiled, wondering why he even needed to have asked such a pointless question.

'I shall send them down to the crew's mess when I have finished with them,' Nicholas decreed. 'Now you may leave the bridge.'

A piercing scream followed by a terrifying laugh prompted Sabrina into the position she thought best to greet the brute. Lubyanka's most infamous gaoler was doing his morning rounds, and that included pleasing himself with the female prisoners.

Disgusted and frightened by him though she was, Sabrina knew she had to find a way to get through to him. The door of the adjoining cell closed with a loud clang and was followed by a stream of shouting and screaming; no doubt the woman was hurling obscenities at what he had just done. Sabrina had no way of knowing and she couldn't understand the language, but what she did understand was the sound of the key in her cell door.

The loathsome brute appeared in the doorway, blocking it completely with his massive bulk. His presence was made all the more frightening by his menacing stance. He was hunched over, and his face carried with it the promise of violence.

Despite this, Sabrina pulled the mattress in front of him and laid back, naked, her knees apart. The brute released a low guttural groan and descended upon her like some feasting Nosferatu. He had no fangs with which to penetrate, having lost most of his teeth to poor dental hygiene, but what he did have was a cock that was comparable in size to his massive bulk.

His shapeless mass crushed her breasts and he made no attempt to support his own weight. He liked to see and feel the girls struggle beneath him, gasping for air as he pounded into them. Sabrina spread herself as far as her legs would allow, granting him deeper access, which his turgid penis took with increasing presence.

'You feel great,' she said straight into his face, and ignoring his foul breath she added, 'you feel like a real bull.' His lips sagged in a wet grin and he increased his efforts, and as uncomfortable as Sabrina was on the torn, soiled mattress, and as disgusting as the man-mountain was grinding on top of her, she managed to feign pleasure, hoping to please him. 'You fuck like an animal,' she whispered, smiling grimly. 'And you stink like one.' He kept grinning. 'You don't understand a word I'm saying, do you? You stinking shit of an excuse for a human.'

No matter what she said he kept up his disgusting grunting and heaving and pounding.

'Do they fuck goats in your village?' She whispered the insult sexily. 'What do you do, bribe them to sleep with you? That's all you're good for…'

'Obviously not,' interrupted a cultured voice.

The loathsome gaoler didn't miss a stroke, but continued humping on the poor girl, and behind him in the doorway, stood Captain Vasili. He was flicking through a small folder that held her documents.

'You owe me one army all-terrain vehicle,' he calmly told her.

Sabrina's body jerked in rhythm with the brute's thrusts. He was moving more frenziedly and she knew he wasn't far from ejaculating, and then he came and despite clinging on to his shoulders and grimacing with disgust as he flooded her, Sabrina felt elated because Vasili offered a chance to get out of the hellhole and away from the utter slob who was lurching on top of her.

'I-I think I'm paying for it, don't you?' she implored.

The captain smiled a knowing smile. 'It was an expensive vehicle, and I had trouble explaining how it was stolen.' He kicked the slumped gaoler and signalled for him to leave with a jerk of a thumb. The fat man stood up and made a big play of putting his cock away, leering down at his lovely victim, then kicked some rotten fruit across the floor and left with the steel bucket to feed the next prisoner.

Sabrina lay still for a moment; exhausted after the ordeal she had just been through. Vasili stood at the door and impassively studied her.

'Quite daring,' he said, after Sabrina had pulled

herself to a sitting position against the cell wall. 'The British are obviously improving their training of spies. Beautiful women seducing Russian officers; officers in the KGB, at that. Very impressive.'

'And your female spies don't sleep with British ministers?' Sabrina countered.

'So you admit you are a spy?'

Despite her previous trials Sabrina felt really terrified. It was a stupid thing to say, and she feared that with that one slip she might have sealed her fate. 'I – I didn't mean that,' she stammered. 'I was just saying that Russian spies probably have to do that. As part of their job, I mean.'

'Like it was part of your job?'

'No.' She stood up, still naked, brushed back her bedraggled hair and stared at the ceiling, realising that what she said next could see her shot. 'Listen,' she whispered in a voice that splintered along with her confidence. 'Everything I said yesterday… to those women with the water.'

'In the bathhouse.'

'Whatever you call it. It was the truth; I'm simply searching for someone.'

'Then why is there no record of you entering the country?'

'Because I didn't come through like most people.'

'Oh,' said Vasili, clearly anxious to learn how the borders of the mother country could be crossed so easily. 'And how did you enter?'

'The first time was—'

'The first time?'

Sabrina considered there was little point in lying; not if she wanted to keep out of the bathhouse, or one of the other rooms she had glimpsed when being dragged to the cell.

'Yes, I was here a year or two ago. We were

delivering a man. The one I was chasing when I crashed the truck... your truck.'

'And what were you doing?'

Sabrina's shoulders slumped. 'You won't believe me.'

'Then you must persuade me. You seem good at that; persuading people.'

'Is that you?'

'Just me,' answered Catherine. 'Who were you expecting, the KGB?' She put down two large bags of groceries on the kitchen worktop and noticed the pristine condition of her typical single girl's flat. Justin was just finishing washing some dishes.

'You don't have to do that,' she told him.

'I want to,' he said, and lightly touched her face with his wet fingers, leaving a small ball of suds on her nose that made her sneeze. 'You do so much for me. Besides, it keeps me busy.' He went to the fridge where he had made up a pitcher of vodka and orange. 'There you go.'

Catherine took a drink and went about putting away the provisions she had bought from the indoor market near the police station. 'I have some news for you,' she announced.

'Good news?'

'I saw Viktor.'

'That's not good news,' Justin said, and he threw the tea towel onto the worktop and collected his own drink.

'I never said it was good news, jealous man.' She pulled his drink from his mouth and replaced it with her lips. She kissed him, and then pulled away to see him give one of his 'I'm sorry' shrugs. 'Perhaps I won't tell you,' she added, 'if you are not happy with Viktor's help.' She picked up her cigarettes and lit one, then busied herself once more with her shopping, and when she reached down into a cupboard next to the sink Justin hugged her around the waist in an attempt to apologise.

'What did he say?' he asked.

'I have forgotten,' she answered sulkily, and pushed past him to reach for an ashtray.

'You said he had news.'

'Who?'

'Viktor.'

'Ha! So you do know his name.'

'Yes, I know his name. And his game.'

'Game? What is this?'

Justin stepped closer and hugged her again. With a sigh he said, 'Look, let's start again. I really do want to know what your Viktor said.'

'Okay then.' She exhaled a cloud of blue tobacco smoke. 'But first, he is not my Viktor. He is my friend. And second, are you sure you want to hear the news?'

'Why?' he asked, suddenly afraid of what she was about to say.

'Because it is about your girlfriend.'

'Sabrina?'

'Yes, Sabrina.' She knocked the ash off her cigarette and took a long thoughtful pull of smoke. When she felt relaxed enough she took a sip of vodka and announced, 'She is in Lubyanka.'

'Great!' exclaimed Justin. 'Then she must have got away... Where's Lubyanka?'

'Moscow.'

Justin missed the flat tone of her voice. 'What, north, south... where?'

'Moscow, Justin. It's a prison. A very bad prison. Many go in. Few come back out. The KGB, it is their prison.'

'Oh, no,' Justin sighed, and Catherine was surprised

171

by the mild manner in which he took the news; she was expecting some sort of emotional outburst. 'I told her,' he went on. 'When she was waving that stupid bloody gun around in that shop. Why didn't she listen? How are we going to get out of this mess?' His body slumped and he made his way into the lounge and sat on the sofa. Catherine picked up her drink and joined him.

'Viktor will find a way,' she told him. 'He has many contacts... many contacts.'

'And what will he want for this help? I suppose he isn't doing it for the benefit of my health.'

'Then you will be right,' she told him. 'He wants me to work for him.'

Justin gave a false laugh. 'And you don't have to tell me what as. I can guess.'

'Then you will be right.'

'You don't have to do this – not for me.'

Catherine took up his empty glass to refill it. 'It's not just for you,' she said. 'He has asked me for a long time. I was going to do it anyway. I need money, I have no job. So I was just waiting to see what he would offer me.'

'But it isn't for you, is it? It's for me.'

'I know,' she said from the kitchen, then came back into the room and gave him his recharged glass. 'But I have nothing I really want. So why not? At least someone gets something.' She paused for a moment and then tried to reassure him. 'I was going to do it anyway. Why not now?'

There was a light bump when the *Olga* jarred into the quay at Amderma. The crew were already busying themselves and David's ski sled swung gently in the netting of a boom crane.

'Very efficient,' he complimented.

'We must hurry,' Leonid replied. 'We don't want to be here too long.'

David smiled. 'I think we are safe now,' he said. 'Well away from Murmansk. The captain's happy.' He looked across to the girls who were kissing a number of the crew farewell. Many of the men were taking the added liberty of running their hands underneath the girls' leather skirts and rubbing their bare bottoms. 'The crew are happy,' he added. 'What can go wrong?' and almost before he had finished his sentence the cold northern air was filled with the terrible scream of a jetfighter swooping low. David ducked by instinct, but the rest hardly seemed to notice.

'Mig 31,' said Leonid impassively. 'Foxhound. The 72nd Fighter Regiment have a base here.'

'No wonder you want out,' said David. 'They frightened the shit out of me.'

'It is not the fighters,' Leonid replied. The sled was landed on the quay and released from its packaging. 'You do not know about Novaya Zemlya?'

They were joined by the girls, who stood either side of David. 'The big island to the north? What about it?'

'Object 700.'

'I thought it was just a happy fishing ground for the tribes.'

'Fish as big as a ship,' laughed Leonid. 'Not that you can eat them.'

David looked at the large Russian for an explanation.

'Object 700,' Leonid went on. 'Was the great motherland's testing ground for nuclear weapons. Everywhere is radioactive.' He lifted up his hands and trembled them. 'It's all buzzing,' he smiled.

'What about them?' asked David, pointing to a group of scientists waiting for the weather equipment they had ordered.

173

'They are in special suits,' Leonid answered. He was stating the obvious because the three men on the quay looked like well-padded polar bears. 'They do two months and are taken off. Then some others come. No one stays longer. You shouldn't.'

'Fucking marvellous,' David moaned. 'Idiots to the west, soldiers to the south and one huge microwave oven to the north.' He looked down to the sled and the long trailer attached to it. 'Your brother did order the supplies I asked for to go on the sled?'

Leonid guided David to the gangway. 'Enough for a month,' he assured him. 'Nicholas was very happy with the journey. He has never seen his crew so content and willing to work. You must not stay in this region longer than you have to. Set off straightaway, or soon you will have no appetite for food at all.' He held out his hand and David took it in his. The Mig screamed overhead again and as David looked up to see it he caught sight of the captain on the bridge, controlling the unloading through a radio. The two men exchanged waves and David and the girls left the ship. As the three pulled away into the dim light of the afternoon the cheers of the crew followed them.

Chapter Ten

Floating in outer space was how Sabrina felt. The darkness was total. There was no front, no back, no up, no down. She lifted her hand and waved it before her face. She couldn't see it, and for a terrifying moment she thought she couldn't even feel it. She didn't even register the chair she had been forced to sit on several hours ago. Her limbs seemed to have detached from her body and she felt herself to be just a brain, or even less, some intangible mass of thought with no substance.

To try to gain some sort of sensation she pinched the soft inside of her thigh, the pain was exhilarating and she felt herself gain some control over her panic.

Then the light came on; a thin pencil beam that hit the top of her head from above and cast shadows beneath her. She was naked, but that didn't bother her. She was more concerned with her immediate future.

The ceiling light had illuminated a small circle on the floor and she found herself studying the circumference of it intently, and was rewarded by the sight of a shiny black patent leather boot stepping into the light. She gasped, and her breath billowed in an icy cloud before her face.

'Comfortable?'

She recognised Vasili's voice. 'Not really,' she replied candidly.

The Russian captain stepped into the light, lit a cigarette and fixed his glare upon Sabrina. 'Then how can we help each other?' he said in a calm, almost soothing voice.

'I will tell you whatever you want to know,' she answered. She had already figured she was probably not going to leave the prison outside of a box at midnight, and she had no desire to spend her last moments in pain.

'I can assure you,' put in Vasili, 'that you would undoubtedly tell us everything.' He paused a moment and took a few paces to the side before returning to his original position. 'But now, now we are not interested.' She didn't asked why, and he was impressed by her silence and control. 'I have to congratulate you on your resilience,' he complimented her. 'Let us hope your friend is as good at surviving as you are. Where he is, he will need it.'

She remained silent, having no way of knowing whether he meant David or Justin. Then Vasili made a mistake by adding that it was only a matter of time before they apprehended her friend from the shop. 'He will be the lucky one,' Vasili added. 'At least he will die here, in the warm.'

So he was talking about David, Sabrina thought. The fight had not completely left her and she found herself desperate to know where David was. 'You call this warm?' she chanced, hoping he wouldn't have some torture prepared for any misdemeanour she committed.

'A lot warmer than where your friend is,' he grinned. 'Perhaps we should concentrate on your other friend, the one who was with you in the trading post. Where is he?'

The fear churned again in Sabrina. She had no knowledge of what had happened to Justin. They wouldn't believe that, she knew. They would simply increase the pressure on her. God knows what they would do after what she had witnessed and experienced in the bathhouse. 'I honestly don't know,' she said with a whimper. 'I would tell you Vasili, you know I would.'

Vasili dropped the stub of his cigarette and ground it firmly into the concrete floor. 'I was hoping you would say that,' he informed her. Suddenly the metal door swung open and clattered against the wall and two men and the gaoler marched in. Without hesitating they strode straight to Sabrina, lifted her out of the chair, forced her arms behind her back and buckled them at the elbows and the wrists. Before she had time to react a cold iron bar was slipped into the gap between her restrained arms and her body, and at one wall the brute released a chain that lowered another chain connected to a metal A-frame. The frame was connected to each end of the bar behind Sabrina's back and she grimaced before the brute had even begun to haul her towards the ceiling. She knew what was coming because she had done it herself, to the women and men who had been to Camelot for training.

The gaoler grinned as he pulled on the chain and his mouth split to display a row of yellow teeth like broken gravestones. If there had been a caring heart in that room witnessing her ordeal it would have melted. Sabrina first struggled against her bonds, and then stood pitifully on tiptoe before he pulled again and she continued her torturous ascent.

'Please,' she pleaded. 'Whatever you want, I will do it. Whatever it is.'

'Information,' Vasili said coolly. 'What is your friend's name?'

'Which one? I don't know which one you mean.'

'Well then.' Vasili lit another cigarette and walked to Sabrina, until he was a few inches in front of her suspended body. He admired the tattoo on her pudenda and remembered the pleasant evening he had spent between the girl's thighs. He blew the cigarette smoke and watched it curl and fold in front of the rampant

177

felines, then looked up into her eyes. 'Let us start with the one who stayed at the hotel *Polarny Zony* and left without paying for his stay. Who is he?'

'David,' Sabrina quickly answered. 'David Harper – but I don't know where he is. Honestly I don't.'

'Shhh,' Vasili soothed. He took hold of her ankles and pulled playfully at them, increasing her distress. 'We know where this David Harper is. One of our planes spotted a supply ship landing a ski sled and a man and two girls at Amderma. We have already sent some men to pick them up.' He tugged her ankles and gave some consideration to her distress, and then he turned to the gaoler and spat some instructions, and a moment later the loathsome slob pushed over a rusty iron box.

Sabrina heard the container being opened and strained to see what horrors it held. It was impossible to see anything, but she knew the clink-clank of metal being knocked against metal.

'Who is he?' Vasili asked. His voice was cold and detached, but his hands were probing Sabrina's vagina.

'I don't know,' she sobbed.

'Where is he?'

Before she could answer she felt him separate her inner labia and pinch each puffy lip between the jaws of a bull clip. Their bite was firm; firmer than she'd had cause to use in her own training school, but she knew the reason for the extra strength. The chain dangling from the clips gave it away.

'Again,' said Vasili. 'Where is he?'

'He must have run away when I crashed the truck.' Her limbs were beginning to warm up as the muscles in her arms began producing lactic acid. This anaerobic process allowed her to withstand the pain of being suspended, but it wouldn't last forever, and she would soon become convulsed with cramps.

'Then where did he go?'

'Back to the hotel I suppose.' She felt him fumble between her legs and braced her body by squeezing the bar behind her back. It helped, a little. Vasili had attached two small weights to the clamps and they pulled down on her vagina. 'Please, Vasili,' she pleaded. 'If I knew I would say. You must know that.' More weights were added and the flesh between the clips distended, forcing the blood to move elsewhere. 'Remember the times we had together,' she whimpered in search of mercy. 'The ice palace... *Uncle Vanya*.'

Another weight brought forth a scream, as Sabrina was tortured from her shoulders to her sex. 'Please,' she begged. 'Listen to me.'

'Perhaps you should have listened to me,' Vasili interrupted. 'You asked me to explain the meaning in *Uncle Vanya*. I said it was devotion. You thought only of human devotion, of love between people. Devotion takes many forms. You will find that more than anything I am devoted to my country. To Russia.'

The sound of Vasili searching the container for more weights brought absolute terror to Sabrina. Her pleas became desperate and she began to tremble with abject fear. The captain ignored her appeals, and she felt the weights lift as he held them to attach yet more.

'That's enough!' The voice echoed around the dank cell.

'But, Major Bokov,' Vasili protested, straightening up indignantly, 'I have not yet finished my interrogation.'

'I have seen enough,' insisted the major.

'But she has yet to tell us where her accomplice is.'

Major Sergei Bokov stepped out of the shadows and into the circle of light. 'I said, enough.'

Captain Vasili Leskov snapped to attention and saluted with evident resentment. 'Yes sir!'

'You are dismissed,' the major continued, and as the captain marched slowly from the room he added, 'Perhaps you are too personally involved with this prisoner. Clearly your irregular loan of the army vehicle has clouded your judgement.' He stepped closer to the suspended Sabrina and took up the weights dangling from her sex lips. 'I shall take over from here.'

Vasili stopped for a moment at the door. 'As you wish,' he said, and left the room.

The major barked more orders and the gaoler lowered Sabrina to the chilled floor. 'Release her and take her to Cheka 3.' The brute removed the bar and bulldog clips, then took Sabrina by the arm and dragged her from the cell, and as she neared the door she called out her thanks to the major several times. He responded by ordering the other two men out of his sight as well, and when the heavy door closed behind them the fifty-year-old major lifted the clips to his nose and breathed in the sweet aroma of the girl.

A black Trabant pulled up outside Catherine's flat and the driver tooted the horn impatiently.

'Cool,' Catherine hissed between gritted teeth. 'Let all of Russia know we have a wanted man in the place.' She smoothed down her stockings and turned her back to Justin, then pulled up her black knee length skirt. 'Okay, good?' Justin followed the lines of her seamed nylons to the top of her thighs, where just a glimpse of beautiful white flesh was visible before the black silk of her French knickers hid her charms once more.

'Perfect,' he answered, and stretched out with searching fingers, but another toot sounded from outside and Catherine slapped away his hand.

'No time for that,' she scolded. 'We must hurry

before everyone is out looking at what that fool is doing.' She slipped a long black woollen coat over her deep blue satin blouse and swept out of the apartment. Justin cursed the driver and followed her through the fresh fall of snow. The two climbed into the car and Catherine exchanged angry words with the driver, who retaliated by waving his arms and gesticulating his displeasure at being kept waiting. When the car finally pulled away Justin looked anxiously out of the rear window and was glad to see nothing but the flurry of snow churned up by the chains on the Trabant's wheels.

'I don't like this,' he said nervously. 'Why does Viktor want to see me?'

'Don't be frightened.'

'I'm not frightened. I just want to know why he wants to see us.'

Catherine lit a cigarette and blew the smoke purposely at the driver. 'You said me,' she pointed out to Justin. 'I think he…' she searched for the word, '…I think he *intimidates* you.'

'Nonsense,' Justin scoffed, unconvincingly. 'I just don't like being summoned like a dog.'

'Like your Sabrina would call you?'

Justin stared out of the window in silence.

'I am sorry,' said Catherine. She pushed her arm through his and cuddled into him. 'I was cruel.'

The car pulled up suddenly but the driver said nothing.

'Is this it?' Catherine asked, and then got out of the car and threw her cigarette into the snow, where it looked dirty and out of place upon the pristine white blanket.

The pair stood in front of a single-storey building that looked like one of Corbusier's modernist designs. It was surrounded by a high metal fence, which closed behind the leaving Trabant.

'He could have sent his other car,' Justin said, with a nod at a sleek black limousine in the garage by the side of the house. They both smiled, pulled up the collar on their coats, and stepped up to the front door to be greeted by a pleasant looking middle-aged woman in a black and white maid's uniform, as worn by Victorian servants.

The inside complemented the exterior to perfection. It was very art deco, quite sparse and open-plan. A burnished teak floor was kept warm by two rugs; one a Siberian tiger, the other a polar bear, replete with smiling heads. At the perpendicular to the flat-faced white marble fireplace ran two Biedermeier sofas upholstered in black leather.

'Hello, Catherine.' It was Viktor in a smart, thinly lapelled jacket and trousers. In his hands were two small schooners of sherry, which he offered to them. Catherine took hers and thanked him in Russian, but Viktor replied by saying, 'Let us speak English tonight. You are not the only guests.' Behind him a short middle-aged man entered, attired in similar fashion to Viktor.

'This is Snejana Radoslavov,' announced the Russian. 'An associate from Burgas, in Bulgaria.' There were polite how-do-you-dos from all, and after the maid took Catherine and Justin's coats they sat down, two on each side, on the Biedermeiers.

When they were comfortable Viktor called for Irina, the maid, who brought in a tray of rolled spicy meats and sweet cakes, which she placed on the coffee table between them. She then removed the Chinoiserie fire screen and lit the fire, revealing that she was wearing stockings as she did so.

'Beautiful view, Justin, don't you think?'

Justin pulled his eyes away from Irina's legs to

answer Viktor. 'It is, yes. It must be marvellous in the summer.'

Viktor leant forward and poured everyone a cup of tea. Handing one to Justin he continued their conversation. 'The winter is much better. Too many mosquitoes when the weather is warm. They are such a bother.'

Justin scanned the room and noted that despite its formality and sparse decoration it was expensive, tasteful, and classy. 'Still,' he said. 'You've got your comforts.'

Sabrina leant across Justin with a hand on his chest and spoke almost directly into his mouth. 'Oh yes, Viktor likes his comforts.' She crossed her stockinged legs, which Snejana observed in appreciative silence.

'Try one of these, Justin. They are good. Irina bakes them herself.' Viktor held out a small china plate. Justin picked up a small slice of cake, took a bite and put it on a spare plate. He saw Viktor awaiting a comment and stated that the cake was indeed very nice.

'Almonds?'

'And sesame,' answered Viktor. 'Irina is very good in the kitchen. She keeps everything simple – the way I like it.' His comments brought a smile from the demure Irina, who gave something akin to a curtsey and left the room. Justin followed her exit with interest and wondered about the relationship between Viktor and his Victorian servant.

'Well,' said Catherine to Snejana, 'how is Burgas?'

'Grimy and full of money,' he replied. 'But I have a lovely little house near Pomorie. You can see the sea from my balcony. It is all very beautiful – as you are. Maybe you would like to see it?'

'I would love to,' Catherine gushed, then Snejana added that he would like to get Viktor's decorator to come to Bulgaria and make his place as wonderful as Viktor's house.

'Have you seen it all?' Catherine asked.

'No, I haven't,' Snejana replied. 'I arrived just a moment before you.'

'Can I show Snejana around, Viktor?'

The Russian gangster smiled and nodded, so Catherine stood up, smoothed down her skirt, and took the Bulgarian by the arm and out of the room. Justin's eyes followed them, and Viktor answered the unasked question.

'She has been here before. Many times.'

Justin's stomach churned with emotion, which Viktor recognised. 'I see you two have a deep friendship.' Justin nodded. 'But you cannot stay here, in Russia. You know that?' Justin nodded again, and Viktor continued. 'Catherine is taking a great personal risk by helping you. Do not put her in any more danger than she already is.'

'I wouldn't dream of it,' said Justin, before Viktor added,

'There are special agents all over Murmansk looking for you. It is only a matter of time before someone notices Catherine buying more food than usual, or a light come on in her flat when they know she is out. People talk, especially when the KGB is asking the questions.'

'But what can I do? I feel like a trapped animal. I can't go out, I can't stay in.'

'Relax,' Viktor advised. 'We must work fast and take the hunters by surprise.'

Justin looked bemused. 'I don't understand.'

'Take a cigarette,' said Viktor, and he pushed a silver box across the coffee table. Justin patted his jacket pockets, thanked the Russian and said he had some on him.

'I think you will find this brand more interesting,' Viktor insisted, Justin got the message, and opened the silver lid. Inside was a small handgun.

'What the...?'

'Walther PPK,' smiled Viktor. 'Just like your James Bond.' He pulled a slim cigarette case from inside his jacket and flicked it open. 'You can be James Bond now.'

Justin took a cigarette with a trembling hand. 'I don't understand,' he said.

Viktor offered him a light and reclined with his own cigarette. 'Your Sabrina is in Cheka 3,' he informed Justin. 'So we may have a chance of a rescue.'

'I thought she was in Lubyanka.'

'Cheka 3 is a department of Lubyanka.'

'How do you know all this?' said a stunned Justin, before adding, 'What is Cheka 3, anyway?'

Viktor smiled and took another cake from the plate. 'Ah,' he grinned between bites, 'Cheka 3 is the KGB's entertainment section. A certain group of the disappeared, used for the pleasure of top politburo officials and high-ranking officers in the military. Mostly women, though there are some men.'

'So, she is safe?'

'Not an adjective I would use,' Viktor said, displaying a greater command of the English language than Justin had given him credit for. 'She is safe for as long as she is required. I know she has been tortured and they are happy with what she has told them. They are still searching for you and apparently they know where your other friend is.'

'Where?' Justin asked.

'I don't know. I have a contact but he cannot ask too many questions without causing suspicion.'

Justin's stomach had settled now, after the shock of the gun and hearing about Sabrina, and he felt a little more relaxed. He took a cake for himself and asked Viktor to disclose his source, fully expecting to be rebuked, but Viktor gave one of his confident smiles just as Catherine guided Snejana to one of the bedrooms that ran off from the open-plan living room. He followed Justin's gaze and smiled again. 'Snejana is my contact,' he said, and waved gently to the man, who waved back as Catherine opened the bedroom door.

Justin's emotions were again in turmoil. He was desperate to hear about Sabrina, but his familiar jealousy over Catherine returned. 'How do you know he's telling the truth?' he hissed, rather ungratefully as beyond Viktor he watched Snejana place his hands on Catherine's hips.

'Let's just say we have an ongoing contract with some people in the military,' said Viktor, but his words failed to regain Justin's attention. He was watching Snejana kiss Catherine fully on the mouth, but proud of his underworld operations Viktor continued. 'You see, Snejana has a haulage fleet in Burgas.' The middle-aged Bulgarian was caressing Catherine's bottom. 'We get our people to contaminate the oil, then we get paid to take it away and dispose of it.' Snejana was now on his knees and gathering up Catherine's skirt, exposing her suspenders and the bottom of her knickers. 'The clever bit is that the oil is only contaminated with water. We just leave the trucks on a hill and wait for the oil and water to separate out.' Catherine's knickers were gathered in a wet knot around her knees. 'Then we transfer the oil to our tankers and sell it on the market.' Viktor stubbed out his cigarette. 'We even sell to the military.' When he sat back his smile was broader than ever. 'That's how Snejana knows about the girl.'

He stood up and walked across to the bedroom.

Catherine was naked from the waist down and the Bulgarian was fucking her over the foot of the bed. Justin looked on impotently as the older man screwed his young Russian love, and then Viktor calmly closed the door and returned to his seat. 'There is always a price to pay,' he told Justin. 'Even for information.'

For the first time Justin picked up the gun and weighed it thoughtfully in his hands. He had never held one before and was surprised how good if felt. As he toyed with the weapon he heard the distinct cries of Catherine's orgasm.

'Bullets?'

'They are elsewhere,' said Viktor. 'Can you use it?'

'I don't know. I suppose I'll have to.'

'Come with me,' Viktor instructed. 'I will show you.'

When the two men passed the bedroom in which the Bulgarian was riding Catherine, moans of sexual ecstasy were reaching a crescendo. Justin paused for a brief moment before Viktor's guiding hand directed him to the rear of the house, where he collected some clips for the gun from a biscuit tin. 'Not very original,' Viktor admitted.

Outside the cold air bit into their faces and began attacking their bare hands. Viktor snapped the clip into the gun, made a brief gesture of showing Justin how to release the safety, and let off three shots into a water butt. Three perfectly round holes spouted water and Viktor handed the gun to Justin. He did like they do in the movies, raised the gun with arms outstretched and emptied the clip into the same water container. The recoil was minimal, as was the report, and Justin felt the rush of excitement from handling the weapon; it was small and yet heavy. He raised the empty gun and trained it once more on the barrel and made the same pretend shooting sounds as he did as a child with the cowboy guns his mother would buy him for Christmas.

'I think you've got the idea,' Viktor told him, and gestured to the house. Justin's face was flushed and the cold was no longer felt.

'How many more clips do you have?'

Viktor reached into the biscuit tin and pulled out another four. 'One thing,' he said, 'if you go around shooting at people, don't be surprised if they shoot back. Russia is not the Wild West. It is not that sophisticated.'

When they returned to the living room Snejana and Catherine were sitting next to each other. She was smoking a cigarette and he had the smile of a cat that had got the cream, which was exactly what he had.

'Everything okay?' Catherine asked.

Justin's feelings slumped at the sight of his girl and the reminder that she'd been with the other man, and he couldn't answer her.

'He will be fine,' Viktor announced as he sat down. 'Now it's time to go over the plan.'

Justin joined him on the settee. 'What plan?'

Snejana leaned forward and rested his elbows on his knees in a conspiratorial fashion, and the others did the same. 'In two days Sabrina will be accompanying Major Sergei Bokov to the theatre. They are to see *Uncle Vanya*.'

'She's seen it,' Justin put in rather stupidly.

'At the Theatre Minsk,' continued the Bulgarian, ignoring the remark. 'It is a new theatre on the outskirts of the city. Cheka 3 has a recreation club in the woods not far from the theatre. There is only one road between the theatre and the club, and it has trees sheltering each side. We have a chance of getting her there. Bokov will be driving so there should not be any bodyguards to worry about.' He leant back, satisfied with his basic plan.

'What about transport, fuel, money?' asked Justin.

A huge wad of roubles landed on the table. 'That will get you to Odessa with few questions,' answered Viktor. 'Then you will have to arrange a boat to Turkey. You are on your own then.'

Justin fondled the gun in his pocket and felt his confidence swell. He turned to Snejana. 'What about your contacts in Burgas? Can't they get me out?'

Snejana laughed. 'And risk my whole operation for two westerners who don't even have any money for insurance?'

'Then just why are you doing this?' Justin asked, with a steely tone to his voice.

Catherine placed a hand on his shoulder. 'Please,' she said, in an attempt to stop the line of conversation, 'they are trying to help you.'

'It's business,' Snejana answered him, then patted Catherine on the inside of her thigh and added, 'for which I have already been partly paid.'

There was no hiding the look of anguish on Justin's face, and he turned away. 'How do I get to Moscow?' he asked.

'Tonight,' said Viktor, 'Snejana is to take you and Catherine.'

'Not Catherine!' Justin gasped. 'What if something goes wrong?'

'She's part of the deal,' Snejana said calmly. 'It costs money to set up this sort of operation. She is coming with me to Burgas. She can make a lot of money down there. Lots of oil-men, lots of sailors.'

'Then she comes to work for me,' Viktor added. 'I have costs too.'

Justin took out the gun and pushed it across the table. 'Forget it,' he spat, and then turned to Catherine. 'I can't let you do this.'

She brushed his cheek with her hand. 'Let's not go over it again,' she said calmly, and dragged the gun back across the table and left it in front of him. 'You have no choice. You must get out of Russia, with or without your bitch friend.' She paused. 'And I have to find a way to live.' She gave him the softest of kisses. 'It was special to meet you.'

Both Viktor and Snejana eyed Catherine with avaricious intent.

'What is it to be?' asked Viktor.

Chapter Eleven

David and the girls had spent a day travelling south along the Gulf of Baydaratskaya. He considered heading across the ice, which never saw the bow of an ice-breaker, but that would keep him nearer to Novaya Zemlya and the high radiation Leonid had told him about when they left the *Olga*. This route was safer and it skirted the Ural Mountains, but it was arduous. The freezing temperature had crept into the caribou-skin tepee last night and the three had huddled under the furs. David knew, if he ever had any doubts, that the push eastwards was going to be hard. He had already used two of his chemical cooking containers, which also heated the tepee. At this rate he wouldn't have enough to see him across to the land of the Chukchi unless the weather began to break. But it was still only March and although the days would start getting lighter from now on, it would only take one severe storm and their insufficient equipment would be unable to keep them alive.

The morning had started off early, but David found himself so exhausted from the previous few days that even the sight of the girls waking with their legs entwined did little to encourage his libido. Old habits die hard, though, so he indulged himself with the girls before they ate some charqui and continued on their way.

It was another Arctic day to contend with, but at least the snow had stayed away. In his haste to put as much distance between him and Amderma he had chosen to cross the frozen Obskaya Guba. It wasn't going well and he'd badly misjudged the distances between shores. So badly in fact, that they had no choice but to make camp on the ice or risk going around in circles and using up their fuel supplies before they got to Norilsk.

The ice was solid but they made camp near a large breathing hole abandoned by some walrus. It hadn't had time to freeze back over yet and David sent Mishka to collect some slushy ice for coffee. The Arctic was almost free of salt and the ice held none at all.

The coffee was very welcome and warming and the three stayed out of the tent to enjoy the night. It wasn't warm by anyone's temperature scale, but it was very much milder than the previous night. Another two chemical heaters were used but David felt more confident; perhaps it was the caffeine.

The night was temperate enough for David and the girls to sit outside on the trailer of the ski sled, though they were wrapped in furs. All around them was ice and some distance away, to the front and rear, was a thick dark line. It cut through the velvet blue sky and delineated the low hills and sparse coniferous trees that had managed to establish themselves in the harsh climate. The three sat in silence with just two feet of opaque ice between them and the murky depths of the Kara Sea.

David looked to the heavens and did his best to remember the few constellations he'd learned in secondary school when Mr Bruce, the maths tutor, insisted on teaching them astronomy instead of trigonometry. The Great Bear dominated the sky – the Russian Bear, David mused, huge, powerful and uncompromising.

The quiet was broken when Teena stood up and walked towards the walrus hole in the ice. In the deathly silence of the northern night she appeared to be the only thing moving, and her actions attracted David and Mishka's attention. They watched impassively as she flicked the protective skins outwards, gathered up her skirt and squatted to pee. The sound of her escaping liquid was quite audible, though her body was in silhouette. David liked to watch the girls urinate; it showed a total openness in their behaviour, an acceptance on their part that they had no secrets and could hide nothing from him, even the most private of functions.

The hair on his neck bristled and an involuntary shiver tingled its way through his body. He thought that was strange. Something was different; it wasn't an excited shiver, it was a frightened tremble.

He peered into the darkness and saw only the dark outline of Teena. He turned to Mishka. Her eyes were wide open and he sensed she felt the same as him. Both of them turned to the squatting girl, and saw it together. There, coming out of the hole in the ice was a shadow. A long thin black pole as long as a walking stick... now twice as long. It tapered to a point, like a spear, now taller than a man. Beneath it a bulbous wet mass bobbed and a high-pitched scream emanated from its leathery body before it released a spume of foam that covered the peeing girl. The sudden splash of icy water took Teena's breath away, but it returned with a strength of its own and her screams rent the Arctic night as she leapt to her feet and scurried back to David and her sister. The three watched the black pole move in a slow circular motion like some bewitched broom handle. Occasionally a sad cry emanated from the creature, but it remained in the black water.

Nerves finally began to settle when all three of them realised the monster was nothing more than a rare narwhal lost beneath the ice and desperate for air. The creature displayed some distress, but there was nothing to be done. Somewhere out there in the vast Kara Sea there must be some open water, but this narwhal had made its way into the inlet and found itself starved of air. Quietly and almost serenely the ivory tusk sank back into the icy depths and hopefully on to free water. David and the girls could only hope.

The sudden appearance of one of nature's most secret creatures was a wonderfully warming experience. The two girls leant on David's shoulder and all three stared at the empty space where the giant tusk had so proudly been displayed just seconds earlier. It was a close moment for everyone, and hands began to explore in an effort to keep the feelings alive. The girls kissed, David fondled breasts and slowly bodies became entwined on the sled trailer above the ice and beneath the star speckled sky.

When Teena kneeled alongside her sister and both girls pushed out their tight bottoms David felt the icy breeze blow across his cock before it was engulfed first in one warm vagina, and after a few wonderfully slippery strokes, the other. His naked back gathered ice particles that heightened every sensation and made every feeling twice as intense. He rode on Mishka's beautifully formed bottom with measured, powerful thrusts while her sister knelt behind him and nuzzled his bloated balls. With one hand she cupped and squeezed them while her other ran sharp nails along his refrigerated skin, raising electric lines of excitement.

When his orgasm came it arrived in a boiling tumult of semen that coated the inside of Teena's sexual sheath. David looked to the heavens, and for no other reason than it felt right, he howled, an animal roar that escaped his straining throat to announce his male prowess.

Teena joined him by wailing at the sky, and all three slumped together. Ignoring the cold they spent the night on the ice, to wake as the dawn was just breaking.

David pulled himself up to the end-bars of the trailer and stretched. As the morning haze left his eyes and the world came into focus it felt good to be alive. He shook the girls awake and hopped off the trailer to relieve himself.

It was then he saw them.

Just a few indistinct blurs near the shore. At first he thought they might have been bears, until the unmistakable blink of a headlight revealed them to be soldiers. They may have been out on exercise – then again, they may not. His mind travelled back to their departure from the *Olga* and the Mig flypast. He couldn't take that chance and barked orders for the girls to break camp. They were also relieving themselves and the sudden shouts from David startled them into a panic. They ran across to him and David immediately pointed to the figures moving through the trees. To his dismay the girls then pointed to another group moving on the opposite bank.

'Fucking great,' he groaned through gritted teeth. He motioned frantically for the girls to pack up and reached for his telescope. The first group were definitely soldiers and he could make out the officer returning his gaze through his own binoculars. The second group were far less easy to distinguish because they kept themselves low behind some rocks. The girls called David to the packed sled, but he had to make a decision about which way to go. The girls made that for him.

'Nentsy,' cried Mishka, pointing towards the second group. 'They Nentsy. Friends.'

They started off as fast as the sled would take them, expecting the first group to take up the chase. They

195

didn't. Initially that worried David, but then he realised they were travelling in a large all-terrain truck. The officer had obviously decided not to trust his vehicle on the ice, fearing it wouldn't take the weight. To travel around the inlet would put almost a day between the pursuing soldiers and them. That allowed David to slow down and contemplate those in front of him.

Some Nentsy lived in the Kolkhoz, the state's collective farms, but others persisted in the old-nomadic ways, living off their deer, fishing and trading. Fortunately, both appeared to hate the Russians, but there was good and bad everywhere and David wondered how much he was worth to the authorities. Was it enough to turn an enemy into a collaborator? He was about to find out.

With less than a hundred yards to go the shore came alive with a dozen shouting men urging them to hurry. David proceeded cautiously, but the girls began waving and shouting in their own language. The sled left the ice and ploughed into thick snow, sending it up in a great flurry. A fallen log upended the sled and all three were sent sprawling, but they were picked up by the Nentsy and dragged away into the trees and out of sight of the soldiers.

'Th-thanks,' David panted, but the man who helped him just grinned until Teena translated his gratitude, then his grin turned into a laugh and David was helped up a nearby hill while others went to fetch his sled and equipment.

Everyone gathered at the top of the hill and David was amazed at the sight before him. A caravan of around thirty mobile Nentsy homes was waiting in line. Each was about the size of a small bus and made of animal skins wrapped over wood, and they were pulled on sleighs by teams of reindeer. Each one also had a little stovepipe in the roof coughing out small clouds of smoke. That meant fire and warmth, and when one of the Nentsy pointed at David and then towards the caravan David eagerly took the cue. He called the girls over and made sure his sled was to come with them, then set off towards the relative comfort of the vans.

Inside everything was cosy and warm and extremely bright. The Nentsy wore bright clothes made mostly of some sort of heavy wool, and not the furs the Lapp girls preferred. The van David found himself in belonged to Fyodor Grabar, a middle-aged man with a young attractive wife who was sitting near a slit in the van's skin. The slit allowed a set of reins in while it stopped the heat from escaping. From her position, on a small wooden bench, Natalya could steer her reindeer. Not that they took much steering, except for the first team in the caravan; after them, each team followed the one in front.

Fyodor's first act was to offer some hot potato soup, which David and the girls devoured in seconds. As they ate Fyodor threw a clump of coal-black peat into the stove, which sparked immediately into life and sent a wave of heat through what was best described as a mobile home on ice.

David and the girls began to relax, when outside came a great cry. Fyodor saw the apprehension on David's face, and spoke to the girls.

'We're moving off,' said Teena. Natalya shook the reins and the vehicle juddered for a foot or so before beginning to glide.

'Thanks for helping us,' said David.

Fyodor smiled broadly, understanding not a word of David's language, but he recognised the tone and knew what was meant.

For the next few hours the caravan swayed like some great well-fed snow snake east towards Norilsk. Inside each van a family busied themselves doing what Nentsy families did. Many of them made belts that signified the life of their families. While some young girls were starting on their first belt, others were adding to ones that had been in the family for generations. David noticed that the pretty Natalya was beginning a new belt, perhaps for a hoped-for addition to the Grabar family.

'How did you find us?' asked David. The girls translated the best they could and there was much laughter between them all as they tried to discover what each was saying. David noticed Natalya hiding her smiles shyly behind her hand, and found it curiously erotic.

The Nentsy had been aware of them for quite some time. Some of the men had been out searching for deer that had strayed away from their small herd, and saw David's party. The men reported to Fyodor, who was one of the tribe elders. He told them to keep watch on them, not knowing if they were Russians on some scientific expedition, 'Coming to see what more they could take from the Nentsy.'

The arrival of the soldiers had confirmed that they were enemies of the Russian state and that was good enough for Fyodor and the other elders, who decided that any enemy of the Russian state was a friend of theirs; hence the rescue.

The van came to a stop, and for a moment David's anxiety returned. Fyodor pulled back the heavy drapes that acted as a door and David could see that night had begun to fall and the group was setting up camp before anyone got lost in the darkness. Like some western movie the other vans began to form a circle and David saw the movement of people between vans, and a number of children appeared on the snow to play in the twilight.

Fyodor dropped from the van and went out, presumably to consult with the other elders, and Natalya followed him to feed and secure the reindeer for the night. While they were gone David surveyed the van. It was cosy and quite spacious. There was the proverbial place for everything and everything in its place. The walls were covered in heavy blankets made from the winter wool of the reindeer. They were brightly decorated with beads of amber, malachite and jade; evidence of the trade the Nentsy conducted with other tribes. Utensils that had clinked happily during the journey now hung silent from hooks hammered into the wooden frame. Everything was silent and David relaxed and motioned for the girls to fetch his drinking horn. He considered there was enough time to take a few drinks before setting up his tent, and sat back on a hair-stuffed mattress to enjoy his vodka. It was warm, just as the van was, but he couldn't allow himself to relax too much; there was still work to do setting up his own camp.

The drapes opened and Natalya climbed inside. She was carrying a slab of meat that trailed blood, which Teena and Mishka looked at expectantly. Their eyes met with Natalya and words were exchanged, and the girls rose and went to fetch a small knife that Natalya pointed to, then all three squatted on the floor of the van and began to remove the small amount of skin still left on the meat.

When Fyodor entered a few moments later the girls were rubbing salt and herbs into the flesh. He smiled and took down a pouch filled with loki, began stuffing it into a long wooden pipe and offered it to David.

David refused, saying that he must set up his camp. The girls repeated what he said and Fyodor shook his hands and head in an exaggerated manner.

'We sleep here,' Mishka said.

David smiled and answered that Fyodor had done enough for them, but Mishka was clever enough to only mention David's gratitude. 'You offend them if we not sleep,' she told him. Relieved that he didn't have to venture out into the falling night, David nodded happily and Fyodor returned his gesture and once again offered the loki. In return David offered his drinking horn.

Natalya left the girls washing some vegetables and went about the van lighting small oil lamps, which flickered and gave off a faint but pleasant scent. The loki pipe went back and forth between the two men until the girls presented them with the food, and laughed when David looked apprehensively at the raw meat. They were as relaxed as him and were having some fun, and David slapped Teena's bottom and pointed to the stove. Natalya looked confused and the girls explained that he only ate his meat cooked. Fyodor laughed too.

'He laughs because white men are strange,' said Mishka. 'You live all together and,' she struggled for the words, 'you eat food in metal tubes. You have to cut it out with a tool. He says why?'

David shrugged his shoulders and Natalya offered him the plate again, but Fyodor picked up the meat and threw it on the stove himself. Then the four Arctic people ate while David waited hungrily on his reindeer steak.

The four chatted amongst themselves quite feverishly and David found himself an onlooker, his thoughts concentrating on Natalya. Her contribution was less than that of the others on account of her innate shyness, which David found very attractive. She looked about the same age as Mishka and Teena, perhaps a bit younger, and her curves were less obvious. She had small breasts and her hips didn't flare out in the way of his girls. She also had her hair cut in a crude bob that gave her an open honest look – a look of innocence that was no doubt a lie, given the age of Fyodor and the fact that she was his woman.

Teena handed David his steak and the contrast between the girls became more obvious as he surveyed her large breasts, a characteristic she shared with her sister. The girls were also wearing fur skins and leather strappings to complement the amber jewellery he loved to see them wear. Natalya wore heavy, brightly coloured woollen clothes, including a high-necked top that encased her slim throat and seemed to mount her head on a pedestal. She noticed him watching her, and for a moment her eyes met his, but David did not look away. His gaze bore through the flicker of defiance she suddenly displayed, and even in the dim lights he could see she had become embarrassed by his attention.

The men handed their empty plates to be cleaned and enjoyed their drink and a smoke while the girls did their chores. It amazed David how two strangers, who could only communicate through gestures and translation, had become so relaxed in each other's company in such a short space of time. Maybe it was what they shared; life experiences that only came with age and the ownership of younger females.

The girls came back to see their men about to pour more vodka, and were handed cups of their own to drink. Teena and Mishka took theirs with a smile and passed each other a knowing look; David rarely gave them alcohol unless he was feeling aroused or wanted them to perform for him. He also offered them some loki and the girls settled at their men's feet – fed, watered and in a dizzy haze.

David watched Natalya grimace at the taste of the strong drink, and she gave a tiny cough when the loki seared her throat. He watched the young Nentsy and wished he could ease that ticklish throat with a tincture of his sperm. He transferred his attention to his own girls and consoled himself in their beauty, and the fact that they would service him more than adequately in the absence of Natalya.

The evening finished with the two men playing backgammon on a homemade board with the tokens made from tusk and antler. As the game drew to a close the girls prepared two beds and secured the door drapes, trapping the layer of loki that hung in a twilight cloud upon the vodka fumes. The board was packed away and David made clear his thanks for all that had been done for them that day by bowing deeply in front of Fyodor. Fyodor returned the gesture, smiled and pointed to the bed, indicating it was lights out soon. David pulled back the heavy covers and bumped into Natalya as he did so.

'Sorry,' he blurted, 'I thought this was ours.' He moved to the other bed and attempted to climb into that, but Natalya was right next to him. He was confused – more so when he heard Teena and Mishka giggle. 'What?' he asked them. 'Am I doing something wrong?' He cast a glance at Fyodor and saw that he also looked puzzled. Then Fyodor called Natalya over and she obeyed by moving to his side. The old man then spoke and his tone was colder than it had been earlier. David turned to the girls.

'What have I done?'

'You hurt him,' Mishka replied.

'How?' David asked. 'What does he want?'

The girls struggled with David's English, then Teena replied, 'He wants nothing.'

'Then what?'

Fyodor showed him what by lifting his young wife's skirt and exposing her to everyone in the van. Natalya's eyes were fixed firmly on a saucepan hanging behind David's head. The penny still never dropped for David, and he noticed that all eyes were upon him. They were obviously expecting him to do something, but all that filled his mind was the dark triangle of pubic tundra that kept Natalya's sex warm through the icy northern climes. He remained motionless and a definite air of tension descended amongst them.

'You must take Natalya,' said Teena. 'Fyodor is upset.'

Slowly the penny began to turn. This was Nentsy hospitality, David realised. He was being offered this beautiful girl for the night simply because he was a guest. The penny hit the floor with an almighty clang. It was an honour and one he was glad to reciprocate. He motioned for the girls to undress and the van was once again a cheery haven. Fyodor spanked Natalya smartly on the bottom and sent her over to David with one push of his hand. The girl fell into his arms, but she refused to look at him. Mishka spoke to her and she answered.

'It is her first time with another man,' Mishka informed him. 'She is scared. You are white. She says what will you do to her.'

For the briefest of moments David considered simply sleeping with her, but Fyodor was already making busy with Teena. He appeared to be very happy with her breasts and seemed to be trying to squeeze the very nipples away from the flesh. His other hand had already found an appreciated spot between Teena's legs and the girl was pulling up her knees to make the old man's access easier. Mishka was not idle either. She had taken the old man's gnarled cock from his trousers and was busy dipping her head over his swollen glans. David wanted some of the same, and though he vowed to himself to take it easy on the girl, it was his lust that always had the last word. He pulled up the tight sweater she was wearing. She stopped him, but Fyodor saw and barked at her angrily. David tried again, and this time she lifted her arms and allowed herself to be stripped.

She really was beautiful, and though she was obviously a Nentsy she shared few of their features. Her body was leaner, and not just through youth; somewhere in the past this girl had an ancestor from warmer latitudes. David ran his hands over the small mounds that formed her breasts. She still refused to look at him, but he detected the telltale shudder of her shoulders and the swell of her nipples. Whether it was her first time to be shared or not, it was a clear indication that her body was preparing itself for sex.

He guided her over to the thick mattress and bent her forward until she had to support herself with her hands, then he set about an intimate examination of her. Despite her earlier apprehension he found her cleft moist and accepting of his probing fingers. He continued working on her from behind as he bent down to smell her sex; he loved the taste and smell of a natural woman. His attentions were arousing the girl and she began to push back against his fingers, forcing them to probe deeper. He helped by using two, and registered how tightly her sheath gripped him.

He took hold of Natalya's small left breast and used it to turn her around and sit her upon the mattress, then pulled up her legs until she was open for viewing. The tight split of her sex lips revealed just the merest hint of the slick pink cavity beyond. David moved her hand and rested it upon her unkempt mound. Disappointment was evident in her face, but her expression changed when he began to undress. She responded by sucking her forefinger and using it to run small circles around her clitoris, alternating her actions with little forays into her vagina and firm caresses of her fattening lips.

Her actions increased when David's cock was revealed, and he noticed a faint smile, the one he found so attractive, return to her face before it melted into a look of intense desire.

David sat beside her and motioned to Natalya to mount him, and this time she didn't need one of the girls to translate. She lifted one of her lithe legs across his and sat demurely in his lap, and now that the moment was upon her she became sweetly nervous again. David took his time and surveyed every inch of her body, before finally lifting her up and adjusted his cock at the target. The girl bit her bottom lip as the fat head nudged aside her labia, but there was resistance. She was so tense that full penetration promised to rip his foreskin. A moment or so later and he would have gladly risked it, but he caught sight of Teena sitting on the mattress opposite. She was naked and her knees were pulled up to her breasts, and David could see the evidence of Fyodor's ejaculation on her inner thighs. For the moment she was pulling on the pipe of loki and enjoying the sight of her sister being fucked.

David called her and pointed to the erection spearing up from his lap. Teena immediately put down the pipe and shuffled across on hands and knees, buried her head between the couple, and sucked it into her mouth, and he allowed her to lubricate him for just a few moments before he grunted for her to stop. She knew what was required next, and parted the girl's sex lips and slipped David's swollen penis up into Natalya. She gasped and lifted herself, but David prevented her from moving and pushed home. She was as tight as a virgin and he felt like he was breaking her in for the first time. After several stabs of his hips he was still only halfway embedded, but despite the discomfort of her tight vagina he continued to pump.

He held out a finger to Teena and grunted for her to suck it. When it was wet enough he fed it up Natalya's puckered and equally tight sphincter, and the absolute shock of having a finger rudely pushed into her bottom had the effect David wanted. As the girl's mind reeled from each new experience she relaxed long enough for him to force his prick fully up into her snug sheath, and with a wail she began to bounce on his member, repeating the same incoherent words over and over.

David took that as encouragement and met her thrust for thrust as she pummelled her way to an orgasm. But he was more patient. He sensed her descent from the sexual heights and adjusted the power and length of his thrusts until he found himself on that wonderful plateau between excitement and unstoppable ejaculation.

Natalya slumped onto his chest to rest and enjoy the rhythm of her first white man. Behind them Teena was still on the floor. She was smiling at her new friend's obvious pleasure, and when David looked at her she pointed between the mating couple's legs. David nodded and enjoyed the sensations of Teena's tongue sliding up his cock to Natalya's cleft.

The Nentsy girl enjoyed it too, especially when Teena's tongue paused over her anus before probing inside. Now that the heavy throb of her orgasm had subsided Natalya lifted herself up from David's chest and looked down at him with a contented smile. He smiled back at her and, holding her waist, began to slowly move the girl up and down his rigid manhood. She took up the rhythm and supported herself with her hands on his shoulders. With every shunt David's cock was revealed and Teena took the opportunity to lap at it, and when Natalya's bottom sank down she licked at her anus and sent tiny sexual shockwaves up to her already over-stimulated brain.

David calmed her momentarily by lifting her off his cock and turning her around to face the others. Remarkably Fyodor had already finished for the second time and he and Mishka lay together on the other mattress, enjoying a smoke and the show.

Entering Natalya again, David picked up the pace and began to thrust with increasing passion. She responded and began to grind on his cock avidly. The others, who were watching in intense silence, enjoyed the sight. Teena climbed to her knees and sucked Natalya's breasts, helping her to another orgasm, and when it came it met with David's groan of ecstasy and shuddering release. His climax was so strong that pearls of his fluid leaked back down his cock and found their way to the grateful lips and tongue of Teena.

It wasn't the first time that Major Sergei Bokov's chauffeur had driven his boss while watching him ride a female in the back of the car. He adjusted his rear-view mirror until it revealed the shaven sex of the major's latest conquest. Sometimes he didn't even bother looking, but this one was something special. She was pert and arrogant, and despite what she must have been through – he was well aware of how the major came by his girls – she was full of confidence.

He drew the mirror upwards, consigning the images of the major's cock slipping in and out of her to memory. Sabrina's face came into view and their eyes met. Her expression was blank and she rode the army officer with the cold dispassionate manner of a cheap whore.

The two watched each other coldly through the mirror until he smiled. She returned his gesture by blowing him a dry kiss with a look of cool disdain. The driver smiled again and concentrated on the road.

The limousine sped along the dark lane that cut its way through forest and led out to the recreation centre for members of Cheka 3. It was to be Sabrina's second consecutive night there. The previous evening she had enjoyed the hospitality of the major and his military cronies and they in turn had enjoyed her, especially when she was made to perform with another of the girls taken there. Under other circumstances she would have actually enjoyed it. The recreation centre was a large stately pile that had been confiscated from the family of some Russian minor aristocracy during the revolution. Obviously the decadent charm hadn't offended the communists so much that they felt compelled to raze it to the ground. Some of the men had also been quite handsome, dressed as they were in their military uniforms. At a different time and under different circumstances, Sabrina would have enjoyed the company of so many powerful men – and the sex too!

The car sped onwards, as did the major. Then, with a mile or two to go, Sabrina felt the vehicle begin to slow down. The major was lost in his own pleasure but Sabrina turned from looking out of a side window and saw there was a vehicle parked precariously at the side of the road. It had one of its doors open and a dark bundle was lying on the light dusting of snow that covered the road. The shape was clearly that of a body.

Only when their car came to a halt did the major finally stop fucking Sabrina and show any interest in the situation. He pushed her off him and she adjusted her dress while he spoke to the driver. They had obviously decided upon caution, because Sabrina noticed the driver unclip his sidearm as he got out of the car. Once outside he drew his pistol and made his way to the bundle in the glare of the headlights. Beyond the car's beam everything was black.

As the driver neared the shape on the ground the major lit up a Belomor and looked on anxiously. He exhaled the acrid smoke from his cigarette and flashed an unsuccessful reassuring grin at Sabrina. She was looking out of the side window when it happened, but the major's shouts and the sound of gunfire instantly seized her attention. There was no longer a bundle on the road outside, just a man grappling with the major's driver. Both were locked together in an embrace that would decide who would live and who would not. Neither had guns. The man on the road had spun over as the driver appeared, but his reflexes were not good enough. The driver had kicked out and sent the gun into the bushes before levelling his own and firing. He missed, and the man managed to pull him over and knock the driver's gun to the road. The struggle was like a silent movie, neither man uttering a word, each concentrating on becoming the victor. Suddenly the stranger swung around and threw the driver to the ground. It was a bad move. The driver wasn't hurt and his gun laid an arm's reach away. He turned and smiled, sensing victory, then reached for the weapon, but as his fingers touched the cold steel he felt the weight of a rock strike his temple with a sickening thud. There was no pain, no real dying, just darkness.

Justin dropped to his knees with exhaustion, and with the realisation that he had been a mere moment away from death if that rock had not been there, or his aim off. He shuddered at the thought, and then remembered his task – Sabrina.

Suddenly he gained new strength and rose to his feet, only to be greeted by the sight of Major Bokov walking towards him with his pistol aimed.

In the car Sabrina saw something black flash past near the trees. She remained where she was, too afraid to move and draw attention to herself. She still had no idea that the man in the road was Justin.

The major was closing down on Sabrina's would-be rescuer. He did not want to shoot at too great a range. He stopped just six feet from his target and levelled his gun. Justin was numb. There was no desire to run or plead. He was almost glad that his Russian nightmare was over; he was ready. As the major took one more step he let his hands drop to his sides and closed his eyes. He never flinched when the gun went off; he simply remained on his feet and felt the batter of warm brains run down his forehead. He opened his eyes and saw the soldier sprawled on the road, and if he still possessed a face Justin would have described him as being face down. Behind him, motionless and in shock, stood Catherine. She was trembling violently, and she held the smoking gun that had been kicked out of Justin's hand a few minutes before. Justin rushed to her and took her in his arms, and squeezing her tight he could not find any appropriate words. Obviously he did want to live, after all.

Suddenly the whole road lit up and the glare brought both Justin and Catherine to their senses. 'Quick!' she gasped. 'You must grab her and get out of here!'

David turned and ran to the major's car while Snejana Radoslavov drove out onto the road, got out and surveyed the scene. In the major's car Sabrina was trying to make herself as small as possible behind the driver's seat.

'Sabrina!'

Slowly the cowering girl turned her head, half expecting to meet with a bullet. But it was Justin's face she saw, and for a short moment she could not say a word. Then it all came out.

'J-Justin?' she stammered in disbelief. 'What are you doing?'

'Rescuing you,' he answered quickly, and stretched out a hand for her to take.

Out on the road Catherine was drawing deeply on a cigarette in an effort to calm her nerves while Snejana was collecting something from the boot of his car. Sabrina surveyed the bodies as Snejana approached.

'Well then,' he said to Justin, 'not so much like James Bond. You like Rambo.'

'What do we do now?' asked Justin, too tense to appreciate the attempt at humour.

Snejana put an arm around Catherine. 'We are going to Burgas,' he said. 'You two are on your own.'

'What about them?' Justin pointed at the two bodies.

'Ah, yes,' Snejana smiled smugly. He took out what he had collected from his car and threw it over the major's head. It was a Chechen flag. 'Let them think it is rebels,' he added, and guided Catherine back to his car.

As she passed Sabrina, Catherine said, 'Look after him.'

'You must be Catherine,' said Sabrina, and Catherine stopped and turned to face her.

'Yes I am.'

Sabrina looked her in the eye, and then surveyed the carnage. She owed these strangers a favour. She didn't know who they were or why they were doing it. 'Thank you,' she said quietly.

As Catherine neared Snejana's car Justin called after her. She stopped and turned and Justin thought he saw the glint of a tear. The two looked into each other's eyes, and then Catherine spoke.

'You must be quick,' she said, wanting him to leave before she burst into tears. 'Someone may come.'

Justin looked at Sabrina and then returned his gaze to the Russian girl who had helped him without fear or thought for herself. 'I will never forget you!' he

211

shouted.

Sabrina allowed Justin a brief moment and then pulled on his sleeve. It was wet from the tussle in the snow and she noticed he had a bloody nose. In the first touching gesture she had extended to him in numerous months she held out her handkerchief and wiped away the blood. He took it from her and turned away towards his car, wiping away a tear as he did so. Sabrina followed and climbed into the passenger seat, and as they too fled the scene she began to gush with a thousand questions, but Justin remained silent and thoughtful as the bodies of the soldiers faded behind the speeding car.

After a very long period of silence Sabrina asked what Justin's next plans were.

'Odessa,' he said simply. 'Then home.'

'How do we get there? Is it all set up?'

Justin turned to her. 'You heard them. We're on our own.'

'And how do we get there?' she asked again, then pointed at the dashboard of the Trabant they were travelling in. 'In this? What about food, clothes? What about fuel?'

Justin reached into his pocket and pulled out the fat wad of roubles he'd been given by Viktor and Snejana. 'That should do us.'

Sabrina thumbed the cash. 'You did it, Justin. All this time I've been thinking you were just a soft wanker and you do this!' She waved the money excitedly in the air and he took the opportunity to take it back from her. 'I was obviously wrong,' she continued. 'You've finally woken up. Perhaps now we can finish what we came to this ice box for.'

Justin careered the car to the side of the road. 'No way!' he barked, displaying his renewed confidence.

'I didn't come through all this to start it all over again.'

The tension had brought a fresh flow of blood from his nose and Sabrina wiped it away tenderly. 'But you can do it. We've got the money, and you…' she sounded excited about him for the first time in a very long time, 'you've got the courage to see it through.'

'No!'

Sabrina dropped her hand into Justin's lap and caressed him. 'You've shown me a side to you I never knew existed.' She unzipped his trousers. 'Things will be different between us.' His cock was soon free and Sabrina slipped it into her mouth. She sucked for a moment and then looked up at him with her girlish brown eyes. 'I promise.'

Justin pulled the car back onto the road and switched on the wipers. It was beginning to snow again, but inside the car the heater was having a relaxing effect on both of them. 'Going to Odessa and getting out that way is just as dangerous as chasing David,' she said, between kissing and rubbing his cock. 'You've shown me now that you hate to lose as much as I do.' A black car containing four uniformed men sped past them in the direction of the carnage they had left behind. It sent the adrenaline rushing back through Justin, and in that brief second he considered their chances of getting out of the country. It was obvious that all borders, ports and airports would be on the look out for them, giving them no choice but to remain in the interior for some time yet. The thought also entered his mind that Snejana or Viktor may well see it in their interests to 'help' the authorities and inform them of their plans.

'There's no point,' he finally said. 'We just need to keep our heads down until we can get out. Besides, we don't know where he is.'

'I do,' said Sabrina, smiling enigmatically. 'Russian

officers just can't shut up when they're in bed,' and with those words she dropped her head once more into Justin's lap.

The sudden jolt of the ice caravan from the forest path on to icy road woke David. During his sleep he had once again been tormented by nightmares. It seemed that every night he was reminded of being held captive by Sabrina and her plans to bring him to northern Russia and sell, or rather hire, his body to the rich women whose men were away in the great Arctic factories. He remembered the girl they had also sold to the islanders of the Orkneys, and how he feared they were going to drown on the rough sea passage to St Petersburg.

Then he recalled his escape and the tortuous months he had spent trying to survive in a strange country with the many different languages. He shook the frightening fog of memories from his mind and accepted the cup of chicory from a smiling Mishka. Fyodor was driving the deer and Natalya was working on her belt. The two Lapps were preparing food and the van smelled wonderful, and it was warm, unlike outside where a snowy squall reduced the visibility to about thirty feet. No one was concerned; they were on the road to Norilsk and a welcome stop for all the tribe, and David too.

Lubyanka was buzzing with the news of the death of Major Sergei Bokov and his driver. Captain Vasili Leskov had been summoned to a special meeting of Cheka 3 and told to find the Chechen rebels who had carried out the assassinations – whatever it took. The captain picked his papers up from the desk and marched from the room. He had been reinstated after the controversy of his damaged vehicle in Murmansk, and he intended to repair his damaged reputation. In the corridor outside the Cheka 3 office his subordinate asked if he should round up all known Chechens in Moscow. The captain replied in the affirmative and added that three men were to be shot as an example to others.

'Once we have found the pigs responsible we shall show them not to fool with the mother country,' said the desperate-to-please soldier.

'You will not find the rebels responsible,' the captain informed him sagely, then in response to the soldier's bemused expression he added, 'There never were any rebels.'

The soldier hurried along beside his captain. 'Then why are we to shoot three men?' he asked.

Captain Leskov turned on his highly polished boots. 'Because,' he said coldly, 'our superiors expect it.'

Chapter Twelve

The Nentsy caravan had formed their usual kraal just outside Norilsk, and the people were setting up all sorts of games to play while the elders went into the town to trade. Some children were racing their dogs against each other, women were teaching girls how to make their traditional belts and clothing, and a number of the men were enjoying a drink and telling tales around a crackling fire of sweet-smelling pine logs.

David and the girls were unloading their sled in preparation for their trip to the town and some trading of their own. The fog had mostly lifted, boiled off by the mid-morning sun, and the snow scurried in tiny vortices from the occasional gust of wind rather than fall from the sky. It was a beautiful day.

There was no such thing as a poor person in Norilsk. It was a mining town and they dug for nickel, copper and, more importantly, platinum. David had little to bargain with. As time had gone by he realised he had to make for Alaska; he had no idea of the whereabouts of Sabrina and Justin, but he did know the Russian military were on his trail. So it was no good trading his amber for roubles; they would be worthless in America. What he wanted, apart from enough fuel and supplies to get him to the Bering Strait, was platinum; something he could exchange for dollars. He squatted on his sled, and with Teena's arms around Mishka who had hers around David, they gave Natalya a cheery wave and set off for the best trading centres in town – the bars, clubs and casinos.

Rich it may have been, clean it wasn't. The whole town was a series of prefabricated buildings and gaudy neon signs that screamed encouragement to the money-laden miners and threatened electrocution as sparks flew from unprotected electrical connections. This was a town without a seedy quarter; it was a seedy town, full stop.

As David's sled made its way along the central street, fur-clad miners meandered from bar to bar seeking out new ways to part with their money. He paused outside one ramshackle structure that deluded itself it was a casino, and peered inside. Two dozen drunken men were dropping roubles into machine slots in an attempt to rid the boredom of the icy wastes. As David suspected, they were being served by just two girls; the only Russian gold diggers brave enough or desperate enough to venture this far north.

He patted his own girls on the thigh. 'Time to clean up,' he said to himself, and motored over to what laughingly described itself as a hotel.

A thousand or so miles away in Berezovo a tired out Trabant entered town. Its long hard drive over the Urals had finally finished its brave little two-stroke engine. A smiling mechanic came out of his garage to administer the last rights as he had done so often to those foolish enough to challenge the unforgiving mountains. Fortunately, a young man who possessed a modicum of English accompanied the mechanic.

After the car had been taken inside an old world war two airplane hangar Justin and Sabrina considered their options. They could wait a few days for the new distributor and head gasket for their car, but delivery times were notoriously variable and that would put time and distance between them and David. They could ask Boris, the mechanic, to replace the damaged parts with those from one of his other Trabants in the hangar, but they were almost as bad as the ones they would replace. That left buying the only good vehicle Boris had left, and good was more of a euphemism than a description. It did have some advantages though. They could at least start off again in the morning and any witnesses, like the four men who had passed them near the Cheka 3 recreation building, would be looking for the wrong vehicle.

The only setback was money. Boris obviously realised that a product was only worth what you could get for it, and for the creaking Opel that had hardly moved in two years, he sensed he could get a lot. The fall of communism had a lot to answer for.

Darkness was also closing fast and they would need somewhere to sleep. As one horse towns went Berezovo didn't register as one with a donkey; there was no hotel. Neither Sabrina nor Justin relished the thought of one more night huddled in the Trabant. The previous night had almost seen them succumb to exposure so they took up the only option available, the back room of the hangar cum garage. It had a potbellied stove that burned peat and there was a number of old settees and chairs for them to sleep on. It did mean though, that they could cook something hot. Boris and the boy, Stepan, had a room on a mezzanine floor that was only slightly more comfortable than the space on offer. It was a take it or leave it choice. They took it.

Darkness had now fallen and the temperature outside had slumped as if in challenge to the coming spring. The three men settled down to an evening of cards, Boris using an old engine block as his seat, and Sabrina found herself busy preparing a meal of soup and bread. It was a drop in status for her, but she was still shocked at the character change Justin had undergone, and she was beginning to realise just how much she needed him.

She carried the food to the table and noticed the glances the two Russian men were casting at her. When she came back to sit with them Boris produced a bottle of homemade vodka. She took a sip from her glass and coughed at its coarseness, prompting laughter from the men.

'What?' she spluttered, and held up the glass. 'It's brake fluid, isn't it?' She took another sip and swallowed it defiantly. 'Or aviation fuel?'

When Justin and Stepan laughed again Boris joined in and refilled everyone's glass. It was a happy atmosphere and Sabrina was quite content to take away the dishes and clean them when Justin told her to, and when she returned the aviation-fuelled vodka was taking effect on the three men. They sat beneath a bare bulb and played their game, and all the time they were whispering, and Sabrina noticed the glances were becoming more frequent and intense.

'Deal me in,' she announced, after noticing the game they were playing was rummy. She held out her hands expectantly but no cards were forthcoming. Boris dealt only to the men.

'I'll play,' Sabrina repeated.

This time Boris grunted some sort of reply and Stepan informed her that women couldn't play cards with men, so she stood up and sulked around the garage, although she remained close enough to the stove to benefit from its warmth.

The garage was scattered with spare parts and tools and she returned to the table and its single bulb before she stubbed her foot on one of the many clumps of metal that lay on the floor. The men continued playing as if she was not there, and tired of being ignored and unfamiliar with not being the centre of things, she broke her silence and interrupted them.

'What are you playing for?' she asked, desperate for any sort of conversation.

'The Opel,' Justin replied.

Sabrina took up the near empty pack of Belomor and removed a cigarette. 'I thought we'd agreed to buy it already,' she said.

He didn't look up from his hand. 'It's too much.'

'We've got the money.'

Justin turned on her, and in a manner that made her feel suddenly and unusually vulnerable he snapped, 'I've got the money. And it's too much.'

Sabrina stood and paced the floor anxiously. 'So what is it? You win the money off him and buy the car with his own money?'

'Sort of.'

'What do you mean, sort of?' she snorted. 'What if you lose? We end up with less money and we still have to buy the car.'

'If I lose,' Justin answered calmly, 'I pay the asking price. If I win I pay half the price and Boris and Stepan get to fuck you.'

The two men stared hungrily at Sabrina.

'What?' she exclaimed. 'What sort of a bet is that?'

Justin put down his cards and took up a second bottle of the homemade drink. 'Just that,' he answered confidently. 'A bet, and I've just won.' He slumped down on a greasy sofa. 'So get ready to pay up.'

Boris and Stepan got to their feet, and Sabrina remained rooted to the spot. Suddenly Boris cleared the table with a sweep of his hand that sent cards and glasses to join the other debris littering the floor. There was no place for Sabrina to run to, and she allowed Stepan to grab her by the neck and move her to the table, where Boris was already unbuckling his belt. Stepan was young and fit and his grip was unrelenting, and as he forced her over the table she saw Justin sitting comfortably. He was pouring himself another vodka and smiling smugly, settling down like a man about to enjoy a movie. He even raised his glass to her as Boris lifted her skirt, and his contempt and indifference to her plight stirred emotions in her that she hadn't felt for him in a long time.

The skirt now lay across her lower back, exposing her pale silk knickers. Boris removed them without Sabrina having to lift a leg; he simply tore them in two and cast them aside. And he did not find her unreceptive; her submissive nature was again coming to the fore, but this time it was Justin who was driving her desire. She wanted him to see her being used, needed him to see her forced.

Stepan increased his grip as the old mechanic sought out her entrance. She felt his entry and spread herself accordingly, only the slight grimace she displayed as his width bullied its way inside her was evidence of what she was enduring. She watched for some emotion on Justin's face. She knew he loved her, rescuing her the way he had was evidence enough of that, but he was looking on impassively. His cold stares frightened and excited Sabrina. She began to respond, began to snatch and strain for Boris's hard cock. She wanted Justin to want her like Boris did. She reached back with searching hands and urged him on. Boris responded briefly before growling and releasing himself into the girl's sheath. His ejaculation was prolonged and copious; he didn't have many outlets for his needs in Berezovo. The only contact between the mechanic and Sabrina had been his cock. He hadn't touched her or even tried to kiss her. His was simply a release, and now he was sated he placed his hand on the girl's neck to keep her pinned to the table. It was time for Stepan to collect.

The youth was in no hurry. For him Berezovo was a happy, if limited, hunting ground. Nonetheless, it was always nice to have a different female, especially if she wasn't even from the same town. He made a great show of removing all his clothes and stroking his impressive penis in front of Sabrina; Stepan's conquests had no cause for complaint in that department. What the girls usually didn't agree to was where Stepan liked to put it.

Unlike his older friend Stepan was very tactile. His hands roamed freely over Sabrina's body and he took the liberties expected of him by Justin. When he had tired of exploring the lovely thing pinned helplessly to the table by the strong mechanic he made his way behind her, and to his favourite orifice. Sabrina tried in vain to glance back, but Boris held her tight to the table. Her only vision was of Justin watching her being abused. She knew he was enjoying it; the way he adjusted his trousers to accommodate his thickening muscle was evidence enough, and that made her enjoy it too. The Russians thought they were holding her against her will but she would have bent over for them anyway. All Justin had to do was tell her. For now though, she would go along with their game. She even yelped when Stepan stung her bottom with several swipes of his hand, and deep down the stinging thrilled her.

No matter how excited her body though, Stepan's intrusion was to prove uncomfortable, at least initially. The girls in the town had always struggled to harbour his girth. It was that which excited him the most, to see them grimace as they struggled to take him, to watch them wince at what they had to accommodate, and he revelled in their shame.

Stepan pulled the cheeks of Sabrina's bottom apart and anointed her sphincter with saliva. It took him several minutes to prise her open, but he was in no hurry. He was enjoying watching her gasp for breath as the mushroom head of his cock pushed its way past her tight ring. Sabrina held her breath and closed her eyes, and then the resistance yielded and Stepan's glans sank into her rectum until his humid groin pressed down on her buttocks.

It was not the first time Sabrina had been buggered, but she had never been impaled on anything quite so big. Her whole being felt like it was under invasion from some great meaty spit from which she had no escape. She instinctively tried to squeeze him out of her bottom, but it was useless. There was only one response for her to make. With each thrust of his gnarled prick she squealed, the way he wanted her to. Her obvious discomfort made him even thicker and she wailed all the more. It was a vicious circle that could not end until he had fired his sperm into her rectum. Sabrina knew that. She knew it would come, and she saved her loudest squeal for that moment, but what Stepan didn't know was that her desperate exclamation hid the onset of her own shattering and exquisite orgasm, the culmination of being treated so ruthlessly.

Stepan collapsed on the settee next to Justin and proudly stroked his wilting cock. Then he swallowed half a glass of fiery vodka, and Sabrina was stunned to see his penis pulse once, then again, and then slowly rise until it stood proudly from his groin once more. He rose from the settee, and as the two rough males closed in on her she gazed at Justin from her position over the table and smiled faintly. The nights in Russia were very long.

Chapter Thirteen

'No roubles!' shouted David. 'Platinum – only platinum.' He dropped another nugget into a pouch beneath his shirt and opened the door to the miner. 'Just platinum!' he hollered again, above the clamouring heads of the milling men wanting entrance to the latest attraction in Norilsk.

Entrance, of course, was the operative word. It didn't take long for rumours to spread of new and freshly available girls. You just had to tell the hotel manager, borrow a room from him and promise him a cut of the takings.

'What's the act?' asked one very well spoken Russian. His clean and smart appearance indicated he was not one of the miners.

'Oh, it's no act,' David answered. 'This is the real thing.'

The man craned his neck over David's shoulder to glimpse some girls carrying trays of drinks. They were topless and were enjoying extra wages from the hotel manager. Some men were also enjoying mouthfuls of lovely Russian breasts as the girls handed out the drinks. David had one night to make as much platinum as he could. Tonight nothing was off the menu, no act too low, no instinct too base.

The man scanned quickly and caught sight of Teena, who was totally naked except for her knee length suede boots and her amber jewellery. She was lying against an upturned table with her shoulders on the carpet, her bottom in the air and her legs folded down to touch the floor in front of her shoulders. In that position her sex was facing a row of men. She was holding herself open in the most lewd manner and the men were trying to lodge small nuggets of platinum in her vagina. It made a change from dropping worthless roubles into gaming machines; on them you just won more useless roubles. If you hit the slot here you got to see the other gorgeous Lapp suck the nugget from her sister and bring it to your mouth with a deep kiss that tasted of sex. If you missed though, your nugget stayed on the floor to be picked up by Mishka. She also held a sealskin whip, which she used to keep the men behind an imaginary line she had drawn on the carpet.

'How much?' asked the eager Russian at the door.

'Half ounce of platinum,' David answered.

The man seemed to slump with disappointment. 'I've only got roubles,' he answered. 'I'm not a miner. I'm on leave from the Kurevka hydro plant. Can't I pay with roubles?'

David shook his head and turned the man away. A moment later he saw him bargaining for some platinum with a miner.

When all who wanted in were in David closed the door and joined the throng. Teena had moved on to her party trick of bending her back even further until she could point her vagina down over the neck of a beer bottle. In that position she was almost able to kiss her own mound. Once the neck of the bottle was nice and deep inside her she clenched and picked it up. Then she lifted the bottle and with her legs pointing towards the ceiling emptied it into herself. The miners watched mesmerised, then roared with pleasure as Teena pushed out the bottle with a vicious squeeze of her powerful muscles. The bottle was quickly followed by several golden fountains of beer that squirted into the air and sprayed the audience. All the men went wild and made desperate attempts to get some of the foam into their mouths. They then took it upon themselves to spray Teena with a shower of platinum.

Kneeling on a makeshift bar was Mishka, who had left her sibling to do her party piece. She had a long red tapered candle sticking out of her bottom, which men were using to light their smokes. Unknown to them she was also clenching a bottle opener inside her sex. Amazed miners were buying beers by the dozen so one of the barmaids could open their bottle in the most bizarre manner, and then they could taste the girl as they drank.

David was also happy to see that one of the hired girls was already down on her knees with a prick in her mouth. He had let in more men than he'd intended and was worried that the girls would have trouble catering for them all. Now that the barmaids were obviously enjoying the whole scene and getting involved, he looked forward to a great night of getting rich.

A few hundred miles outside Norilsk Sabrina and Justin were in trouble. The Opel had begun to make worrying noises a hundred miles earlier, but they were in the middle of nowhere and had no choice but to head for the nearest centre of population.

And that was, purely by chance, for Norilsk.

The car had grown steadily worse until it let out a metallic bark and ground to a halt.

Justin slammed the bonnet back down and jumped into the car with Sabrina, who immediately threw several large blankets over him. 'If God wanted to give the world an enema, he'd stick the pipe in this fucking country,' he grumbled.

Sabrina winced and shifted her bottom playfully. 'Don't talk about having things shoved up your bottom after what you three did to me in Berezovo,' she smiled.

Justin pulled the blanket up to his chin to maintain as much heat as he could. 'At least it kept you warm,' he replied.

She snuggled into him and began to fondle his penis. 'It still is,' she said.

Justin reclined his seat and watched as the windscreen whitened over with the falling snow, and Sabrina ducked under the blankets and suckled on his swelling cock. It made them both warm and she knew that if she kept on sucking Justin would soon make some snow of his own.

It had taken far too long to organise, but the Sikorksy finally arrived to pick up Captain Vasili Leskov. He was several days behind his prey, but he knew they were somewhere in central Siberia. He had sent a contingent of soldiers in pursuit, but they had lost them on the ice of the Obskaya Guba bight. It was up to him to find them and exact vengeance for the murder of Major Sergei Bokov and the slight the westerners had brought to Russia. He gave the thumbs up to the pilot and a flurry of excited snow signalled their departure north.

Everything was bright and totally white in the Opel when Justin and Sabrina awoke.

'We must have slept through a snowstorm,' said Justin unnecessarily. He tried his door, but it wouldn't budge. Sabrina's side was the same.

'We're trapped,' she announced, a hint of panic in her voice. 'What are we going to do?'

Justin didn't honestly know, but he tried to remain calm and reassuring. In his head he was trying to work out what was going on outside. 'Let's wait awhile,' he said. 'The sun might thin it out.'

'But what if it's still snowing?' she suggested. 'Things may be getting worse.'

He knew she was right, but the simple matter was they were trapped and it was down to nature to blow or melt the snow away.

Sabrina started trying to wind down the window, but Justin reached out and stopped her. 'What are you doing?' he challenged.

'I'm trying to get us out of here,' she said.

'But we don't know how deep it is,' he said.

'Then we better make a start.' She had regained some composure now she'd decided on a course of action. 'Can't you feel it?' she added.

'Feel what?'

'The heat. It's warm in here and we're covered in snow.'

'I think it's supposed to be,' Justin told her. 'I've read about people caught in avalanches. They reckon it keeps them warm. You must have seen films when farmers pull sheep out from snowdrifts.'

'We're not sheep,' she snapped. 'Look, we don't know how long the car has been under the snow. It might be hot because we are running out of air.'

The moment she said that Justin's lungs tightened and he began to take conscious control of his breathing. Slowly he took away his restraining hand while he considered what she had said. 'You're right,' he eventually acknowledged. 'What have we got to lose?'

The window didn't budge until Justin reached across and pressed the flats of his hands to the glass. It finally lowered and left a pure sheet of compressed snow in its place.

'Ready?' Sabrina asked.

Justin nodded and she punched into the wall of white, and immediately a huge fall of icy snow fell into the car and she gasped at the cold. It fell into the footwell and onto her lap, and then more dropped through the open window and the car began to fill up.

'Close the window!' Justin shouted. It was jammed, and Sabrina's cold fingers began to find it difficult to grip the winder handle. Justin panicked and tried it himself. It was no use. Another fall of snow and Sabrina screamed that she was cold. Panic gripped Justin: options raced through his mind. Even if they got the window closed they would be sitting in melting snow with their air running out. If they carried on trying to tunnel they might bring in more snow. They had no choice. Unable to make much headway on Sabrina's side he opened his own window. More snow came in and he climbed onto his seat and began to dig frantically. Then came more powdery, cold and unforgiving snow. It pushed him back into the car. Sabrina wasn't moving. The snow was up to her middle. He climbed into the back of the car and tried again. The same result. He cowered in the one remaining clear corner, his chest tightening. Was the air fading…?

The white snow gave way to spiralling blackness.

There was noise; he heard it. And smells… food!

Justin wasn't dead. He could smile but he couldn't move, and his eyes remained closed. He faded again, for how long he couldn't know, but the next sense to return was touch. He felt them. Someone was laying next him. They were naked! *He* was naked!

His eyes opened to reveal a picture of loveliness; a girl with long perfectly straight and jet-black hair. She returned his smile and cuddled into him. He remained perfectly stiff – in every way. The girl lifted a leg to wrap around him and it brushed his erect penis. She noticed it and looked at him with that smile again. Justin was mortified. What was happening to him?

He lay there quietly studying the heavy tarpaulin ceiling and praying that his erection would subside. Oh no, he thought to himself, her hand had just touched him. He noted with relief that there was no intent; the girl was getting up.

'Shh,' she hushed, and held up a finger to her lips. 'Just rest.'

She could speak English. She climbed out from beneath the furs and displayed a perfectly formed physique. She was in her mid-twenties with a nipped waist, small but wonderfully shaped breasts and a thick mat of hair between her legs, and she clearly wasn't embarrassed about nudity.

Though he didn't move his head Justin followed her athletic form with his eyes as she left him. In his attempt to keep sight of her he saw a mound a few feet away. Then he noticed the motion; they were moving. As clarity returned to his head he realised they were in some sort of covered wagon. He could feel the warmth of a fire, though he couldn't see one. Something moved in the opposite mound. It was a person, a young boy of about fifteen. The boy smiled – everyone seemed to smile. He lifted his head and Justin could see an unconscious Sabrina lying beside him. She was on her back, but alive. Someone else was with her and the boy. On the far side an older woman raised herself up. It was the girl's mother, that was obvious.

The girl returned with a mug of soup. She helped him up onto his elbows and held the mug to his mouth. The soup was hot and he could feel the life-giving warmth racing through his body. He had so many questions, but they would have to wait until he had finished.

'Where am I?' he eventually asked.

'We are Komi,' the girl answered. 'I am Irena and

this is my mother and brother.' Justin smiled in acknowledgement. Smiling was becoming contagious. 'And that is my father.' She pointed to the front of the wagon and Justin saw a weather-beaten face, also smiling.

'How did you find us?'

'We passed you. You were like a huge snowball by the side of the road. We dug you out.'

'Thank God you did,' Justin said sincerely. 'I thought we were dead.'

'Almost,' Irena confirmed. 'Your friend is still asleep. She is very ill.'

'Is she going to be all right?'

'I think so. My mother is very good. She has seen people in the snow before. We are trying to get her warm.'

Justin flopped back down, exhausted. 'How long have we been here?' he asked weakly.

'Two days. We are going to Norilsk. You can get help there.'

Justin didn't hear the reply – he was already asleep again.

By the time they arrived in Norilsk Sabrina had come round. She had taken some soup, and although she was weak she refused to seek help. They simply couldn't run the risk of alerting the authorities. Irena was confused, but accepted her decision. She was further confused at the offer of money for rescuing them.

'It is Komi hospitality,' she told them. 'We did not do it for money.'

'I know,' Sabrina said. 'But it would make us feel better.'

'Where we come from,' Justin added, 'no one would help.'

Irena, who was talking on behalf of the family, was resolute. 'We have all we want,' she said.

Justin and Sabrina looked at the stark wagon they had been living in for the last three days. It was listing to one side and in need of repair. Irena saw them looking and knew what was going through their minds.

'Westerners; you want cars and homes. We are trying to build a better place for our people, so that people can have nice things and still live together.'

'I hope it works,' said Justin.

Irena was still firm, she had a mind to match her body. 'It will,' she answered. 'My family run a school for our children. That is why I speak such good English. We are showing our children what man can do, both good and bad. We are here to see the council for ethnic people. To get them to support us.'

Sabrina held out the money again. 'Well take this,' she pleaded. 'You can buy some things for your school. Do some of the things you're talking about.'

Irena considered what they were saying and accepted the money. 'You are very kind,' she said, and kissed them both, then climbed back onto the wagon and added, 'Will you be all right?'

'We'll find a hotel and rest,' answered Sabrina.

The father shook the reins from inside the wagon and it trundled its way along Norilsk main street, and Sabrina and Justin turned and went in search of a hotel.

There were plenty of them in the town and they all looked similar. They signed in and ordered a bottle of vodka without even going to their room, and then they sat by the fire to take stock of their experiences. Sabrina seemed particularly anxious to get as near to the heat as possible.

'I will never forget that cold again,' she told Justin. 'I was so numb.'

'We were so lucky,' added Justin, throwing another

log on the fire. 'Imagine if they hadn't come along, at that exact time, on that particular road.'

'There is only one road,' Sabrina pointed out.

'Still,' Justin added, 'what if?'

They fell quiet then, enjoying their drinks and good fortune.

'So what do we do now?' Justin asked, after a few minutes of contemplating. 'Press on?'

For the first time in this whole adventure Sabrina wavered. 'We've lost several days on him.' She refilled her glass and added in exasperation, 'I never knew how big this country is. Are they still going east? David's a clever bastard; he could double back, drop south and head for somewhere warmer.' She rubbed her legs vigorously. 'And who could blame him.'

The sound of heavy boots on the bare pine floor drew Justin's attention and he looked into the window at the reflection of the wearer.

'Fucking hell,' he whispered. 'Get down.'

Sabrina immediately dropped in her seat and fought a desperate urge to see who Justin was so afraid of. It was then she saw the reflection for herself – the green uniform, the brass buttons and braid, the glinting insignia on the cap. It was Captain Vasili Leskov.

Fortunately for Sabrina and Justin the chairs they were in were both facing away from the reception counter. Nonetheless, they both pulled their legs up under their chins to make it look like no one was in them. Then they waited.

The conversation between the captain and the hotel manager began quietly enough. Within a few moments, though, it was clear that all was not well. Vasili shouted; the manager shouted back. Vasili shouted louder and the manager was suddenly subdued. Then the conversation resumed in a more civil tone until Vasili shouted once more, spun on his heels and marched out of the room.

The manager waited until the soldier was well clear and then spat in his direction and released a verbal torrent. You didn't have to be a translator to realise he wasn't wishing him a good day. When he had calmed down he began violently polishing the counter, the first time he had ever done so. As he rubbed away at the dull wood he noticed the strange sight of his two guests quietly returning their feet to the floor.

'Well, well,' said Sabrina quietly. 'The tide of destiny.'

'Sorry?'

'Doctor Zhivago, you know,' said Sabrina. 'Why would Vasili be here if David wasn't somewhere near.'

'Nowhere is near in this country,' Justin reminded her.

'Another bottle?' It was the hotel manager. 'Food?'

'Yes, both,' stammered Justin, surprised at his sudden appearance. 'Whatever you've got.'

He returned with a bottle of crystal-clear vodka and two cabbage turnovers. 'May I?' he said, inviting himself to sit down.

A nervous Justin motioned towards a couch on the other side of the fireplace.

'Have you been in Russia long?' he asked straightaway.

'A while, yes,' said Sabrina. 'It's a lovely country. We're setting up some trading links. Komi and Lapp products; clothing, trinkets, that sort of thing. We want to sell them back in Britain.' She got all that out first so that Justin would know what story to sell.

'That's very good news,' said the manager, apparently sincerely. 'Many of the Komi are very poor.' He rose to leave and then added, 'I'm sorry, I forgot to ask for your passports when you booked in.'

'They... they're in our rooms,' Justin blurted. 'I'll

drop them down later.'

'You haven't been to your rooms,' the manager calmly pointed out.

'That's right,' Sabrina put in. 'They're outside in our car.'

The manager went to the window and looked up and down the snow swept street. 'I think your car has been stolen,' he said, then smiled broadly at the look of panic on their faces and sat back down. 'Do not worry,' he continued. 'That soldier, he is looking for you, isn't he?'

'Captain Vasili Leskov,' said a resigned Sabrina. 'Yes.'

'I will not tell,' the manager said to great relief. 'The military,' he added with disgust. 'Strutting around in their uniforms. They do not know what a day's work is. No, they only know how to force others to work for them.' He was in full flow and issuing a tirade of abuse against the state, which, it turned out, sent his family to Siberia in Stalin's time. 'And your friend David, he is wanted also. Is he not?'

Sabrina and Justin sat up and took notice. 'David?' she said, trying to hide her excitement. 'He's been here?'

'Yes,' the manager said, 'with his two girls. We had great fun.' He winked at Justin. 'They were very friendly. He said they could only stay a day, but what fun we had. They stayed for a few days. He only left yesterday morning. You have just missed him.'

Sabrina filled up her glass and pushed it towards their new friend. 'What a shame,' she groaned. 'We keep missing each other.'

'It is a big country,' said a rapidly inebriating manager.

'Tell us about it,' she persisted. 'Did he say where he was going?'

'East,' was the reply, and he grabbed for the bottle.

'Any particular east?' Justin asked.

The manager seemed to magically sober up. 'I told him not to go,' he said. 'Very dangerous.'

'Did you tell the captain where David was going?'

'Of course,' he said with false dignity and his hand on his heart. 'I told him they were going south – to Kazakhstan.' He held a finger to his lips and then motioned them forward as if about to impart some secret. 'It was a little lie.'

Sabrina leaned forward and put her hand on his knee. 'Where is it very dangerous?' she asked soothingly. 'We want to help David.' She looked at Justin and added contemptuously, 'and his little Lapp girls.'

'Chukotskiy Poluostrov,' he finally managed to disclose, along with a loud smelly belch. 'You say Bering Strait, I think. That is where Chukotskiy Poluostrov is.'

'What of the danger?' asked Justin, always the more cautious of the two, but before he could receive an answer the manager fell asleep.

Chapter Fourteen

For two whole weeks, it could have been more but David had lost count, they struggled ever eastward. On through central Siberia and into the east. Across endless tracts of tundra and the bleak, almost nondescript landscape of the far Arctic north. When only five days out from Norilsk David had considered turning back, but he thought they must be nearing the Bering Strait and freedom, and so he pushed on.

He was wrong, and when it seemed that the whole country of Russia was behind him another huge expanse always seemed to lie in front. Supplies of food and fuel were running low, and he'd noticed the engine on the ski sled was beginning to tug on occasion – a bad portent.

For their part the girls were faring well. More at home in the ice than he, they had taken the monotonous landscape in their stride. David was not so well equipped. Each morning he woke he saw only the same scenery and was no longer able to discern any difference in the featureless wastes. It took all his character to continue on or even to believe in his own decision-making. For several mornings now the girls had risen to find their master, unshaven and unkempt, staring intently to the horizon, wondering when the end would come. He longed for the sight of the ocean, frozen over with a magical bridge of ice. Russia, for David, had become a nightmare and he hungered for the land of the free – for America.

The travelling was no different for Justin and Sabrina,

but at least they had the thrill of the hunt. They had left Norilsk the following day after using Justin's money to equip themselves well for the journey. After a few days they had realised that tracking their prey was not as difficult as they had thought. Paths through the ice were often self-evident, there being only one way through. With increasing confidence they pushed on.

For his part David had given up any thoughts of being pursued and his journey lost momentum, sometimes making only half the distance in a day that they would have normally. Then, on the fifth morning, Justin spotted some marks in the ice. They looked quite nondescript at first, but as they travelled he noticed they were uniform and appeared to follow the same path as they were travelling.

'What do you think of those?' he asked Sabrina.

Desperate for any sort of stimulus she jumped to the obvious conclusion. 'We're getting near.' She let out a whoop and punched the air, then looked forward, her face a study in determination. Justin also found himself smiling. His newly found confidence had him more outgoing, more aggressive. When they set up camp at night he had started to take Sabrina without request. She was no longer cold towards him and welcomed his nightly attentions. Strangely though, Justin's desire for her had changed. She was still very important to him and he would always thank her for strengthening his character, but it was a one-dimensional strength; one that knew only aggression and selfishness. Catherine had shown him that he could be strong and still be a decent human being; compassion was not a sign of weakness. Although he enjoyed sex with Sabrina it had lost the intensity it once had. He was no longer the pursuer of her; she was beginning to need him.

The excitement created by the sight of the tracks increased several-fold when the pair came across an obvious camp. There was blood on the ground where a meal had clearly been prepared and, worryingly, Justin spotted a bullet casing. David obviously had a rifle. He and Sabrina had thought them unarmed and so they only carried the side arms from the assault at Cheka 3. Their pace accelerated.

For the next two nights Justin found himself peculiarly aroused from the pursuit. During these nights his treatment of Sabrina had been quite brutal. The previous evening he suspended her naked from the roof of their tent. He watched her for a long time in the flickering of the fire, as she dangled helplessly in front of him. He realised then that they were in the middle of nowhere, literally. Some parts of the region did not even have adequate maps. He had a naked woman suspended and at his mercy. There was no one to rescue her, no one to prosecute or condemn him. It was an incredibly powerful and stimulating thought. When Sabrina, who enjoyed being subjugated, had asked to be let down because her arms were beginning to ache, Justin got up from his bed of furs and simply gagged her with a leather strip. He then sat down again and continued to eat and drink.

When he finished he wiped his hunting knife on his trousers and closed in on Sabrina. She saw the knife pointed threateningly towards her and experienced exactly the same thoughts of isolation that Justin had. The knife had one very sharp edge, which terminated in a pointed tip. Justin touched the tip lightly on Sabrina's clitoris. She understood perfectly the need not to move. Justin dropped to his knees and took hold of her sex lips. He squeezed the two together, and Sabrina screwed her eyes shut and endured the discomfort of being dry-shaved.

When he had finished Justin rubbed a generous amount of horse liniment into her tender mound. It burned so badly that she screamed into the gag, and again when Justin prodded a finger coated with the embrocation into her vagina. With a sex that felt on fire Sabrina began to writhe in her bonds. To increase her discomfort Justin gripped her legs firmly and tied them together with a belt. The lips of her sex were now rubbing together and she had no way of relieving the heat between her legs. All she could do was swing her joined legs backwards and forwards in an effort to distract her mind.

Justin watched closely, enjoying her suffer for the torments she had put him through, and finally Sabrina's flailing subsided and her head fell forward in a faint. Several hefty slaps on her bottom failed to revive her, but she was clearly unharmed. Justin then remembered a story he had read about the French aristocracy. If a lady fainted it was the custom for some kindly gent to blow tobacco smoke up her bottom. Just how this was discovered Justin didn't know. He was also ignorant as to whether the operation was performed in some private room or the woman's bloomers simply pulled down in full gaze of everyone and the perfunctory cloud of smoke blown bowel-wards. He decided to discover if the French were leaders in circulatory medicine or simply perverts who took their chance to sniff a rich woman's arse, no matter what the excuse.

Taking his knife, Justin cut Sabrina down from her restraints. Unconscious she was a deadweight, but he managed to arrange her into position and hogtie her with her knees drawn against her chest and her wrists tied to her ankles. In this way he could prop her up on her knees with her breasts and face pressed to the fur-strewn floor. He left her in that position while he retrieved his tobacco pouch and set about rolling a cigarette. When he was done he leant against one of the travelling rucksacks and enjoyed a few pulls on his smoke while he observed Sabrina's tight bottom. She was a remarkable young woman, a beautiful young woman, and she was now learning to accept him as the dominant one in their relationship. Her sex lips protruded rudely between her legs. 'How many men got between them in Lubyanka?' he asked himself, before deciding he didn't really want to know.

He leaned forward and caressed her taut and very smooth skin. Slowly he parted her bottom to reveal the dark pursed muscle of her anus. He inhaled a lungful of smoke and blew into her bowels. It was a difficult procedure and he didn't even know if any smoke had gone up inside her. He reclined back against the sack and noticed tiny wisps of smoke curling out of her bottom. Sabrina stirred and proved the Frenchmen right, although it still didn't explain how they discovered it. It also failed to relieve the heat burning within the girl's vagina and she began to squirm again, only this time her bonds were even tighter.

Sabrina's eyes ran with tears and she pleaded beneath the gag for some release. Finally Justin relented and went outside to collect some snow, and when he returned he fed the icy particles into her simmering pouch. The relief was instant, but the shock of the cold released a stream of urine that soaked one of the furs. Justin decided that she needed a belt for that, and proceeded to unleash a torrent of strokes that raised several red weals on her bottom. When he was done he untied her and took her outside to sit upon the ice.

The next day Sabrina was very attentive towards him, smiling every time she saw him glance at her and touching him affectionately whenever she got the chance. He felt strong and in control again, and it was he who became the major force in the pursuit – a pursuit that had paid off when, across the great flat wastelands of the north, they spied a small group several miles in front of them.

Justin and Sabrina hurriedly ducked behind a snowdrift in case they were themselves spotted.

'This is it,' he gasped, then poked his head above the snow and peered through his binoculars.

'Is it them?' Sabrina asked agitatedly.

'It's them,' he confirmed, then reached into his heavy Arctic coat and pulled out his gun. Sabrina did likewise.

'What now?' she asked, proving that she really had relinquished dominance in the relationship; not long ago it would have been her who made the decisions.

'We wait,' Justin decided. 'Keep behind them and out of sight. If David sees us he could let fly with that rifle and we'd never get near him. Let's wait until they make camp. When he's snuggled up nice to his girls we'll move in.' He replaced his gun, satisfied it was all okay. 'Give them a few minutes to get over the horizon and we'll follow.'

Light turned to dusk and the pair closed in nearer to David and the girls in case they lost them in the dark. The night was crisp and clear and the stars blinked down from a cloudless sky. There was a crescent moon that gave some light, and the snow reflected it in shades of deep blue. The pair edged closer to their prey, finding them camped in a depression in the ice. Outside David's tent hung an eerily glowing chemical light. A lime green phosphorescence glowed from it, illuminating the surrounding area like some secret ray from a flying saucer.

Sabrina and Justin kept up their watch. Everything was silent; the world appeared cold and dead.

Then there was movement in the camp. It was Mishka, tall, dark-haired and beautiful. She was swathed in furs and studded with amber jewellery. The hunters waited and watched. Mishka went to the sled, threw back the protective leather covers and took a piece of jerky from a bag. She bit on the strip of beef and walked to the edge of the light, where she squatted and relieved herself while still chewing nonchalantly. On the way back to the tent she picked up the bag and took it with her.

'It's going to be a while yet,' Justin informed Sabrina. She looked frustrated and moaned before curling up into a ball to wait it out.

Justin let her sleep. There was no point in both of them keeping watch, and she wouldn't complain this way.

Another two hours passed and the cold was beginning to creep through his clothing. The camp was perfectly still and the chemical light continued to burn. It was time. Justin stretched out his arms and legs to relieve the cramps and shook Sabrina. She was slow in coming round, so he gave her a moment or two.

'Ready?' he whispered.

Sabrina didn't answer, and Justin turned to ask again. She was staring out into the darkness, eyes wide open, as was her mouth.

'What's the matter?' Justin hissed. 'We've got to do it now.'

There was no response. Suddenly he felt the hairs on the back of his neck begin to rise. Something was wrong. Slowly he turned, and pointed at his neck was a vicious barbed bone tethered to a short pole. To move would have meant death.

Justin and Sabrina were force-marched for over an

hour at the tip of bone spears. The Chukchi tribesmen had arrived silently, as if out of nowhere. Justin had not even the time to consider his gun before he was disarmed, tethered and made to walk. Sabrina was tied in similar fashion and the two were urged up a hill by sharp jabs of the spears. Escape did not look an option. At the top of the hill they saw what David had been racing to find – the Bering Strait. It was frozen over, an icy bridge between America and Russia. In a week or so the ice would begin to break up and the connection lost. Already the lengthening days were beginning, unseen, to soften its crystalline structure. It looked like David was going to make it after all.

What was to happen to them Justin could only surmise, although the treatment they had so far received didn't augur well. The pair were marched down to a beach where the Chukchi had made camp of a dozen or so tepees huddled beneath the bluff and illuminated by several fires of washed-up wood that burned blue-green. It was savage, frightening, and very isolated.

Justin and Sabrina were thrust into a tepee and the flap closed behind them. A thin vein of morning light threaded down into the tent from the smoke escape. It revealed a bare floor of stone and sand and a bundle of dried seaweed that was intended as bedding. A few large stones became seats, until tiredness overcame them and they moved silently onto the bed and fell into troubled sleep.

Justin was the first to wake, and through the gap in the top of the tent he noticed that the night sky had returned. Something was obviously happening out on the beach. Raised voices that faded on the fresh wind and feet that stumbled over icy pebbles alerted him first. The sounds grew louder and Sabrina must have heard them too, because she stirred and finally opened her eyes. She soon realised her predicament and a groan escaped her lips.

'Why did I wake up?' she complained, and sluggishly sat up. 'I just can't take much more of this country.' She got to her feet and made to leave the tent, but a spear met her head and she retreated quickly.

'I want to take a piss!' she shouted, but there was no reply and she was forced to pee on the floor.

'Did you see anything?' Justin asked.

'They've picked up our sled. It's over by the large tent.'

'Good,' Justin said. 'Then we've got a chance at least. What's the noise all about?'

'I don't know. There's an avenue of fires leading to the big tent. But it's dark out there.' Sabrina finished peeing and took up a seat on one of the large stones. 'How long have we slept?'

'Must be all day,' Justin guessed.

Sabrina took his hand. 'Sorry about this,' she whispered sincerely. 'I should have listened to you.'

'Well, it's too late now,' he said. Then he heard the grinding of pebbles as someone approached. The tent flap was thrown open with a flourish and a short stocky Chukchi entered with the ever-present spear, which he waved in the direction of the tent opening. They passed the unkempt and wild looking tribesmen and stepped into the icy evening air. The Chukchi stabbed menacingly in the direction of the large tent and Justin and Sabrina made their way to the avenue of fires.

'At least it's going to be warm in there,' Justin smiled unconvincingly, but his words were met with a heavy thump from the tribesman. There was no use retaliating because there were another four men, all armed, behind him.

They made their way along the avenue of fire to the ever-increasing sound of a drum thumping monotonously, and as they drew nearer to the tent Sabrina's heart seemed to beat in time with it. Her chest hammered a growing rhythm, then all but stopped as the screech of a terrified woman rent the air. She looked at Justin, silently pleading with him to do something, but it was useless. The savages thumped them in the back and forced them onwards.

Both stepped into the tent drenched with fear. The heat hit them straightaway, as did the thick acrid air. All was screams and drumbeats and noise. Chukchi tribesmen were spinning on the spot and reaching for the ground before stretching for the sky.

'It's a fucking nightmare,' screamed Sabrina, and her words were met with another blow from the spears which launched her forwards into the tent. Justin was also pushed to stand beside her. In front of them sat a Buddha-like figure. He was cross-legged on a mound of silver furs.

Suddenly the noise stopped and Sabrina looked around. Justin did the same, and their eyes came to rest on him at the same time.

It was David!

A leather thong was tied around the guiche ring piercing his scrotum, and another thong was wrapped about his neck. It looked as if the thong was pulling him backwards, but he was unable to fall because a hook had been pushed through each of his nipples and they were attached to thick fishing lines suspended over a frame. He was obviously in excruciating pain, but the leather strap about his neck stopped him from screaming. His forehead pulsated with a blue vein that looked about to burst, and the pressure he had to build in his neck had bulged his eyes and made him feel faint, but if he did faint and collapse his nipples and the surrounding flesh would be torn from his chest.

Justin tore his eyes away from his onetime friend,

and for the briefest of moments wondered what madness had brought them to this inferno in the ice. His wandering eyes then found David's girls. They were naked, no jewellery, no furs; pegged down on a bed of seaweed and being continually taken by Chukchi after Chukchi, who fell on them in twos and threes and took what they wanted. Occasionally one would scream, only to be silenced by a hand or a penis. There were no Chukchi women in the group; this was an all male hunting party, and they had found their prey.

The chief spoke and two men stepped forward and began cutting Justin's clothes from his body. He asked them to stop, but they never even registered his words. A thong was placed around his neck and he knew the rest.

'Please,' he begged. 'We are British. We have money. Take what you want.' His cries were met with laughter and their laughter was met with screams as first one, and then two long barbless fishing hooks pierced his nipples. The hooks were pulled tight and the strap around his neck drew his head back.

Sabrina saw the two girls and noted the savagery of the tribesmen, but consoled herself that she had been through it all before, in Lubyanka. She would survive; she knew she was strong enough for that.

Other Chukchi descended upon her and she was stripped as expected. She remained silent and accepting; to fight would be to anger or excite them. She didn't want either. All she was expecting was the prod of a penis, probably the chief's, who would naturally take precedence.

Her arms were fastened behind her back. Then the four men picked her up and carried her face down to a fire. Now she did struggle, and less than two feet below her were the glowing embers. The heat scorched her face and the dry air desiccated her lungs with each agonising gasp. Slowly she was lifted upwards and tied to the same frame from which hung David and Justin. Her head flopped down, but with all her effort she raised it and stared at the fat Chukchi chief.

'I hope you die in fucking agony,' she cursed, as calmly as she could muster.

The chief continued smiling and pulled out a pouch, from which he took a wad of loki and filled a bone pipe. As he smoked one of his men threw a large bundle of loki twigs onto the fire, and the wet leaves began smoking immediately and the cloud of pain-relieving vapours hit Sabrina. She breathed deeply, inhaling as much as she could, and the pain turned to a peculiar buzzing sensation. The fire caressed her skin and her whole body felt aglow within wave after wave of sexual sensations.

The chief got up and lumbered behind her, positioned between her suspended legs. He opened them easily and nudged his cock towards her vulnerable entrance. Sabrina was ready, the pain and the ecstasy had prepared her for this.

She was penetrated with one aggressive lunge. She loved it, loved the sensation of being rocked back and forth on the frame, revelled in the torment her body could endure.

Her orgasm came with the crack of a gun and the deadweight of the Chukchi chief upon her back. His extra weight was too much for her restraints and she plunged into the fire, but fortunately the damp leaves had taken away much of the heat. She crawled from beneath his body and brushed the ashes from her skin. There was more gunfire and more screaming – only now it wasn't the Chukchi captives, it was the Chukchi themselves.

Russian soldiers poured into the camp and were

firing at anything that moved. Sabrina grabbed a knife from the chief's belt and bounded towards Justin to cut him down.

'What about David?' he cried over the cackle of gunfire.

'We haven't got time!' she screamed. 'Let's get out of here!'

Justin watched her run to their clothes, but he couldn't leave his friend to be tortured. She had seen what they had done. How could she be so heartless? Sabrina threw his clothes at him and told him to hurry.

'I'm going to release David,' he shouted through all the mayhem.

David heard what Justin said and for a moment believed he had a chance, but Justin stopped in his tracks as Captain Vasili Leskov walked into the tent.

'What the…!' shouted Justin. 'Doesn't he ever give in?'

'Come on!' Sabrina screamed. 'We've got to save ourselves.'

Through a half strangled throat David managed to screech Justin's name, but it was no good. Sabrina had cut a hole in the tent wall and they were gone.

Gunfire reverberated everywhere. Chukchi were throwing themselves on armed soldiers like devils. Somewhere behind David a bullet had passed through the lung of a Chukchi and hit the frame that held him. The frame collapsed, pulling him forward and straining his neck as the leather thong bit into him. On the verge of passing out the thong broke and David fell to the ground, minus a nipple. He crawled forward as tracer bullets whizzed over his head and sought a burning ember. With gritted teeth he lowered his hands onto the flame until it burned its way through his bonds – and he was free!

His initial thought was safety, but he remembered

the girls. They were safe too. Huddled in the seaweed they watched the soldiers cut down the tribesmen who had grinned and laughed as they abused them. David dragged them out and they made for the hole, grabbing furs and what was left of their clothing as they did so. But the captain had seen them. As David threw himself out of the tent a shot rang out from Vasili. It missed. David made for his sled and found the keys in the ignition. The sound of the engine brought more soldiers running, more shouting, more gunfire. David steered for the frozen Bering Strait, dodging boulders as he did so. They hit the ice and the sled picked up speed. He could hear Vasili shouting orders from the beach and he saw Justin and Sabrina running in front of him. He passed them at speed, Sabrina's screams for help fading in the rush of cold air that bit into his wounds.

On the beach Vasili called for the rocket launcher, ripped out the safety lanyard and aimed. It missed the sled by several feet and exploded into the ice. The soldiers set off in pursuit as Sabrina and Justin fell into the freezing waters that were gushing around the broken ice. David heard their screams and despite the urging voices of Mishka and Teena he stopped the sled. The Russians were bearing down on them. David went back. By the time he got there Justin was out of the water and gasping for air on his knees. David gestured for him to get on the sled. Sabrina saw her friend's rescue and screamed for help too. David considered her plight. The Russians were coming. David looked at Justin... who said nothing. The sled sped away and, looking back, Justin saw her hand waving pitifully above the ice. Vasili was standing on the broken floe as it bobbed up and down on the disturbed sea. The Russian sank down on his knees and addressed the woman who had brought him so much calamity.

'The tide of fate has brought you back to me,' he said, and held out his hand. Sabrina reached out and grabbed it. The two shattered masses of ice began to move back together, like enormous frozen scissors.

Vasili grinned. 'Come to Uncle Vanya,' he said.

More exciting titles available from Chimera

* * *

All **Chimera** titles are/will be available from your local bookshop or newsagent, or direct from our mail order department. Please send your order with a cheque or postal order (made payable to *Chimera Publishing Ltd*) to: **Chimera Publishing Ltd., PO Box 152, Waterlooville, Hants, PO8 9FS**. If you would prefer to pay by credit card, email us at: **chimera@fdn.co.uk** or call our **24 hour telephone/fax credit card hotline: +44 (0)23 92 783037** (Visa, Mastercard, Switch, JCB and Solo only).

To order, send: Title, author, ISBN number and price for each book ordered, your full name and address, cheque or postal order for the total amount, and include the following for postage and packing:
UK and BFPO: £1.00 for the first book, and 50p for each additional book to a maximum of £3.50.
Overseas and Eire: £2.00 for the first book, £1.00 for the second and 50p for each additional book.

*Titles £5.99. All others £4.99

For a copy of our free catalogue please write to:

Chimera Publishing Ltd
Readers' Services
PO Box 152
Waterlooville
Hants
PO8 9FS

Or visit our Website for details of all our superb titles
www.chimerabooks.co.uk